THE LAW'S DELAY

JANE STUBBS

Richmond Press

Richmond Press

ISBN: 979 8 39068 535 8

CHAPTER 1

It was the custom for the doctor in attendance at a birth to present the new arrival to the father first. On this occasion the doctor had a problem. Two men hovered on the landing anxiously waiting for news. The older man was the father of Dorothea, who had just squeezed out the tiny scrap of humanity lying in the doctor's hands. As the father of Dorothea, Mr Woodward was undoubtedly the grandfather of the new arrival. Next to him stood his son-in-law, Edward Carter, the lawful husband of the newly-delivered mother. After the briefest blink of hesitation the doctor turned to offer the child to the grandfather, Mr Kenneth Woodward, owner of coal mines and cotton mills, respected member of the Methodist Church and four-times mayor of Atherley.

'It's a girl,' said the doctor. His choice showed he placed the ties of blood above the letter of the law which ruled that, until there was evidence to the contrary, the husband was the father of any children of the marriage. While there was no doubt that Mr Woodward was the grandfather to the child, there were serious reservations about the role of the other man in the proceedings. Edward Carter might be married to Dorothea, but no-one believed him to be the father of her child.

Mrs Woodward arrived to take up her new role of grandmother. She managed to hide her disappointment that the new arrival was female and in a rare display of tact pointed out that the baby's jet-black hair was just like Dorothea's. She refrained from pointing out that the child bore not the slightest resemblance to the blonde and blue-eyed Edward.

An ear-splitting scream came from the bedroom behind the doctor. It so shocked Mr Woodward that he almost dropped the child. His wife lunged forward to catch her. The doctor rushed back to his patient. The door slammed behind him. It could not keep out the screams of Dorothea or the nature of some of the words she used to ease her agony.

Mrs Woodward sat in a chair and cradled the baby in her arms. Mr Woodward paced the floor, his face distraught; he could not bear Dorothea to be in pain and he was shocked by some of the words that escaped from her and through the walls of the bedroom. Edward put a hand on his father-in-law's shoulder and quietly suggested they retreat to his study for a medicinal brandy. This was the second time Dorothea that had driven her teetotal father to drink. 'It's not every day you become a grandfather,' Edward consoled the older man as he poured him a generous slug of golden liquid. He screwed the top on the bottle and hid it back in the drawer.

There was a tap on the door. A smiling maid brought an urgent summons from the doctor. Mr Woodward leapt to his feet, his face white. The maid gestured to the tell-tale glasses on the desk. 'You might like to take some of that for the doctor. He looks as if he could do with it.' She winked at Edward as she turned on her heel and slipped through the open door.

Upstairs the doctor was waiting for them. 'Well, that was a surprise,' he said mopping his brow as he held out what looked like a bundle of bedding. He offered it to Edward Carter, who automatically held out his arms to receive it. He looked down in puzzlement as the bundle heaved and wriggled, revealing a small, red, and apparently furious baby.

'Where's this come from?'

'Same place as the other one,' said the doctor. 'That was a girl. This is a boy. I didn't realise it was twins.'

Edward looked down at a head as bald and as pale as an egg. The tiny living thing squirmed and opened its eyes. They were as blue as Edward's own. He turned to Mr Woodward and held out the child for the older man to take.

'It looks as if one day it will be Carter-Woodward and Son.'

Tears streamed from the older man's eyes.

———————————————

The arrival of the two babies transformed the older Woodwards. From a hag-ridden depressive, reliant on laudanum, Mrs Woodward became a brisk and doting grandmother. The arrival of a son in the Woodward mansion filled her with joy. The feat that had so long eluded her, had been achieved by her daughter almost as an afterthought.

Mr Woodward forgot his embarrassment at the manner of the twins' conception in the satisfaction of having an heir apparent for his business empire. He looked forward to having another little girl to coo over. No warning message against indulging this child as outrageously as he had spoilt Dorothea flashed across his mind.

Between them the Woodwards hired – and fired – nurses with extravagant abandon. There was no-one good enough to look after the two precious babes. Mrs Woodward fretted that the boy was not putting on weight fast enough. The maternity nurse, who was booked for the 6 weeks of Dorothea's lying-in, begged to differ. Voices were raised and tears were shed. A white-faced Mr Woodward gave the nurse her marching orders. The grandparents spent a tense night in the nursery, while a replacement was found. When she arrived, she took a firm hand with the pair of them.

'I think we are worrying too much,' she told the senior Woodwards and gave them a fierce look. The starch in her apron crackled as she tucked a child under each arm and headed to Dorothea's bedroom. 'Door, please,' she shouted and Mr Woodward, captain of industry, four-times mayor and well-known car-owner leapt to obey.

No-one knew what the nurse said to Dorothea. No sound trickled out through the closed door. Half an hour later the nurse emerged with a series of instructions. The cheery maid was to go into town to buy feeding bottles and baby food immediately. To avoid delay Edward was summoned to drive her there in the car. Mr and Mrs Woodward were informed that the children would be brought to the drawing room at six o'clock, as was the custom. That evening two contented-looking babies were brought for inspection before dinner.

'Mother and I have reached an understanding,' the nurse announced. 'If you are agreeable, I am prepared to continue to look after Mother and the babies for the remainder of the 6 weeks.' She looked to Mr Woodward. He swallowed hard before obediently nodding in her direction. A smile of satisfaction flitted across the nurse's face. 'Good. We can go into details tomorrow. The twins and I will be sleeping in the night nursery. Mother needs her rest.' No-one raised any objections.

Some days later the doctor came in his pony cart to check on his patients. It was not a very satisfactory visit from his point of view, but it helped to justify his fee. He knew much less about babies than the starchy nurse, and his adult patient held him personally responsible for the pain of childbirth. Dorothea did nothing to soothe his ego. 'You might have warned me there were two of the creatures,' she complained.

The doctor pulled out his watch and pretended to take her pulse while he worked on his defence. His reputation was at stake. Dorothea had been the subject of intense scrutiny among the comfortable middle-class ladies of Atherley. These were the very ladies the doctor wanted as his patients. So much more rewarding than tending the grubby poor. The doctor put his watch away; he had his story ready.

'Of course I didn't tell you. It would have worried you dreadfully. It isn't good practice to share every scrap of information with the patient,' he told Dorothea. 'There is always a risk with twins. Better a pleasant surprise than a bitter disappointment. Your father is delighted to have a grandson. Ignorance is bliss.' He waffled on as he picked up his black bag.

His excuse of medical discretion was not enough to pacify the gossips. Dorothea had been the centre of frantic speculation since her return from France. She had brazened out her sudden secretive wedding and refused to display the shame that society thought compulsory for young women who anticipate matrimony. While her mother lay prostrate in her bed, Dorothea took over her role as queen of the town's Nonconformists. On 'at home' days she teased the ladies with titbits of false information. As they watched her waistline and counted the months on their fingers, Dorothea took pleasure in lacing her corsets tight and dropping wildly different estimates of her due date into the murky pond of gossip.

'Is there any way I can avoid going through this dreadful childbirth business again?' she demanded and stopped the doctor in his tracks as he tried to make his escape. He flushed and stammered at the unexpected question. Most women were too taken up with their new baby to think of such things, never mind speak about them.

The doctor wiped a finger between his collar and his neck. 'Er… er… much too soon to think about, er… that sort of thing.' Had the baggage no shame? It seemed Dorothea did not. She went on. 'My father always says there is no time like the present. Prevention is better than cure. He's big on proverbs.'

The doctor lifted his bag up to his chest like a shield and turned towards the door. 'I don't know anything about that sort of thing,' he muttered. When his hand was on the handle and his escape route was secure, he took courage. 'In a word,' he said and turned to address Dorothea. 'Abstain.'

He fled down the stairs. In the hall, Edward stopped him and asked for a word in private. The doctor rolled his eyes to heaven and prayed for mercy. The usual reason a husband wanted a private word at this time, was to know when he could return to his wife's bed. Perhaps he had been unwise in being so emphatic on abstention to Dorothea.

'I should warn you, young Mrs Carter will need time to recover from the birth,' he began. 'It will be some time before it is safe to return to… er …'. He sought an appropriate word that a grammar school-educated boy would understand. He rejected 'coitus' in favour of 'marital relations.'

Edward waved a dismissive hand. He had drunk his fill at that particular well. 'There are two babies.'

The doctor gave a dry little cough. 'Er. Yes. I thought it better to keep the second one as a bit of surprise. They don't always survive.'

'They are not twins. Identical twins, I mean?'

'Obviously not.'

'So, what kind of twins are they?'

'Ah!'. The doctor was on firmer ground now. 'Identical twins are formed by an egg splitting. Your babies come from two separate eggs. It is unusual but not without precedent. It is an extra strain on the mother to carry two infants.' Edward said nothing. 'That is probably why they were born so early,' the doctor added diplomatically. Edward moved to show the doctor to the front door. 'I should warn you,' said the doctor, 'that your wife may take some time to recover.'

Edward gave him the kind of strained smile that a man who has been given bad news is supposed to produce. He guessed that the doctor was following Dorothea's bidding rather than giving a professional opinion. As the doctor climbed into his trap, flicked the reins and drove off, Edward's smile split into a wide grin. Two separate eggs. The second one is mine, thought Edward. I knew it the minute I looked into his little face. He went to see Dorothea who was lying-in as custom dictated. She was surrounded by bouquets and notes of congratulation. As he went to kiss her she turned so he could reach only her cheek, not her lips. He could hardly blame her.

'I have to do this lying-in thing for 10 more days. Not that I'm grumbling.' She patted the front of her nightgown to see if it was damp. 'The nurse has bound my breasts up. I think they've stopped leaking now she's taken both those brats to the nursery. They are in there if you wish to see them.'

Edward did. He found the starched nurse and Mrs Woodward each with a feeding bottle in a hand and a baby on a knee. Mrs Woodward smiled at him. Real joy shone in her eyes. He was inexplicably touched that she was feeding the boy, his son, as he now believed him to be. He had drilled deep enough into Dorothea in the days of his lust. It was not beyond imagining that the child was his.

The Carter family had provided no template of fatherhood for him to follow. All the Carter boys were in such deep awe of their mother that a father seemed superfluous. Much as he admired Mr Woodward as an employer and engineer, Edward could not put his hand on his heart and claim that his business partner was an ideal father. He had indulged Dorothea disgracefully.

In the world that Edward knew there was only one man who had steered a steady course between kindness and firmness with his children. And that was John Truesdale, the Registrar of Births, Marriages and Deaths in Atherley, the man who had conducted the brief and uncomfortable ceremony that transformed Edward and Dorothea into husband and wife while bestowing on the bridegroom a half share in his father in law's business empire.

They would meet again when Edward went to register the twins' births. He took comfort from the thought of John's kindness; he would not snigger at the briefness of the pregnancy or reminisce about the rushed and shameful wedding. This was the man who brought up a up a stranger's child with as much care as the children of his own flesh. The little girl abandoned by the man who stole John's bicycle was Jenny, the love of Edward's life, the other half of his being. His heart thumped as he thought of her. He took a breath to control it – and his thoughts. He must not think of her. He had made a deal and must stick to it. Her father had set him an example to follow. The law ruled the twins to be his. He would treat them as his own. Both of them.

He watched as the children sucked eagerly on the bottle, then let go of the rubber teat. The women held them upright and gently rubbed their bendy backs until their mouths opened again in search of nourishment. Reluctant to interrupt Mrs Woodward, happily feeding a boy child at last, he approached the formidable nurse. Would she let him try feeding his daughter? The nurse kept her face impassive as she handed the baby over. The fragility of the tiny body took Edward by surprise as she lay like thistledown in one of his capable man's hands. She sucked happily for several minutes before turning her face away. The nurse came to reassure him that there was nothing wrong.

'The child simply needs winding,' she said as she grasped the girl and straightened her back. A huge burp and a dollop of regurgitated milk followed.

'I think I'd better leave it to the professionals', said Edward and stood watching as the nurse took over. After a few minutes he had worked it out. 'I see now why you have to keep stopping. The child makes a vacuum in the bottle.' He treated them to his disarming smile and left.

'In all my years,' the starchy nurse began. She said it again for emphasis. 'In all my years as a nurse, I've never seen a father do that.'

When there were only 2 more days of lying-in to endure Dorothea fell back against the pillows and examined the too familiar wallpaper of her bedroom. And this is how it's going to be, she decided. My bedroom. Edward had moved out before the birth and that was how it was going to stay. There was to be no more of this childbearing. An awkward imp popped up in her head to remind her how much she enjoyed sex. What was it Aleksy had said? 'You are a natural. You have rhythm'. She put that problem to one side. She would deal with that later.'

Now she had mentally barred the door of her bedroom, its flowery walls felt more like a prison than a place of refuge. She had come home from France before she realised she was pregnant. Once back in Atherley the trap closed round her. The child – children – inexorably growing in her belly held her captive. Society with its endless rules, restrictions and punishments wrapped her in its silken cords. Her family pulled the knots tighter. Marriage to Edward was her father's choice. Now that tiresome pregnancy was finished Dorothea looked for a way out. Her eyes scanned the horizon in search of an escape route.

The nurse and her mother arrived, each bearing a baby that was both clean and fed.

'We've come to visit Mama,' said Mrs Woodward as she gently laid her little bundle next to Dorothea on the bed. The nurse did the same on the other side. She didn't waste her breath in encouraging Dorothea to be motherly. She and Dorothea had come to a thorough understanding of each other on their first meeting.

Dorothea looked down at the two little scraps of humanity. She tried to feel the famous surge of maternal love. It did not happen, although the room was full of the treacly stuff. Her mother dripped with it. Even the starchy nurse had a soft smile on her formidable lips.

Mr Woodward arrived. He carried roses which he laid at the foot of the bed as if at a shrine. He went to stand behind his wife and laid a hand on her shoulder. Mother and father beamed on their daughter with pride and joy. Their dismay at her failure to be chaste, the hasty wedding and her stained reputation were all forgotten, as they gazed at the babies, small messengers of hope.

Edward came and stood beside the nurse. The grin that had caught many a girl's eye flashed briefly across his features. Dorothea saw that his eyes were blue, like one of those blithering babies. 'That's not possible,' she told herself. 'Lots of babies have blue eyes at first.' While her parents cooed over their grandchildren, Dorothea studied the husband her father had provided. Pleasuring him – and herself – in the bedroom had kept him tame for the duration of her pregnancy. She had assumed him to be some convenient hireling who would disappear to the factory and the pub when his role as putative father was completed.

Her theory was proving wrong. While she took over mother's place in society, snarled at her father and spent hours punishing the piano, Edward had, as the locals put it, got his feet under the table. Her parents stood smiling at his side. Edward smiled down at her, friendly but cool. There was a glint of steel in those blue eyes.

'We've come to discuss names,' he said. 'My mother always wanted a girl. I'd like my daughter to have her name. Your mother has kindly agreed with me.'

Dorothea heard the clang as the prison door shut. 'Dear God,' she thought, 'I am surrounded.'

CHAPTER 2

While Dorothea fretted and sulked, her mother, the starchy nurse and an army of domestics fed, bathed and cared for the twins. When they were three months old their grandmother decided the time had come to show them off to the ladies of the town. She sent notes inviting all the ladies with social ambitions to an afternoon tea party. Mrs Anna Mainwearing did not quite qualify as a member of the comfortable leisured class but Mrs Woodward sent her a pressing invitation. Anna had been kind to her in the days of her despair when she could not raise her head from the pillow or endure the pain in her mind without the solace of laudanum.

It took all Anna's courage to walk up the hill to the Woodward mansion and let the heavy brass knocker thud on the door. 'Mrs Mainwearing,' announced the maid, pronouncing the name as it was spelt. Anna did not correct her as her late and not very lamented husband would have done, by hissing, 'It's pronounced Mannering,' into the maid's heedless ear. Anna did not wear her surname with pride or affection. The name she longed for but could not claim was, Truesdale, Mrs John Truesdale to be precise. Anna's sister, Florence, had been married to John Truesdale. After her death in childbirth, Anna fulfilled the duty expected of her by coming to help the distraught widower run his household and raise his family – his daughter Margaret, the foundling, Jenny and little Tommy, the new arrival who survived his mother.

As John recovered from his loss, he and Anna fell in love. They would have married, with joy in their hearts and had children of their own, if an act of Parliament had not specifically forbidden a man to marry his late wife's sister. Events drove Anna to flee from the impossible situation. She later conformed to the rules of a society which saw marriage as the only suitable role for a woman. She married George Mainwearing, a man who was fussy about the pronunciation of his name but not about the welfare of the wife who was soon to be his widow. After his death Anna returned to the shelter of John's home where they found they could not restrain their desire. They loved in secret, fearful of an accidental pregnancy which would advertise their illegal love-making to a disapproving world. Fate twisted the knife in their hearts by arousing in Anna a gut-wrenching urge to carry John's child. She feared the presence of the twins would bring the urge she had worked so hard to quash back into vibrant life.

A quick inspection of the Woodward drawing room reassured her. There were twenty women but no sign of the famous babies. On the advice of the starchy nurse, the twins were to remain in the nursery until the maids had finished pouring the scalding tea and delivering cakes. The nurse explained to Mrs Woodward that it was a scientific fact that disease was spread by germs on peoples' hands and by coughs and sneezes. The twins were not to be offered to guests, to be oohed and aahed over, kissed and cuddled, and passed from hand to hand. Mrs Woodward had said goodbye too soon and too often to the baby boys she had brought into this world to argue. Accordingly when the dangerous hot tea pots were cleared away, she rang the bell to summon the starchy nurse and the two nursery maids each carrying a baby round the room at a brisk pace, like soldiers presenting arms.

Mrs Woodward scarcely had time to point out Clare's black hair – so like Dorothea's – and the sweet nature of the sleeping boy - before the starchy nurse had them though the door and on their way to the sanctuary of the nursery.

Anna sighed with relief. It was clear there would be no risk of kissing a smooth cheek, touching a tiny hand , or inhaling that unique smell of baby. In the evening she told Jenny of her trip to the Woodward mansion. John took refuge behind his newspaper but kept a discreet ear on their talk. He knew babies were a dangerous topic of conversation for Anna just as Edward Carter was for Jenny. He was relieved to hear that the tone of their talk was brisk and business-like; they carefully avoided stirring up strong and hopeless passions. Both women were too well-acquainted with being denied their heart's desire. Anna could not marry and have a child by the man she loved. Jenny could not have Edward, the man she had loved form her schooldays. Marriage to Dorothea and the arrival of the twins had rendered him unobtainable.

11

'How did the news go down at work?' Anna asked Jenny who worked as the finance officer in the Carter-Woodward office. 'Was there much sniggering among the men?'

'If there was, they did it behind their hands. Given a choice between pretending Edward is the father and admitting some pesky foreigner had his way with the boss's daughter, most people stick to what it says on the hymn sheet. They know who butters their bread.'

Anna chuckled at this triumph of common sense over the evidence. Jenny went on. 'Mr Woodward came in today and called the men together. Stood next to Edward and announced he had been blessed with two grandchildren. Slapped Edward on the back and looked forward to the day when it would be Carter-Woodward and Son. Promised them and their families a picnic in the summer. In the countryside. Special train. The works.'

'He didn't want them toasting the new arrivals in the pub,' guessed Anna.

'Exactly. We haven't seen much of him in the office recently. He arrives late. Leaves early. Edward takes most of the decisions now. The men are getting used to him running things.'

'Not everything?' asked Anna with a sly smile.

Jenny grinned. 'True. The men don't get to make all the decisions. I keep a tight grip on the money. Mr Woodward is after a typist to do the letters but I'm pretending that we can't afford one. I'm not quite ready to share my very own flushing toilet with another woman just yet.' She giggled at this frivolous exercise of power. Such moments were rare for a woman. Behind his newspaper John smiled, relieved to hear the conversation end in laughter, not tears.

The next day Jenny left her office at dinner time to stroll through the town. She passed the school where she had been a pupil. Then it had fitted into a discreet gentleman's residence. Now it had spread into the neighbouring houses and a white noticeboard proudly proclaimed it to be Miss Fossil's Academy. Girls in white blouses and identical grey skirts emerged, chattering from one of the doors. Jenny inspected them closely; yes, they were wearing a uniform.

Gone were the days of competitive dressing; the game that Dorothea had played so fiercely.

We won that one with our white blouses, thought Jenny. It was a small consolation for the catastrophic defeat that Dorothea had inflicted on her by snatching away Edward Carter. Jenny was sure that in a perfect world Edward would be her husband. In the deepest part of her being she knew that she and Edward belonged together. She was not disturbed by jealous images of Edward kissing Dorothea or doing whatever it was that husbands and wives did in the privacy of their bedroom. Jenny wasn't too sure exactly what was involved in marital relations, but she was confident that Dorothea had only the outward husk of Edward. His heart was hers.

Her footsteps took her round the corner and into the churchyard where there grew the only green living things to be found in the stony heart of Atherley. As so often happened when she thought of Edward Carter, she found herself near him. He was wandering round the gravestones, swishing his hat at the waving heads of the tall weeds, a sure sign he was working on a problem. When he saw Jenny he raised his hand in greeting. She stopped walking and for several seconds they stood and looked at each other, exchanging their feelings with their eyes. There were no ecstatic greetings, no attempts to embrace, merely dignified nods of the head and an upward lift of the lips. They remained a respectable distance apart until by silent agreement they set off to stroll around the graves. Nothing in their manner gave ammunition to the gossips or betrayed the happy turmoil of their feelings. They had not met face to face since the birth of the twins.

'The twins,' Jenny began. 'They are well?'

'Growing fast.'

Jenny nodded. She spared him the conventional congratulations on his fatherhood. They both knew that Dorothea was already pregnant when Edward married her in exchange for a half share in her father's business.

'We're working on names. It's proving difficult.' Edward decapitated a leggy stalk of ragged robin and thanked whatever instinct had brought him to the churchyard and whatever god had

13

arranged for Jenny to arrive. There was nothing like talking to Jenny to set his mind straight. 'The girl's not the problem. She's to be Clare after my mother.'

'That must be a nice change for her. After all you boys.' Jenny laughed, remembering from school the legendary tribe of Carter boys. 'Are the Woodwards all right with that?'

He nodded. 'The debate is about the boy. Novelty I suppose. They've never named a boy before.'

The names of boys rattled through Jenny's mind. She dismissed Edward's own name out of hand. Who was he kidding? John? The name of the man who replaced the father she never knew. John Carter? Too bland and undistinguished. At school the pupils had called her Spinning Jenny. Partly because she was so fast on her feet and partly for the invention that launched the industrial revolution and brought prosperity to the north of England. A name connected to engineering would be just the thing for the boy Edward must regard as his son. Telford? He was Thomas. The lad would quickly become Tommy. Anyway, her family, the Truesdales had their own Tommy.

'Brunel,' she gasped. 'What's his Christian name?'

'Isambard. Isambard Kingdom to be precise.'

'You can skip the Kingdom, but Isambard Carter sounds about right to me.'

Edward wanted to embrace her but had to content himself with waving his hat in the air. What a girl she was! As long as he could control his desire they could have these chance meetings that consoled his heart and calmed his mind. They parted swiftly.

Edward whistled as he returned to work. The boy with his blue eyes would be Isambard. Mr Woodward had been hurt by Dorothea's emphatic rejection of his own name, Kenneth, but the name of an engineer would appeal to him. Edward did not think Dorothea would object to the name Isambard for too long. As her main tactic when she disagreed with anything was to withdraw to her bedroom and sulk, Edward was happy to let her do so. For weeks if necessary.

Babies grow quickly. The helpless bundle in a shawl grows teeth and begins to demand more than milk. This fact of life was brought home to Mr Woodward by the starchy nurse when she knocked on his study door one morning. It was the first time she had ever felt it necessary to consult him. Since her arrival, peace and harmony had reigned throughout the whole household which she organised with the calm and remote authority of a Roman emperor. Surprise and respect kept him on his feet as a matter of courtesy.

'I've come to remind you Mr Woodward, that my contract came to an end some months ago.'

Mr Woodward nodded his head and waited for the request for a pay rise that usually followed such a reminder. It did not. The silence lengthened until the nurse grew impatient at the denseness of her employer. It was clear she would have to explain everything to him. 'I am a maternity nurse. A monthly nurse. I specialise in those perilous first weeks of life when both mother and baby need skilled care to establish feeding for the child and to allow the mother to rest and recuperate. I have on several occasions pointed out to both Mrs Woodward and Mrs Carter that those critical weeks are long past. The twins are flourishing, and Mother is in robust health. It is time for me to go to attend a new mother and for you to make other arrangements for the children.'

Mr Woodward gaped and felt a sudden need to sit down. In the past he had gone to work to escape the problems of his home. Now he neglected his business empire to enjoy spending time with his family. His wife smiling at the breakfast table. Dorothea playing the piano and singing. The babies laughing and chuckling. Edward shaping up to be the son he never had.

The nurse interrupted these pleasant images. 'As I said, Mr Woodward, I am a monthly nurse. The twins are coming up to their first birthday. You'll be wanting to make other arrangements for them.' Mr Woodward shook his head in the hope that his ears had scrambled the nurse's message. Surely the twins were not a year old.

The nurse saw he needed time. 'I expect you'll want to talk to Mrs Woodward and Mother too.' She bobbed him a bit of a curtsy and left.

Mr Woodward put his head in his hands and restrained a strong desire to weep. Nurse leaving! Her arrival had ushered in a time of hope and tranquil mealtimes. Would all this domestic harmony disappear with her? Would he be back to tears and tantrums, slamming doors and flying crockery? Conventional wisdom claimed that motherhood softened a woman, helped her mature and grow less selfish. Where his daughter was concerned Mr Woodward had no faith in this belief; all the evidence was to the contrary.

Dorothea spent her days in piano lessons, singing practice and the occasional public performance. Any spare time was spent in malicious gossip, buying new clothes, and scoring points against the ladies of the neighbourhood. Her children were of no interest to her; the nurse and the maids looked after them. On occasions the starchy nurse would show her disapproval and challenge Dorothea when she judged her to have gone too far.

'If you could postpone your piano lesson to 3 o'clock, Mother,' the nurse would say, 'then the children could have their nap without interruption. Small children need their sleep.' Dorothea would pull a face, but she'd send a telegram to her tutor to re-arrange the lesson without throwing a full-scale tantrum.

Mr Woodward, after due consideration, decided it was in everyone's interests to persuade nurse to stay.

'A special, treat tonight,' said the nurse when she brought the children to the drawing room for the hour before dinner. 'Mother is here.' She beamed at Dorothea and gave Mr Woodward a significant look.

Watching the twins distracted Mr Woodward from thinking about the nurse leaving. Little Clare, holding tight to Edward's hand was taking her first experimental steps along the length and breadth of the drawing room. Izzy careered about the floor on all fours until his energy ran out. When he grew grizzly and chewed his fist, Mrs Woodward picked him up and consoled him by singing nursery rhymes into his ear. Dorothea worked her way through several magazines until the nurse came to take the children up to the night nursery..

When they finished saying good night and the door was safely closed on them, Mr Woodward used the quiet moment to announce that the nurse had told him to make other arrangements as she was leaving. He was greeted by a stunned silence followed by an ear-splitting shriek.

'No. She can't leave. That's not possible.' Dorothea's trained voice cracked like a whip across the room. She was on her feet, her white skin chalky with shock. 'You'll have to do something to keep her,' she shouted, stabbing her finger at her father.

'I suppose we have kept her longer than we planned,' said Mrs Woodward who, as usual, was thinking of Isambard. 'This little man will be walking soon. I suppose we could manage with another nursery maid.'

'You don't understand,' Dorothea shrieked at her mother. 'I can't manage without her. I rely on her. I've got used to her, dealing with ...' Her lips moved and her arms flailed as she groped for a word. She found it. 'Them.'

'Who?' demanded Mr Woodward. 'Who are you talking about?'

'Them.' Dorothea pointed to the ceiling and the night nursery beyond it. 'Them.' Her chest heaved, with a breath so deep it set her corsets creaking. 'I've only just got over…' She swiped her hand down her torso to remind her family where their precious babies came from.

Mr Woodward was speechless. Half of him was horrified that Dorothea appeared not to remember the names of her children. The other half was amazed to see her show such feeling for another human being. She had never shown a pang at parting from anyone before, though she had been the reason for several servants handing in their notice in the past.

Dorothea barged into her father's muddled thoughts with an urgent command, 'You'll have to raise her wages. Find a way to make her stay.' His money had solved her problems in the past and she assumed that it would do so this time. She looked round the room for support.

'It's not just a question of a better wage. Nurse specialises in the newborn,' Mr Woodward began.

'And the mother. She looks after the mother. That's what she told me when she arrived.' Dorothea sniffed back tears. 'That she is responsible for the welfare of the mother as well as the infant, or in my case infants.' An uncomfortable silence filled the room as several consciences twitched. Their attention had been fixed on the babies rather than their mother.

Dorothea's face softened as she remembered how the nurse had sent Edward racing into town to buy baby food. She had expected stern words of reproach at her refusal to persevere with breastfeeding. The nurse had simply bound up Dorothea's swollen and painful breasts; she had put her needs above those of the babies. No-one else had ever done that. 'You get your rest,' the nurse had commanded as she picked up the twins. 'I'll take them away for the night. It will help your milk to dry up quickly.'

Now her saviour was thinking of leaving. Without the nurse the fragile structure of Dorothea's life crumbled. Her musical ambitions, so resolutely guarded, lay on the floor in shattered shards.

'You cannot let her leave.' Inspiration struck her. 'You must promote her to nanny,' she told her father.

'What's a nanny, apart from a goat?' Edward wondered. He knew nothing of the complex staffing of a wealthy middle-class household.

'They have them in Southport,' Dorothea said, looking at her mother. Mention of the town of her birth tended to guarantee a favourable reaction from Mrs Woodward. 'All the girls at finishing school had nannies.'

Finishing school. The words struck a chill in Mr Woodward's heart. It was there that Dorothea fell into temptation and the twins were conceived. He sought a little help from the Almighty who assured him he had turned that catastrophe round and could do so again. The man of business, the captain of industry regained control. 'We have two new members of the household. It is only to be expected that things must change to accommodate them and their needs.' He beamed as he thought of Clare and Izzy and looked round the room for support.

Edward seized the opportunity. 'It feels extravagant, but would you consider a second car? Perhaps a smaller one for getting to work. Then Dorothea, and her mother, and hopefully the nurse and

18

the children, can use the big car while we are at work. I would be happy to buy a small one.'

'Who would drive them?'

Edward took a breath and mentally crossed his fingers. 'We could get a chauffeur.' Mr Woodward's face stiffened. 'Just while your leg's bad,' added Edward diplomatically. The family conspired to blame his sciatica for Mr Woodward's failure to master the complex gear changes involved in driving the car; he went along with the fiction.

'Until then,' said Edward preparing to play his ace, 'we could employ a chauffeur. He could drive Dorothea to her music lessons or concerts. It would be good to know that she was with a reliable driver rather than some random hackney carriage from the town.'

Mr Woodward's face cleared. His precious Dorothea safe. That was an important consideration. A new car. It would be expensive but he could afford it. He beamed with pleasure at the prospect. The bell rang for dinner. He'd let the women sort out this nanny business. Servants were women's work, after all. Machinery was for men.

The next day Dorothea and Mrs Woodward in a rare moment of unity went to ask the nurse to continue as the twin's nanny. In the evening, as the twins slept and the second nursery maid brought her cocoa, the nurse pretended to consider her answer. In truth, her mind was made up. She liked the Woodward household. She did not have to watch how she spoke as carefully as she did in aristocratic homes. Here the same manner of speech did for both the family and her fellow servants. She liked the household's cheese-paring ways with food and their extravagant use of the coal that kept her warm in the winter. It suited her to be near the town and the railway rather than in a remote draughty mansion where the only passers-by in winter were pink-coated huntsmen in pursuit of a fox.

The wages they offered were good. Professional pride demanded she ask for a little more. She was sure to get it. A quick calculation told her that by the time the boy left for school and the girl acquired a governess she would have saved enough to retire. Of course, it was the rarity of twins that clinched it; they seldom both survived so raising a boy and a girl together would be an interesting challenge. And Mother wouldn't be a problem. Dorothea was genuinely indifferent to her children. Cold-hearted mother and doting grandparents. The poor mites could do with someone with a bit of common sense in charge.

The next morning Mr Woodward found a deputation of his wife and daughter on the threshold of his study. They had come for his stamp of approval on the new domestic arrangements. He harrumphed a bit at the cost, as was customary, but beamed with relief that the maternity nurse had agreed to set aside her starched apron and put on a grey alpaca dress with white collar and cuffs and be called Nanny.

There was only one thing that irked the new nanny. To identify nannies they were mostly known by the surname of the family they worked for. Nanny considered using her own surname. She could insist on Nanny Parfitt but it would be a struggle. The might of the Woodward name would win every time even though, technically, she was Nanny Carter, the surname of the children in her care. After due reflection, Miss Parfitt decided to become Nanny Woodward with two maids to do her bidding, a warm home, a healthy income and a free hand with the two children. What more could a woman ask?

While the women dealt with these weighty matters, Edward and Mr Woodward threw themselves with enthusiasm into investigating cars. Edward made plans for a garage on the piece of land at the far side of the paddock. He was confident that they could find a chauffeur; young men were keen to pursue this promising new career.

Everyone was happy. Soon the only arguments at the breakfast table were about who could have the car and when. Mrs Woodward had one reservation about the new arrangements. She confided to Nanny that it was about time Edward moved back into the bedroom he used to share with Dorothea.

Nanny looked her employer straight in the eye. She tapped a finger gently on the back of Mrs Woodward's hand. 'I think on such matters Mother knows best.'

CHAPTER 3

While Mr Woodward was distracted by Dorothea's pregnancy and the unexpected delight of being a grandfather, Jenny found she had a free hand with the finances of Carter-Woodward. She took the opportunity to build up a hefty reserve, ready for the day when Mr Woodward remembered that he had a business empire to run. She surmised that when his mind returned to his business responsibilities he would want to make some startling innovation to remind everybody that he was the boss and that he was back in charge. He would want an expensive piece of new equipment or a dramatic change in the pattern of work. Jenny had the perfect project in mind for him; it involved both a new machine and a new member of staff. The trick was to let Mr Woodward think of the idea himself.

Old Mr Samuel had been in charge of all the correspondence for years. Mr Woodward would give him instructions in the morning, and he would disappear into a cubby-hole where he laboriously wrote all the letters by hand in an elegant flowing script. Edward cursed this antiquated system as he struggled to keep abreast of the correspondence while Mr Woodward stayed at home playing Happy Families.

Jenny started her campaign with old Mr Samuel himself. His daughter was the mother of two young boys. Like his employer, Mr Samuel enjoyed being a grandfather, but he could not afford to retire. Jenny checked his records and found that he qualified for a half pension in 6 months' time. Then she started to collect evidence to show that other firms used typewriters. She filed examples of typewritten documents in a blue folder.

When Mr Woodward returned, he found the backlog of unanswered letters piled on his desk next to the blue folder. In horror he shouted for Mr Samuel, who was downstairs taking his coat off. Jenny arrived first. 'Poor Mr Samuel,' she lamented. 'He's finding the stairs difficult.' As they waited, they heard the old man wheezing up the spiral metal staircase that led to their offices on the first floor. Jenny used the time to build her case. 'Poor chap, his eyes are failing and sometimes his hand just freezes.' She curled her fingers up like a bird's claw and let her pencil slip to the floor. After retrieving it, she went to her office next door and left Mr Woodward with the still breathless Mr Samuel and a lot of tedious correspondence.

It was not long before Mr Woodward offered Mr Samuel his half pension and the gift of a carriage clock. A sudden improvement in his eyesight enabled him to take a part-time job in a book shop. His only regret was leaving Mr Woodward with so many unanswered letters. Primed by Jenny, he suggested that his former employer accompany young Mr Carter on a visit to the Mechanics' Institute. There he would see in action the machine that would more than fill the place left by his faithful old clerk.

The first-year students at the Mechanics' Institute fixed their eyes on a document, their fingers on their typewriters and hammered away, producing a noise like rapid gunfire. Within minutes they were able to peel the paper from the roller and display identical letters.

'That's copy-typing,' said the tutor with a smug smile. 'If you think that's fast you should see what they do after another 6 months.' The students, mostly girls, giggled.

Mr Woodward decided that the office needed a secretary who could type. Within a week he had bought a magnificent black and gold machine with a bell that pinged loudly at the end of each line. Edward suggested that they involve Jenny in the process of recruitment. 'You'll have noticed, sir, that most of the typists we saw at the Mechanics' Institute were female. Good job we built that new cloakroom. Perhaps Miss Truesdale will not object to sharing it.'

Jenny acted surprised when Mr Woodward came to ask her to arrange an advertisement for a typist in the next edition of the local paper. He coughed several times and shuffled his feet as he approached a delicate matter. 'I hope you won't mind sharing the rather splendid cloakroom we built for you, Miss Truesdale. We are hoping to spend no more than £50 a year. I expect most of the candidates to be …er…female.'

'Yes. That's a reasonable assumption,' said Jenny.

'So, we thought you might like to sit in on the interviews.'

Jenny noted that there was no mention of her being involved in the decision-making process. Nevertheless, it was a step in the right direction. 'Shall I find a test piece for the candidates? Then you can judge them by results?'

Mr Woodward was so impressed by Jenny's idea that he left the exact wording of the advertisement to her.

As the only woman working in the offices of Carter-Woodward, Jenny missed feminine company. While her sister, Margaret, was away at Owens College in Manchester Jenny climbed the second flight of stairs to her attic bedroom on her own each night. Though Margaret's thoughts seldom strayed far from the Romans and their language Jenny missed their bedtime chats. Perhaps it would be worth losing exclusive use of the ladies cloakroom in exchange for the company of another woman in the office. If she had to share her treasured facility, who better to share it with than Mavis. It was Mavis who had cheerfully trudged up and down the hill with her to the classes at the Mechanics' Institute. There Jenny studied Commercial Finance while Mavis worked at Office Practice. It was Mavis's presence that convinced John Truesdale to allow Jenny to continue her studies there. He could not allow his daughter to be the only female walking through the dark streets with all those young men. It was true he had his suspicions of 'that Mavis' as he always called her but there was no conclusive evidence against her. She always stood sedately at the foot of the steps to his house when she called for Jenny to keep her company on the way to class.

The real Mavis was a breath of fresh air in Jenny's sheltered life. With no father to control her and a mother with a very relaxed attitude to female behaviour, Mavis was a compulsive flirt in the company of young men. She would laugh raucously at their jokes, which Jenny did not always understand. If a lad took her fancy she would slip off with him into a dark doorway till the others grew restless and shouted at them to hurry up. Mavis was not just rough and ready, she was bright. She qualified as a typist and a year later she was selected to work at the Post Office where she sat at the counter next to Jenny. There the female staff had been provided with a flushing toilet, a rare moment of forward thinking by the powers that be. It had inspired Jenny to insist on one before she went to work at Carter-Woodward.

Jenny decided that this was a moment to show female solidarity. She put on her hat and went to buy a stamp. Mavis in a high-necked white blouse sat behind a metal grille. 'I have something that you might be interested in.' Jenny kept her voice low. Private conversations were not encouraged during working hours. 'Cup of tea after work?'

Mavis checked no supervisor was looking. 'As long as we can go to Cozy Corner and you're paying. I warn you, it's expensive,' she murmured before counting out five pennies in exchange for Jenny's sixpence. Cozy Corner followed the example of Lyon's Corner Houses, where there was a section reserved exclusively for women. Now that women were finding jobs in shops and offices there was a demand for places where they could go after work for a light meal or a cup of tea without risking their reputations. Cozy Corner had been opened to attract such customers.

As she put the pennies in her purse Jenny felt peeved. She had looked forward to making her first visit to the much talked-about Cozy Corner. Typical of Mavis to get there first.

Dusk was approaching when Jenny arrived at Cozy Corner. The 'Ladies only' section hummed with conversation. The little tables with their snow-white tablecloths were topped with ornate cake-stands and silver teapots. A few solitary men in overcoats were scattered about the rest of the café. They read their newspapers as they stretched back in their chairs, taking things easy after their day's work. My word, things have changed, thought Jenny. Two young women going out after dark without a male chaperon and no-one raising an eyebrow. Even so she hoped her father would not see her. He would be sure to question her closely as to what she was doing with 'that Mavis'. John Truesdale thought Jenny had made a mistake in leaving her job at the Post Office to go to work at Carter-Woodward. He persisted in reminding her how sensible 'that Mavis' was to stick to her job, given her unconventional origins in the grubbier end of town.

The waitress was delivering a toasted teacake when Mavis arrived. This was not the Mavis who wore the uniform of the working girl, who tied her hair back severely and spent hours imprisoned behind a counter at the Post Office. This was the real Mavis. She greeted her friend with a friendly thump on the shoulder and a loud, 'All right then.' It was not a question, more a statement of a fact that she challenged you to deny. Her plain black and white clothes were adorned with swathes of chiffon scarves in lilac and purple. Earrings flashed and rings twinkled as Mavis took her seat and settled her skirts. Perfume wafted across the table almost – but not quite − obliterating the fragrant spicy smell of the buttery teacake.

'My word. That looks good,' Mavis bellowed, her eyes on the teacake. Jenny asked the waitress for another one. While they waited Jenny took the opportunity to study her friend. Mavis's lips were suspiciously pink and her complexion suspiciously smooth. When she turned to look round the room, Jenny saw that as well as the traditional ribbon, the brim of her straw boater was trimmed with bunches of purple violets.

'It is nice here,' said Mavis, looking round at the fresh white paint and the flowered cups and saucers.

'And it's respectable. I can come here without my father frothing at the mouth about my being out on my own.'

Mavis gave her sideways smile as she looked round the room. 'That's not a problem I suffer from.' Her teacake arrived. As she picked up the little knife and fork, she said, 'It seems ages since we worked together.'

'I'm hoping we might do so again. I'm to put an advert in the local paper next week. For a typist. Thought you might like to apply.'

Mavis pursed her lips. 'That depends. How much will it pay?'

Jenny took a sip of her tea to avoid answering. She was hurt that Mavis's first thought was of the money rather than the compliment of being invited to apply.

'I have to know,' Mavis explained. 'My mother isn't getting any younger and we have rent to pay.'

'I can't say. Mr Woodward won't say exactly. I'm going to write something about a commensurate salary for the right candidate.'

'I'd need to know before I even try. I don't want a blot on my record at the Post Office.'

'I warned Mr Woodward that they'd be paying you £60 a year and he'd have to match that to get a typist.'

'I don't type letters at work. We just deliver them.'

Jenny grew earnest. 'Anyone who went to school can weigh letters and calculate the cost of three tuppenny stamps. But typing, Mavis, that is a real skill. All those evenings you trudged up the hill to get your qualifications.'

'I don't have the speed now. No typewriter to practise on.'

'You could go back to evening classes.'

'Thank you very much for taking up my spare time.' Mavis bridled. She put down her teacup and said, 'I have more useful things to do with my evenings.'

Jenny never gave up at the first fence. She persisted in urging Mavis to brush up her typing skills, and maybe learn shorthand. If she helped Mr Woodward deal with the pile of neglected correspondence and showed him how business was done in the 20th century – with typewriters and telephones, not wax tablets and carrier pigeons – she could be his secretary within a year. That was a position more usually filled by a man. It would come with a man's salary and had real prospects of power and promotion.

Mavis stopped listening; she had other plans. Her ears were closed but her eyes were busy; they roamed past Jenny and around the other occupants of the café. When Jenny had no more career advice to offer, Mavis was mild but firm with her.

'Face it, Jenny, I can't take the risk. I'm sticking with the Post Office. They're rock-solid employers. Not long now and I'll have done 6 years. And you know what that means.' She gave Jenny an exaggerated wink and a significant look. After 6 years a female employee who left to get married was paid a dowry.

Jenny refused to be impressed. 'It might be nice to get a lump sum. But does it make up for losing your job? You know you can't work after you marry.' Like many employers the Post Office did not employ married women on the assumption that they would soon be pregnant

Jenny started to ask who the lucky man was. Mavis raised a finger to silence her. She leant across the table to avoid being overheard. 'There isn't one. I have a plan to get the dowry without the bother of being married.'

'How're you going to manage that?'

Mavis tapped the side of her nose to warn Jenny not to ask any more questions. 'That's my secret. My mother had a baby without a husband. I bet I can get my dowry without one.' Mavis had a wardrobeful of explanations as to how she arrived in this world without the benefit of a father.

Jenny changed the subject. 'How is your mother?'

'She's not getting any younger. She's got to stop dressmaking. Her hands are crippled. That's why we're saving up. Going to buy a house of our own.'

Jenny's eyes popped at this ambitious plan. Two women buying a house. No man involved! For a moment she was speechless, which was just as well as now Mavis had started on her plan, there was no stopping her.

'We're going to take in lodgers. Mam can still cook. We've had enough of paying through the nose for poxy rooms with mould on the walls and rats rampaging round at night. The minute you move in the landlord puts the rent up. He can throw you on the street any time the fancy takes him. And don't get me started on the neighbours. Two women living alone! I don't know what's worse. The men sneaking round hoping for a quick feel or their wives telling the world we're no better than we ought to be.' Mavis followed this theme for a long time before she ran out of breath.

Jenny left Mavis a space in case there was more she wanted to say. There was. 'It's all right for you, Jenny. You've got a father. People treat you with respect when there's a man to answer the door.'

Jenny nodded her understanding. 'I see why you can't come to us. Carter-Woodward aren't paying dowries.' Not that there is any chance of that for me, she thought.

'Thank you for the offer, Jenny. It's a nice idea, but no.' Mavis rose to go. She scanned the café and gave an almost imperceptible nod to someone sitting at a table behind Jenny who asked, 'Someone you know?'

Mavis shook her head. 'Not really. I hope we can meet up again. I've enjoyed our chat. I can't offer to pay the bill, but I won't have a teacake next time.'

'Don't bother about that. This has been a real treat for me.' Jenny's social life was very limited. It was the price she paid for loving an unobtainable married man.

Mavis disappeared with a swirl of violet perfume. Jenny gestured for the bill. As she counted out the coins for the waitress's tip, she did not see the man, from a table behind her. He folded up his newspaper, tucked it under his arm, and followed her friend out into the street.

In the evening Jenny told the people she regarded as her parents about meeting Mavis. She told them how the two women were saving up for a house. She left out the imaginary bridegroom

'That Mavis is showing a lot of common sense in sticking with the Post Office,' said John. 'Mark my words, you'll regret leaving them one day.' Jenny rolled her eyes. John never missed an opportunity to voice his reservations about her job at Carter-Woodward. His duty done, he shook open the pages of his newspaper and let the events of the wide world claim his attention. Jenny had intended to tell him that she was glad she had a father to stand between her and the world, but she decided against it. He would have to stop criticizing her employer first.

Now that John was not listening closely Jenny told Anna about the excess of perfume, the flamboyant violets and her suspicion that Mavis was wearing face powder and something pink and shiny on her lips. Worst of all was her dismay at her friend's point-blank refusal to consider applying for the typist job. Jenny saw it as a missed opportunity for someone who had no relatives to help her.

'What exactly is it that you want Mavis to do?' asked Anna, who had an uncanny knack of finding the right question.

'We need someone to do letters for Mr Woodward and Mr Carter – and me.' Where work was involved, Jenny never referred to Edward. He was always Mr Carter. 'And to type up contracts.'

'Like a secretary?' Where would this person work?'

'There's room for a desk on the landing outside our office doors.'

'Does it have to be a woman? I thought men were secretaries usually.'

'I don't know. Women are cheaper and I thought it would be nice to have Mavis. We always enjoyed working together. And I'm used to sharing a cloakroom with her.'

Anna chuckled. 'It's that precious toilet that's the problem.' Behind his newspaper John grimaced. He was under increasing pressure from his womenfolk to install a flushing toilet at home. They mocked mercilessly his determined refusal of modern amenities.

That night Jenny wondered why she was so disappointed that Mavis was not interested in working for Carter-Woodward. Eventually she pinned down her reason. It was jealousy or rather the avoidance of that unpleasant emotion. She never saw Edward with his wife. There were no lingering looks or affectionate exchanges to upset her. Like every well brought up girl of her time she had only the vaguest idea of what it was that married couples did in the privacy of their bedroom. Her ignorance spared her the fuel to feed her jealousy. The arrival of an attractive young woman in the office might be a different matter. Mr Carter might smile on her. Edward had never smiled upon Mavis; he thought her loud and silly.

Jenny seized a pencil and started drafting an advertisement for a typist to help with correspondence. She carefully avoided saying 'he' or 'she'. With luck she might continue to be the only woman in Edward's working life and the sole user of the ladies' cloakroom.

Mr Woodward expected flocks of young women to apply to work for his firm. He was disappointed. The young women he had seen at the Mechanics' Institute wanted to work in clean offices for eligible lawyers and professional men. A factory with a smoking

29

chimney and a work force of men in grimy overalls held no attraction for them.

Two people applied to be interviewed and came to do a test on the new typewriter. The young woman proved she could copy type quickly, but nothing more. The young man, on the other hand, could type at speed, rustle up a letter from a few notes and write shorthand. To prove his point, he made strange hieroglyphic marks in a notebook while Edward read some complicated clauses from a contract. Then he transformed the squiggles into a typed copy of the original document. Edward was amazed to have his exact words reproduced in print as if by magic; it was strangely unsettling.

Mr Woodward was silent until he bid the young man a brusque farewell. Then he beckoned Edward to accompany him to the machine shop, something he only did when he had a problem. To a background of wailing drills and thudding steam hammers, each man shouted thoughts that the other man could not hear above the din of machinery. By some mysterious alchemy they emerged with Mr Woodward's problem solved and his mind made up.

'You'll have to persuade Miss Truesdale that it's going to cost more than I thought,' said Mr Woodward. 'I can't for shame offer this chap the job at the woman's rate. Good job the advert didn't give an exact figure.'

'You'll have to add at least a third for the man's rate. You can say that it's for the shorthand.'

'Amazing stuff. All those sticks and squiggles. Do you think we'll get him for £90?'

'Yes, I think he'll be happy to get his foot in the door.' Like I did, thought Edward. 'Young Friedrich looks the quietly ambitious sort.' Like me, thought Edward.

'Freed-rick. What sort of a name is that?' Mr Woodward complained.

'It's German. For Frederick. Could be handy if he speaks the language. Lot of business to be done there.'

'Will he be all right on the spiral stair? He's got a bit of a limp. Sort of drags his leg.'

'Yes. I asked him if it was an injury. He said it was polio, that disease children get. Sometimes it's fatal. He was lucky. Left him with a bit of a withered leg; he wears a calliper.'

'All right. Mr Samuel can write a last letter in copperplate to tell Mr Frederick he's got the job. And that's what we'll be calling him. Frederick. I can't be doing with all this foreign nonsense.

Edward looked forward to telling Miss Truesdale, as he had to call her in office hours, that she could keep the cloakroom for her sole use.

Mr Woodward made a final valiant attempt to master the skill of driving the car. It ended up in the rose bushes. He blamed his sciatica, the steering wheel, the colour of the leather seats, and the phases of the moon. Once he had vented his feelings Edward set about finding a chauffeur. He consulted the Mechanics' Institute who produced a stubby man called Higgs, who demonstrated that he knew his way round an engine and could drive smoothly without crashing into the shrubbery. He quickly became a favourite with the ladies of the house.

Nanny found synchronising the availability of the chauffeur with her employers' social lives to be one of her more important tasks. She would say to Mrs Woodward, 'Well, ma'am, we can take the children to Mrs Openshaw's at home on Tuesday afternoon as long as we can drop Miss Dorothea off at her singing lesson for 3 p.m.' When Mrs Woodward and Miss Dorothea nodded their agreement, Nanny would make a note with her pencil. 'Shall I tell Higgs to be ready at half past 2?'

Mrs Woodward could then look forward to a most satisfactory afternoon. There was nothing she enjoyed more than showing off her two well-mannered and toilet-trained grandchildren to the ladies of the town. Their jealousy was palpable. Mrs Woodward smoothed it, like an ointment, on the bruises inflicted on her ego when her shame at her daughter's pregnancy kept her confined to her bedroom.

'Would you like me to accompany you?' asked Nanny.

'Absolutely.' Mrs Woodward relied on Nanny to maintain the image of a model family. No child was sick when Nanny travelled in the car. Nanny's hanky combined with Nanny spit removed strawberry jam and chocolate from white linen clothes. Her eagle-eyed presence prevented any untimely puddles on the carpet. If the worse came to the worst Nanny's raised finger and a lift of her eyebrow would bring a swift halt to any crying or temper tantrum.

The roar of a car engine disrupted their talk. The children ran to the window and pulled themselves up to look out at the drive. 'Daddy's home early,' they squealed with delight. There on the gravel stood a gleaming green sports car. A tall man in goggles climbed out of the driver's seat, removed his goggles, and looked up to the nursery windows where his children clung to the bars that kept them from falling out. He beckoned them down.

'Can we, Nanny? Can we?' pleaded Isambard.

'If your grandmother agrees,' said Nanny, the master diplomat. 'It's not often that your father arrives home before your tea.'

The children ran down the stairs and were wrapped round their father's knees by the time the two adults caught up with them. Edward swept the ladies a bow and asked if he might take the children in his new car. He would drive very slowly and carefully.

With the children in the back seat, Edward drove to the garage at the far end of the paddock. 'This is where the car sleeps,' he told the children round-eyed with the wonder of it all.

'Is this car all yours?' asked Isambard. He stretched out a hand to fondle the silver radiator cap.

'Careful. That's hot,' said Edward. 'And yes, the car is mine.' The words gave him great satisfaction. He added some more items to his list of possessions: the patch of ground beneath his feet and the modest little extension to the garage that would provide shelter for the car's owner. There was not a brick or a blade of grass that didn't belong to him. Mr Woodward's writ did not run on this corner of the estate.

CHAPTER 4

Who is that excitable little man?' asked the soprano behind her as the audience applauded. 'He seems particularly keen to catch your attention, Dorothea.'

The rotund little man in evening dress was clapping like a seal. While his arms flapped about, his gaze was directed straight at Dorothea. He stood out among the sea of sober-suited dignitaries and their fleshy wives like a cork bobbing in the ocean. Dorothea looked closer. There was something familiar about his buoyant movements. He cupped his hands round his mouth and bellowed, 'Brava, Signorina,' several times.

It had to be Signor Martelli. No Mancunian would dream of shouting in Italian at the end of Handel's *Messiah*. Dorothea cast her mind back to the school concert when Signor Martelli had hoodwinked the other acts to enable her to sing her solo as the finale. That was the moment she discovered her power to hold an audience entranced. The memory of it sent a thrill running through her body, a sensation she had not felt for a long time.

A lot had happened since then. Signor Martelli had disappeared from Atherley, and Dorothea had learned the facts of life the hard way. Since the arrival of the twins, she had contrived to sing in chapel and occasional private concerts to raise money for good causes. Never again had she experienced the sense of power that came from commanding a large audience. She spent hours practising and studied with the best teachers her father's money could find, yet the years plodded past without any relief from the grey monotony of her cramped life. How many years? Dorothea tried to recall the age of her children and failed.

As the singers put on their wraps and assembled in the foyer of the Free Trade Hall, her mother and father came to congratulate her and bask in the admiration and goodwill showered upon the amateur singers. Mr Woodward felt as if his heart would burst with pride. His daughter a soloist in the *Messiah*! In Manchester! And thanks to the miracle of the combustion engine and the expertise of the chauffeur he was able to be present at the event.

'Ah. Signor Woodward. You must be so proud. Was she not wonderful?' Dorothea's parents found themselves besieged by a capering little man who sounded foreign. Their smiles faded into expressions of puzzlement which threatened to settle into stern lines of disapproval.

'You must remember me. It was I who first spotted Miss Dorothea's talent. Tell them, Miss Dorothea. It was the school concert. You remember Miss Dorothea.'

She did. Her toes curled with pleasure as she relived that moment of discovery. The breathless hush as the last note faded. The applause. That was what she called living.

'This is Signor Martelli, papa. From Miss Fossil's school, you remember.'

'No longer a humble schoolteacher.' Signor Martelli bowed as far as his girth allowed, 'Now I am impresario.' He beamed with satisfaction and started patting at the pockets of his evening suit. 'My card. I must give you my card. I seek professional singers. Find them work. London, Leeds. All over the country.' His hands moved frantically in pursuit of an elusive piece of cardboard.

Mr Woodward went deaf the moment he heard the word 'London'. His precious Dorothea was not going to put a foot outside Lancashire. Never again would he let her go to foreign parts as he called anywhere beyond the border of his home county. A tap on his arm distracted his attention. The chauffeur had arrived to guide them to their car. Mr Woodward set about gathering his family and their coats together. Higgs was busy wrapping Mrs Woodward in an unwieldy cloak while Dorothea stood smiling and looking into space. Her eyes were on a distant horizon. It wasn't Leeds or Liverpool she was thinking of, but rather the lights of London, Paris and New York that dazzled her. Her father arrived with her shawl in his hands.

'Oh, Dorothea, it is good to see you smiling again,' he said as he draped it round her shoulders. He put a hand on her elbow to lead her away from temptation.

'Allora,' cried Signor Martelli who had at last tracked down his card. He waved it in the air. Too late. The Woodwards had gone. He tucked it regretfully in his waistcoat pocket. Perhaps some other time.

Mr Frederick slipped into working at Carter-Woodward's as smoothly as a hot knife through butter. Slightly built and with mousy brown hair, nature had designed him to be unobtrusive. Always neat in his grey suit and gleaming black shoes, he sat with his back to the office doors of Edward, Mr Woodward and Jenny. His desk with its black and gold typewriter was the focal point of the first-floor landing.

Mr Woodward soon mastered the new way of working. In the morning he supplied Mr Frederick with his decisions and left the younger man to mould them into polite, business-like letters. Mr Frederick would ask a few questions and write some squiggles in his notebook. Later he would present the typed letters for signature. There was not an 'I beg to remain' or 'Your obedient servant' in sight.

Jenny found the prospect of having a man sit and write down her words unnerving. She soon convinced Mr Frederick that standard letters would be more efficient. They agreed on the wording of a series of letters to late payers. Each one a little more forceful than the previous. All they had to do was fill in the dates and the amounts. There were increasingly ominous threats for determined non-payers. Between them they updated Mr Samuel's old-fashioned style. Mr Frederick would look up at the grubby skylight above their heads as he listened to Jenny's suggestions. As time passed and their trust in each other grew, Jenny took to bringing some of her more complicated calculations for him to check before she risked showing them to a wider audience. Men so love to point out any error found in a woman's work.

One morning Edward was summoned urgently to the coal mine. The barometer had dropped; there were concerns about the ventilation in the pit. He went to supervise the taking of necessary measurements. On his return, hot and grimy, he climbed the spiral staircase. What he saw at the top took the wind out of him. Jenny and Mr Frederick were sitting with their heads close together over a document.

Mr Frederick, as neat and dapper as ever rose politely to his feet. Jenny looked up to see Edward, his shirt sleeves rolled up and a shocked look on his face.

'Are you all right? Is something wrong at the pit?' she blurted out.

'No. All well there. No casualties, thank the Lord.' He wiped a grimy hand across his face. 'It was hot down there. I'm fine.' Edward was not telling the truth. He was suddenly cold and felt he had been kicked in the stomach.

'Thank God,' said Mr Frederick. He wafted his fingers skywards to show respect for the Almighty.

Jenny recovered her documents – and her composure. 'Would you like some tea, Mr Carter? You look as if you could do with some.' She was pleased to see him grin and nod her a yes. He showed her his grubby hands and mimed washing them. Speech seemed to be beyond him.

It was Mr Frederick who went to put the kettle on.

In the cloakroom Edward washed off the worst of the coal dust. It had given him a turn, seeing Jenny so close and so comfortable with Mr Frederick. He cursed his stupidity in agreeing to employ the man. Of course, he would fall for Jenny. Any man would. He looked at his reflection in the mirror above the sink and raked his fingers through his hair. 'Go carefully,' he told his mottled image as the words of the solicitor he had secretly consulted came to his mind. He checked his appearance before leaving the cloakroom. Not as neat as Mr Frederick, but it would have to do.

Three mugs of tea sat beside Mr Frederick's typewriter. Edward took his by the handle and waved it at the grubby skylight.

'I'll send a boy up to get that clean. Can't think why we've put up with it so long."

'I see you managed to keep the cloakroom for yourself.' Mavis told Jenny and several other ladies sitting in the Cozy Corner café, as she flapped about, moving her chair and pleating her skirts to fit under the table in the tea shop. She gave Jenny's shoulder a playful shove.

'All part of my secret plan to get a better rate for the job,' said Jenny. 'You'll be grateful when you come to your senses and decide to come and work for us.'

'How much more exactly?' Mavis slapped her gloves and the question on the table like a challenge.

Jenny avoided answering. Better to keep the exact amount from Mavis. 'You had your chance. One day perhaps. If Mr Frederick leaves.'

'Is that likely?'

'Not very.'

'Oh well! In that case you can pay for the tea again. I'm saving up for a house, remember.'

Jenny tried to guess how much it cost to buy a house and was annoyed to discover that she had no idea. At work she had at her fingertips the hourly rates for each grade of worker, the price of copper and the cost of corn for the pit ponies. At home she knew the exact price of a loaf, a pint of milk or 4 ounces of tea. But a house? Her mind went an annoying blank. It took her a moment to reason it out. She did not know the cost of housing because respectable girls never lived alone. They lived with their father until they went to live with their husband. In the event of accidents, any handy male relative had to take them in. Mavis and her mother were different. They had no male relative to guarantee their respectability.

'How much does it cost? A house, I mean?'

'More than £100.'

Jenny spluttered over her tea with shock. When she recovered she did some calculations. She added Mavis's wages from the Post Office to the pittance earned by her dressmaker mother. It would take some serious economy for the two women to accumulate anything approaching £100. Jenny wondered how much Mavis had actually managed to tuck away. The thought of her own good fortune made her generous. She ordered two toasted teacakes.

Mavis set about her food with a will. As she ate, Jenny studied her friend. Once again, she wore colourful accessories to soften her sober working clothes. The cosmetics were discreet, but they were clearly there – a trace of pink on the napkin gave the game away. She was sure Mavis had lampblack on her eyelashes, something Jenny never dared to do though she had read about it in magazines. Strangely, the effect of the cosmetics was to make Mavis look older. Jenny looked like a girl while Mavis looked like a woman.

Mavis gave a contented sigh as she finished the teacake. 'Another 6 months. Then I'll be able to afford my own teacake. It's a good job I've got a foolproof plan for getting my dowry,' said Mavis with a cheerful grin.

'Which is?'

'That'd be telling.' Mavis touched a finger to her lips and shook her head to show that she was determined to keep her secret. To divert Jenny's attention she suddenly demanded, 'Tell me about this Mr Frederick, Jenny, the one you're not sharing your cloakroom with.'

Jenny found herself curiously reluctant to discuss her new friend. 'He's nice. He's very efficient. Very polite. Very quiet.'

'Just like me,' said Mavis and guffawed loudly.

Signor Martelli patted his left-hand waistcoat pocket for reassurance. Ever since he had failed to give his business card to Dorothea's father, he made sure that one was always within easy reach. With one swift movement he could press the words 'Franco Martelli Impresario' into the hand of any promising musician he came across. The rectangles of pasteboard had done sterling work. Six sopranos, four contraltos and several tenors, all fine singers, were now his clients. He had lost count of the mediocre choral singers and humdrum piano players on his books.

Today was different. Today he was in pursuit of a real star, someone with that special talent to wrap the audience in magic and make their senses tingle. He was going to persuade, seduce, inveigle – there was no single word to describe the complicated process he envisaged – someone he was confident he could mould and direct into a stellar career. His target was Dorothea Woodward.

Signor Martelli had taken care to provide himself with a powerful ally on this mission. To approach a family of such standing as the Woodwards, he needed more than some successful placements in the music halls and a growing reputation with the provincial opera houses. What he wanted was the support of an organisation of substance and reputation. Now he had found one.

On his visits to theatres, he sometimes found the piano with its lid raised and its innards exposed. The air would be full of strange noises while a man with a tuning fork and the precision of a surgeon tweaked the strings to return the instrument to perfect pitch. The man would invariably be blind. It did not take Signor Martelli long to discover where the blind piano tuners learned their exacting profession. It was at Henshaw's Asylum for the Blind, a respected charity with an enviable reputation for the musical education it provided. Their students not only tuned pianos, they also mastered the art of playing them. The complicated organs of churches bowed to the commands of their swift fingers and flying feet, and the Henshaw's choirs made the rafters ring in many a church and place of worship.

Signor Martelli tapped the breast pocket of his jacket and was reassured by the faint crackle of paper. Close to his heart he carried a letter from Henshaw's commissioning him to arrange a concert in Manchester to raise funds. There was also a note from Mr Woodward agreeing to a meeting that afternoon.

Mr Woodward had chosen a time when his wife, daughter and grandchildren would be out making social calls. He wanted to vet Signor Martelli in private first. His desire to please his beloved Dorothea was strong, but his suspicion of foreigners, especially flamboyant musical ones, ran deep.

The sweat of mental effort ran down Signor Martelli's back as he presented himself to Mr Woodward in his study. He stood as stiff as a soldier with his arms clamped to his sides. He knew that these northern men of business did not take kindly to operatic gestures. As serious as an undertaker presenting a bill, he smoothed out the letter from Henshaw's and slid it across the desk. Mr Woodward read the letter and then took it to the window and held it up to the light to inspect the watermark as if checking for a forgery.

Whilst Mr Woodward pretended to know about paper manufacture Signor Martelli took the opportunity to describe the great concert he planned. There would be a full orchestra, two separate choirs of men and women, not all of them blind. The music would range from simple traditional songs to full choral works. The works of the mighty Handel would be included of course. For practical reasons the choir of blind children would provide the final act of the first half of the concert; they could not be kept longer from their beds.

At this point Signor Martelli's discipline snapped. He leapt to his feet and waved his arms. 'There is nothing in this world more touching than the sound of children's voices, so pure and sweet, singing about the baby Jesus. And then you remember that these poor innocent children cannot see.' He produced a white handkerchief and wiped his eyes. It took several deep breaths, juddering through his huge chest before he could continue.

'So, you see the problem, dear Mr Woodward. What can we offer after the angel voices of children? There has to be a decent interval for refreshments.' Signor Martelli was careful to refer to refreshments rather than drinks for the famously teetotal Mr Woodward. 'When that is over, we must have something exciting, something electrifying to offer the audience. Otherwise, they will all go home to an early bed.'

Mr Woodward could see nothing wrong with an early finish, but continued to listen to Signor Martelli. The ambitious impresario explained why the final act was so important. 'If it is mediocre, the audience leave feeling glum and disappointed. They hurry past the collection boxes with their heads down and their eyes on the floor. We do not want that, Mr Woodward, do we?' Signor Martelli held out his hands in appeal as he provided the answer to his own question. 'No, we want them uplifted by beautiful music, their hearts singing with joy and generosity. There is only one person in the whole city who has the skill, the artistry and the voice to touch their emotions and send their hands into their pockets. And that is Miss Dorothea. It has to be Miss Dorothea. I saw her do it at the school concert. It is a rare gift. She can do it again in a full-size Manchester theatre. I will provide the support of the best musicians the city has to offer.' Signor Martelli sank into his chair. A good showman, he knew when to stop.

Mr Woodward gazed unseeing out of the window, his head filled with the memory of Dorothea's smile after she had sung in the *Messiah*. He didn't see her smiling very often these days in spite of the money he lavished on music teachers and piano lessons. Much as he liked Dorothea to be happy, there was something in him that baulked at her performing on the public stage in Manchester, as if she was an actress, a notoriously rackety profession. He could not forget the last time he had launched her into the world beyond Atherley. The gossips had certainly not forgotten. They would shake their heads and remind each other of the rushed marriage and the brief pregnancy. He went to sit behind his desk and stared into space as he considered the problem.

A frown crinkled Signor Martelli's brow as he asked, 'Do you think there is a chance that Miss Dorothea will help with this good cause?'

Mr Woodward cleared his throat. 'Perhaps I should bring you up to date, Mr Martelli.' He refused to call him Signor. 'Miss Dorothea is no longer Miss Dorothea. She is married.' He skipped hastily on to the next bit. 'She is Mrs Carter now and the mother of twins.'

'Oh.' The little Italian sank down onto his seat, his stomach resting on his knees. Had he wasted all his honeyed words on the wrong man?

Mr Woodward was busy with some rapid thinking. Dorothea did not know that he was meeting her old music master or why. If – or rather when – she discovered he had denied her the chance to perform in a Manchester theatre, his life would not be worth living. He was saved by the sound of a car arriving. Edward was back from work.

'Ah! This will be her husband. He may have reservations about his wife taking such a public role. Let us find out what he thinks about this business.'

As was his custom, Edward came straight to his father-in-law's study to bring him up to date with events at work. For once Mr Woodward was not interested in business. He commanded Signor Martelli to repeat his proposal. The impresario ran quickly through the main points: the plight of blind children, the beauty of Dorothea's voice and the possible benefit that would result if she were persuaded to perform in public.

When he finished Edward looked at the two men, his eyes flicking from face to face as he tried to read their minds. The rotund little Italian sat silent and tense, ready to explode into action. The normally decisive Mr Woodward had a woolly messianic look about him.

It was clear to Edward that both men wanted Dorothea to sing at the concert. Mr Martelli had set out his reasons, but Mr Woodward had not. He was too modest to admit that he wanted the world to share his boundless adoration of his daughter and her dazzling talent, but he had tried to step beyond the boundaries of Atherley before and it had all gone wrong.

Traditionally, when a father led his daughter down the aisle responsibility for her welfare passed to the husband. Edward saw exactly what his father-in-law was doing. He wanted Edward to give permission for Dorothea to take this daring leap into unknown territory so he would bear the blame if it all went wrong. In effect his father-in-law had handed him a bomb, primed to explode. He tossed it from hand to hand as he worked out what to do with it. He looked at the two men in front of him, then inspiration struck him. He decided to lob the bomb back at them.

'What does Dorothea say? Surely her opinion is the most important thing?'

Signor Martelli exhaled with relief and bobbed about with delight; he was sure that Dorothea would agree. Mr Woodward felt a burden drop from his shoulders; he would be spared Dorothea's wrath. He rang the bell and summoned the cheery maid to go and find Dorothea. The sound of the piano made it clear where she was.

The words, 'Your father would like to see you in his study straightaway,' made Dorothea jump from the piano stool. The memory of her many trespasses ran through her mind. The dressmakers' bills. The truancy from school. The servants slapped. Worst of all the pregnancy. At the door she turned and looked to the normally cheery maid for reassurance. She got none. Just a solemn face and a slow shake of the head to refuse any further information. When her mistress had gone, the maid's face broke into a satisfied smile. Let the bad-tempered brat sweat for a bit. She'd caused enough trouble in her time. The maid looked forward to finding out what exactly was going on at the servants' supper that evening.

Once she understood the reason for her summons, Dorothea said, 'Yes. Yes. Yes.' She smiled on Signor Martelli and embraced her father. 'The time has come, Papa, for me to stop practising and start performing. You will see that all the money you spent on those teachers was not wasted.'

They tackled the practical matters, discussing dates and times and possible venues for rehearsal. Signor Martelli explained they would have to take place in Manchester.

'We had better warn Higgs, he is going to be busy,' said Mr Woodward and pulled a face. He was sure his wife would complain at losing her jolly afternoon jaunts in the car with the twins.

It was left to Edward to ask, 'And what about Clare and Issy?' He did not really think the children would miss their mother, as they seldom saw her, but he thought it important that they should be considered.

'Thank God for Nanny.' Dorothea's voice throbbed with genuine gratitude. With Nanny's help and co-operation she could make this venture a triumphant success without those beastly brats clinging to her skirts and dragging her down. 'Now I think about it I'll just pop up to the nursery for a chat with Nanny. Let her know what's going on.'

Before she left, she held out her hand for Signor Martelli to kiss. Her heart gave a little skip as his lips brushed her knuckles; it was a sensation she had not felt since her time at finishing school.

When they were alone, Edward brought his boss up to date on events at work. Mr Woodward made a few suggestions, but his heart wasn't in it.

43

'Sorry I didn't warn you about Signor Martelli. I wanted to check him out first. Before Dorothea got wind of it. She doesn't take disappointment well.'

Edward managed to keep his face straight at this massive understatement. Dorothea's tantrums were legendary. 'Quite right,' said Edward. 'This way she got a wonderful surprise.'

Dorothea was not the only one to get a surprise that day.

Edward was in his room unbuttoning his shirt when the cheery maid arrived with the hot water — and a mission. She had decided to redress the balance of the Carters' marriage. As he struggled with a sleeve, she claimed one of the buttons on his shirt cuff was caught on a thread. She came to prise it free, standing close and contriving for his hand to rest on her breasts. It took a lot gentle manoeuvring to coax his arm out of the sleeve and the rest of his shirt soon followed.

Edward was now in his early twenties, eating well at the Woodward's table and working hard. It showed in his physique. The maid found his shoulders irresistible and massaged them with her hands. He made no protest.

Soon their bodies and their breath were entwined as they were both gripped by a sudden animal lust. There were no murmured endearments, no protestations of affection, just voracious kisses and the grunts and groans of intense pleasure. Suddenly the maid raised her head to look him in the eyes. 'I don't talk.' she said. She took his strangled silence as agreement and plunged her hand into his trousers where matters proved satisfactory. Edward wasted no more time before pressing her against the wall and lifting up her skirts.

When it was finished, and she was busily rearranging her dress and tucking her breasts back in her corset, she turned business-like. 'No-one's got me up the duff yet — and there's several have tried — so you are safe there. I am not a professional,' she warned him. 'Just one gentleman at a time. That's not to say the odd 10 bob note wouldn't go amiss.'

She picked up the hot water jug, dropped him a curtsy and asked, 'Will that be all, sir?'

'For the moment.'

CHAPTER 5

As well as being a Methodist, Mr Woodward was a practical man. He saved his prayers for times of desperate need such as flooding in the colliery, his wife's nervous collapse or a sudden rise in the price of cotton. By far the most frequent cause to send him to his knees, calling on his Maker for help, was Dorothea. Her extravagance, her lies, and her disregard for society's rules had regularly made him question his faith and wring his hands in wordless despair.

This Sunday morning, he put on his best suit and looked through the window at the blue sky. It had rained in the night so the air felt fresh and newly washed. Down in the valley, Atherley, blessedly free of its usual pall of black smoke, gleamed as the sun dried the rain from the roofs. His wife smiled as she presided at the breakfast table. His son-in-law put down his knife and fork and started to rise from his chair. Mr Woodward waved a hand to show him that the mark of respect was not necessary. The younger man had carried the burden of the business the entire week; he deserved to eat his bacon and eggs without interruption.

'Dorothea having her breakfast in bed?' asked Mr Woodward as he took the top off his boiled egg. 'Good. She must save her strength for the concert next Saturday.' He beamed round the table. The yolk was runny as he liked it. Nothing could dent his good humour. And this was how it had been for weeks. Harmony had ruled in the Woodward household, ever since Dorothea had started rehearsing for the concert for Henshaw's.

There had been a tricky moment when it dawned on Mrs Woodward that Higgs and the car would be taking Dorothea to Manchester on most days. Nanny had resolved the problem by suggesting a hansom cab for afternoons out. The children had fallen in love with the horse and were busy growing carrots for him. Now they pulled faces of disappointment when they found they were to travel by car.

At first Mr Woodward claimed the right of the backer to attend rehearsals. After all he was the man providing the money and his suspicion of Signor Martelli ran deep, however as the weeks went by he saw how happy Dorothea was. She argued with Signor Martelli sometimes, over phrasing or the choice of music, but not for long. Never once did she flounce off or throw things. Perhaps it was the presence of so many blind people, reminding her of how lucky she was to be able to see.

When he judged Mr Woodward sufficiently mellowed, Signor Martelli started to give a young tenor from the choir more opportunities to sing alone. 'He is good is he not?' he would ask and look round for agreement. 'I am hoping he will be noticed. There will be talent scouts in the audience.' Dorothea said nothing but tucked his words away in her memory as he intended she should. He tapped the side of his nose and winked at her. 'I have taken the precaution of signing him as a client first.'

So subtly did he work that Mr Woodward, kept his reservations about his daughter singing a love duet with the young tenor for the finale to himself. He did, however, after much throat clearing confide to Edward, 'I should warn you, there's some kissing at the end. He's not a bad looking chap. But blind of course.'

Mr Woodward underestimated Neville's physical charms: he was strikingly good-looking, with chiselled features, wavy brown hair and the body of a Greek athlete.

Edward pursed his lips and looked thoughtful until his father-in-law hurriedly added, 'I think she dies soon afterwards. Opera doesn't have many happy endings you know.'

Edward let his face clear. His mind was working through the three things beginning with C that the lawyer had told him to avoid at all costs. Could allowing his wife to kiss a man on stage count as collusion? Or conniving? He thought not. After all her father was present. He frowned as he struggled to remember the last of the three Cs.

The weeks of rehearsal passed with a pleasant sense of achievement. Elaborate travel arrangements were made for the day of the concert so all the members of the family could share in what they hoped would be a triumph for Dorothea. She had worked hard for it. Mr Woodward had booked a compartment for Nanny, the two nursemaids and his grandchildren to travel in comfort by train to Manchester. Clare and Izzy were excited by their first journey by rail. At Manchester Victoria they took a horse-drawn cab to the theatre. They were to leave at the end of the first half, as would the blind children who sang in the choir.

Higgs drove Dorothea and her mother and father to the theatre. There Dorothea found herself in possession of a real theatre dressing room for the first time. It was disappointingly drab and dingy but nonetheless thrilling. If I was singing in an opera, thought Dorotha, there would be bouquets of flowers and glasses of champagne. Men would come to kiss my hand and beg to take me to supper. As it was, her mother produced a packet of sandwiches and a flask of tea. Signor Martelli arrived, overflowing with compliments and airy kisses. He quickly transformed it from a Sunday school picnic into a theatrical first night. Edward arrived with red roses, which earned him a peck on the cheek. It had been Mr Frederick's suggestion; he knew that flowers for the leading lady were a well-established convention.

The concert went exactly as Signor Martelli planned. He played on the audience's emotions, by beginning gently and alternating sad songs with cheerful dance tunes. Dressed in black with a white collar, Dorothea blended in obediently with the Henshaw's women's choir. The innocent voices of the children's choir shredded the audience's heartstrings and dampened their handkerchiefs. They flocked to the refreshments and the sociable chatter of the interval to recover their composure. Afterwards the male choir sang sea shanties and stamped their feet. When they trooped off, the stage went dark while the scenery was shifted. The light returned to reveal a moonlit garden, the haunting strains of the violin hinted at something altogether deeper and more passionate to come.

Dorothea, no longer an anonymous member of the choir, wore a ball gown in her favourite scarlet. Neville wore evening dress with the nonchalance of a man born with a silver spoon in his mouth as well as a golden voice. Though they sang in Italian the audience could tell they were guilty lovers, irresistibly drawn together, only to

48

spring apart at the gnawing of their consciences, their movements mirroring the ebb and flow of the music.

Signor Martelli had rehearsed them well, counting the strides for the blind tenor and building into the routine little touches on his arm by Dorothea to ensure that he took the right direction. What he had not rehearsed in Mr Woodward's presence was the final passionate embrace. As the last notes died away the tenor found Dorothea's lips with unerring precision. The kiss was taken up with apparent enthusiasm by both singers. The audience held their breath while an intense silence took possession of the auditorium. It hung quivering in the air like a shard of ice. Then it broke and the applause started. There were raw shouts from men who knew no other way to express their emotion. They were all aware they had just experienced something very special.

Mr and Mrs Woodward sat in shocked silence as they watched the audience file out. The steady clink of coins in the collection boxes and the verdict of 'Best concert ever,' rang in the air. They were stunned by the power Dorothea had unleashed. Sturdy, stubby Higgs escorted them to the car. There he wrapped them in rugs and passed on the good reports he had overheard on the street. 'They are saying there are two new stars in the sky over Manchester,' he told them.

From his seat in the circle, Edward watched and wondered what a real husband would feel. He did not love Dorothea; he did not even like her very much, and he felt no jealousy of the tenor. He could kiss Dorothea to his heart's content. But a new sensation was growing in him with regard to his wife. It was small, gnarled and stunted but he recognised it for what it was. It was respect. This evening did not just happen; she had worked for it.

Edward had come straight from work in his business suit. The doorman led him backstage and dropped a word of advice in his ear. He could see that Edward was not a regular at the theatre and might not realise what a triumph tonight's concert had been. On such occasions, he hinted, it was usual to have champagne. For a consideration the doorman offered to arrange this traditional refreshment. Edward passed him some cash and asked, 'Any chance of a sandwich?'

Dorothea's dressing room looked like a painting. The black and white evening clothes of the men contrasted with two great splashes of red – the roses and Dorothea's dress. Edward felt as out of place as a dog at his master's funeral. Signor Martelli and the tenor, Neville, had come to congratulate Dorothea. Several ambitious singers from the choir had come along in the hope of being noticed by the little Italian impresario. The air was loud with men's voices and the clink of glasses as they toasted the new diva. She grew radiant from their praise while Edward fell upon his ham sandwich and accepted the doorman's offer of what proved to be a very expensive paper of chips.

After he scraped the last chip from the greaseproof paper Edward turned his attention to the champagne in his glass. It was his first taste of the legendary wine and it was likely to be his last. Dorothea's father would not let a theatrical tradition take precedence over the word of the Lord. He would be appalled to see his daughter drinking champagne with her plentiful bosom on display. It was ironic that most of the men in the room could not enjoy the sight.

Edward felt it was his responsibility to call an end to the proceedings. He took a breath and was about to warn Dorothea that her parents had left earlier and would worry when he was saved by a tap on the door. The guide had come to help the blind singers to their lodgings. Somehow the glasses were collected and a line was deftly arranged so that each man had a hand on the shoulder of the man in front.. The tenor was last to leave. In the corridor his smile flashed bright in the darkness that meant nothing to him.

Signor Martelli was deep in conversation with Dorothea when she rose to leave. 'Remember,' he said and wagged a finger at her. Edward wrapped her in a shawl and packed her into the car without protest; she was still in the golden afterglow of her performance and the champagne. Her trance-like state lasted for several miles. Then Edward spoke. 'You were amazing on stage, Dorothea.'

The storm broke. 'I know, I know,' she screamed and beat her face and breast with her fists. 'You don't need to tell me. I know. I know.'

Edward drove on while she raged and sobbed. Even Dorothea ran out of breath eventually. After the anger came the complaints. She would be so much better if she could work with professionals, take acting lessons, be free to take bookings, live in the city instead of being brought home like a child from school. The list went on. She did not cite her parents and her children as drags and impediments to her singing. Even Dorothea retained enough Victorian training to be wary of exploding the myth of the wife and mother as the angel on the hearth.

Her rage exhausted, Dorothea, fell into a fitful sleep. Edward peered into the darkness at the road ahead. Once out of the city the roads were conveniently empty and inconveniently dark. There must be a way out of this, he thought.

When they next met Edward gave the Woodwards a heavily censored account of the after-performance celebrations. He concentrated on the praise lavished on Dorothea by the members of the blind choir. 'They said that she was a Diva. Apparently that's high praise indeed.' They looked at him doubtfully. He asked how much money had been raised. The final figures were not in but Mr Woodward was optimistic.

Edward set about finding evidence to support the new direction he planned to take. Two Manchester newspapers mentioned Dorothea's debut with warm praise. The cuttings passed from hand to hand at the Woodward dining table. 'A fine voice' and 'an impressive stage presence.' Her mother complained that the tenor had more column inches and her father explained that was only to be expected. When the grand total of the funds raised came in Mr Woodward was gratified to find it was a record amount for Henshaw's. A daughter kissing on the stage no longer seemed so outrageous. Money talks.

After the success of the Henshaw's concert Edward consciously changed his behaviour. At family meals he would make a point of asking Dorothea if she had any more engagements or offers from Mr Martelli. Would tuition in acting help? Should the piano be tuned? There was a concert at the Free Trade Hall. Would she like to go? Would her parents like to accompany them?

51

The answer to these questions was frequently, 'Yes,' or, 'Yes, please,' if the children were within earshot; Nanny was very strict about 'please' and 'thank you'. The household soon became accustomed to Dorothea travelling to Manchester. If anyone queried the purpose of her visit, she would claim she was going for coaching for her voice or her acting. If her mother raised her eyebrows preparatory to asking awkward questions about chaperons and the avoidance of scandal, the mention of Henshaw's smoothed her brow and closed her lips. It was not long before the name of Mr Martelli had the same effect, so closely had he become associated with that admirable institution. With unaccustomed tact Dorothea refrained from referring to him as Signor Martelli when she was in her father's house. There he was always Mr Martelli.

It was not often that Dorothea joined the rest of the Woodward family at the breakfast table; she preferred a tray in bed. Her appearance early one morning therefore piqued their curiosity.

'I have an important meeting in Manchester,' she explained. She turned to the cheery maid who was busy pouring tea. 'Tell Higgs that I'll be leaving in an hour. Get my best suit ready and make sure my blouse is pressed. Then you can come and help me with my hair.' The maid went off to do her bidding. She soon returned to whisper a message into Mr Woodward's ear. He leapt from his chair and gestured for Edward to follow him. The cheery maid disappeared into the kitchen to refresh the teapot and avoid answering the question Dorothea was sure to ask.

'What on earth is going on?' demanded Dorothea of her mother, the toast rack and the empty air. She continued to demand explanations until male voices in animated discussion announced the return of her husband and her father. They had taken their jackets off and rolled up their shirt sleeves and were looking annoyingly cheerful as they told her the car would not be going anywhere today. They were enjoying the belief that they had correctly diagnosed a problem that had defeated Higgs. Diagnosed, but not cured. A vital spare part was needed before the car would work again.

Dorothea did some quick thinking. She turned to Edward. 'You can take me to Manchester in your car.'

'That depends,' he countered. 'Perhaps be best if I use my car to go for the spare part.' He watched her eyebrows lunge into a scowl before adding casually, 'I could take you to the station. You could catch the train.' He watched the dismay grow on her face before he turned to his father-in-law for his opinion. He wanted to show Dorothea that he was not a paid chauffeur and the car in question belonged to him, not her father.

Dorothea tutted at the thought of travelling by train like an ordinary mortal. Her father looked at the ceiling and gave the impression of thinking hard. It was a sham, a doomed exercise in saving face.

'Well,' he drawled, 'if you, Edward, take Dorothea to the station, afterwards you could go to check the drainage in number three shaft. I don't want to leave it any longer.' He looked for and found Edward's approving grin. 'In that case I will have a leisurely morning here with the accounts. Then if the weather's fine we'll get a hansom cab and take *your* children for a drive, Dorothea.'

His daughter ignored the emphasis on 'your' as completely as she ignored her children. She buttered a piece of toast, confident that she would at least get to Manchester though not by chauffeur-driven car. Mrs Woodward, emboldened by her husband's failure to agree instantly to Dorothea's request, joined the fray.

'Exactly what kind of business takes you to Manchester? Usually people write a letter or come to the house if they want you for a concert.'

Dorothea finished chewing her toast. 'If you must know, and I suppose you must,' she looked round the table, 'I am going to meet Mr Martelli. He says that he has several professional engagements lined up for me. Well paid ones. We are going to discuss them over lunch.'

'Where?' demanded Mrs Woodward.

'At a restaurant. It is a public place. It is perfectly acceptable behaviour in Manchester. There is no need for a chaperon.' What she did not say, was that the restaurant was in the very hotel where Mr Martelli was spending his nights. Mrs Woodward was busy choking on her tea. The cheery maid thumped her between the shoulder blades while enjoying every minute of the family drama unfolding before her eyes.

'Does this restaurant have a name?' Edward was deceptively casual. It had better not be The Midland, was the thought thrumming in his brain. He had it in his mind to take Jenny to the famous new hotel, reputed to have cost a million pounds. He didn't want Dorothea to be the first there.

Dorothea shrugged, 'I've got it written down somewhere.' She downed a cup of tea and rose to her feet. At her full height she was a commanding figure. She looked round the three silent faces at the table; the challenge in her gaze was unmistakeable.

'Lay out my dark grey suit,' she told the cheery maid. 'Then I'll want you to do my hair.'

Mr Woodward, seeing the determination in her face, was seized by a sudden panic. His darling girl, in Manchester, alone except for some foreign music master. He avoided catching Edward's eye. Too late to ask him to go with her; a man has his pride. There was one commodity that had solved most of Dorothea's problems in the past. Perhaps it would help today. 'Do you have enough money?' he asked her.

'Oh. I forgot about that.' She flapped her hands, the very picture of female helplessness.

'Come to the study, you silly girl.' He shepherded her to his study, where he rummaged in his desk drawer as he worked through her likely expenses. 'There's your train fare. You will need a cab. You can always send a telegram.' From his desk he took a roll of sovereigns wrapped in paper and pressed it into her hand. 'Do be careful, dear girl.'

'I will, papa.' Dorothea knew he was not urging economy on her. His sole concern was for the safety of her person.

In the dining room Mrs Woodward warned of scandal. 'A married woman in a restaurant without her husband! I never heard of such a thing. You must go with her, Edward.'

'No. I will do no such thing. I will go to my work. Let Dorothea have her way. She has worked for these professional engagements.

I doubt she'll ever earn her own living. She'll soon find out which side her bread is buttered.'

Dorothea heard him from the hallway. She touched the roll of sovereigns in her pocket. Her bread for today was thoroughly buttered. 'I'm going up to get ready, Edward. I won't be long.'

Edward nodded but did not move. A woman's hair could take an inordinate amount of time. He sent a maid for more bacon. When he had finished eating it he strolled off, whistling.

'It's a pity she is not more maternal,' said Mrs Woodward to her husband.

'Is it?' wondered Mr Woodward. He was looking forward to a leisurely afternoon in a carriage behind a horse, with his two grandchildren bouncing along beside him, marvelling at the birds, the trees, the world as they jogged along. His wife had the same thought. Their faces softened into fond smiles.

CHAPTER 6

Edward wandered round the paddock whistling happily and dashing off a mental sketch of the house he would one day build there. No point in going into detail until he could share his ideas with Jenny. Once he started to think of her he found that his legs carried him an unexpectedly long way from the house. Dorothea needed the full power of her highly trained voice to summon him back to fulfil his promise to take her to the railway station.

Edward had to make several attempts at swinging the starting handle before the engine decided to start. Dorothea's bad temper was proving contagious to machinery. He climbed in next to his impatient wife.

'Don't fret,' he told her, 'I'll get you to the station in no time.' He put his foot on the accelerator and roared off. A glance out of the side of his eye showed a spasm of terror on her face. He grinned with pleasure. Her eyes popped but she didn't scream. He'd give her full marks for that. A proper husband would quiz her about her rendezvous with Mr Martelli. Edward kept silent, though for all he knew he was speeding her on her way to cuckolding him that very afternoon. His indifference to that possibility was complete. He felt no emotional tie to his wife. They had a contract and he kept his side of it. The rewards were considerable. Not only was he a man of wealth, but he still had the friendship – as he called it – of Jenny and the cheery maid provided him with consolation of another kind. A smile flittered across his face as he recalled his first encounter with her; she had been very business-like.

'What are you smiling at?' demanded Dorothea as he pulled in at the station.

'Ah! If only there was time to tell you. You'll have to rush to catch your train.' There were no pecks at cheeks, no lingering glances of farewell. Dorothea headed straight to the ticket office and Edward turned his car towards his work and wondered where to get the spare part and if the drainage in number 3 shaft was as bad as Mr Woodward feared.

56

In a modest restaurant on Deansgate, Signor Martelli, as everyone in his adopted city called him, looked appraisingly at Dorothea. Bad temper had brought a flush to her cheeks and the light of battle to her eyes. She'd had great hopes of this meeting; Signor Martelli had talked of signing contracts for appearances and duets with Neville, the blind tenor. Now her whole day was going wrong. The car not starting. The train crowded. The long queue for a cab at Victoria station. The ordinariness of the restaurant and the subdued nature of Signor Martelli's greeting. No cries of 'Bellissima' and no flamboyant kissing of her hand. And now he was examining her like a specimen in a laboratory.

'Have a glass of wine, dear lady. It will help you recover your spirits. I want to talk seriously about your career.'

The word 'career' electrified Dorothea. No-one had ever used that word to her before. She took a swig of the wine. Given her Methodist upbringing it was an act of revolution. The effect on her was immediate. She heard Signor Martelli's voice in her ear, but she did not listen. The details of fees, venues and dates floated past the woolly cloud that was her mind at that moment. The only part with real significance for her was the chance to sing in concerts with Neville. Signor Martelli explained that Neville had signed, and the pianist and the venues were booked. The only doubts he entertained were for Dorothea. Such a nuisance she was married and had children.

'This is only the beginning,' he assured her. He pulled out the contract and laid it on the table in front of her. 'You have discussed this with your family?' he enquired. 'It is a legally binding contract.'

'Of course,' she lied and promptly signed. She would have signed it in her own blood if asked.

Now that he had landed his fish Signor Martelli looked at his catch with satisfaction. She was beautiful, even in that depressing colour she was wearing. Her breasts when displayed in an evening gown were magnificent, but you can have too much of a good thing. How to raise such a delicate matter? He took a breath and started.

'These concerts will bring you to the eye of men with influence and with power. You have natural beauty.' Dorothea sensed the

'But' that was coming. 'You must exploit it. There is fierce competition among sopranos.'

'You're saying I need a bit of polish.' Dorothea looked down at her sober suit. Perfect for going to chapel of a Sunday in Atherley, but not exactly stylish.

'You should wear strong colours. Fitted close.' He made the shape of an hourglass with his hands. She understood the unspoken message. Where had her 18-inch waist gone? Those wretched babies were responsible for that. They had put pounds on her. She remembered her time at finishing school where they had put her on small portions and plucked her eyebrows. She put down her knife and fork and pushed her plate to one side.

'And the eyebrows?' she asked. He nodded.

'Perhaps even a little maquillage,' he suggested. 'The stage lights can be very draining.' She showed her agreement.

When she rose to leave he gave her a copy of her contract. She pushed it into her pocket where it met the roll of sovereigns that her father had given her. Her brain swirled as she walked out on to the street, surrounded by the smart shops of Manchester with money in her pocket. A dizzying combination.

She strolled round the department stores and studied the other women. It was a humiliating experience. She looked like the country cousin who had come to town for the day. She decided to buy nothing because in 6 weeks' time the new clothes would be too big for her. What she did buy was the maquillage Signor Martelli had suggested. It was safe to do that in the anonymity of the city. In Atherley it would be talked about for weeks.

As she wandered along, thinking about the pot of rouge that she had bought with her father's money, she bumped into a man emerging from an office on to the street. As he went through the necessary apologies and hat-raising she spotted the brass plate on the building behind him. Beneath several names was written SOLICITORS.

Dorothea revised her opinion of the day that had begun so badly. Perhaps fate was on her side after all. She strode in and requested an interview. A junior solicitor was available.

Within minutes she was sitting in an office with a sandy-haired young man who was shielded by a huge oak desk. He beamed at her; she was the most attractive woman he had seen for a long time. Such a pleasant interruption to a day of drafting wills, codicils and leases. He spotted the wedding ring and envied the husband. A lucky chap to have a wife so glowing with health and good looks. Whatever she had come for, it could not be a matrimonial problem. Women with marital difficulties usually had brutal husbands, withered faces and hidden bruises. They hung their heads to avoid his eyes and kneaded damp handkerchiefs with nervous fingers.

'How can I help?' he enquired.

Dorothea came directly to the point. 'You can tell me how I can be free of my husband.'

Shock made the young man cough and splutter. It took a large white handkerchief and a glass of water before his throat cleared. He swivelled his chair round to the window, while he recovered his composure. Ladies never began in such a business-like way. They had complaints, accusations and many attempts at justification to work through before the dreadful serpent of divorce was allowed to slip its flickering tongue into the conversation. This client had been direct. He would return the compliment. He swivelled his chair back to her and asked.

'Do you know if your husband has broken his marriage vows?'

Dorothea felt the need to be careful with her answer. Was it some kind of trick question? Better to avoid a straightforward Yes or No. She wondered which vow exactly the solicitor referred to and cast her mind back to the marriage ceremony. 'There was a lot about honouring,' she offered. 'And obeying.'

'That part is only for the bride,' said the solicitor without a trace of embarrassment. 'No-one expects a husband to obey'. He marvelled at his client's ignorance. 'What I need to know is whether your husband has committed adultery. You do know what that is?'

Dorothea did. She thought quickly. Was this the key to unlock the chains of her marriage? She decided to keep the possibility in play. 'I have serious suspicions,' she announced with all the conviction of the practised liar.

'If they prove to be true, then you have cleared the first hurdle,' said the solicitor. Dorothea gave a satisfied grin. It pained the solicitor to take the smile from her face.

'Unfortunately,' he paused to warn her of the bad news on its way, 'unfortunately, adultery alone is not enough to enable a wife to divorce a husband.' Dorothea took the bad news without flinching while the solicitor braced himself to ask the next question. 'Does he perform unnatural acts?' An uncomprehending Dorothea stared at the solicitor who grew pink with embarrassment. He saw no point in explaining in full detail at this stage so gave her a clue. 'It begins with B.'

Dorothea shook her head. The solicitor decided that was a No, not a Don't Know.

'Is he cruel to you? Does he beat you?'

Again Dorothea shook her head.

The solicitor sat back in his chair. 'That is the A B C of divorce,' he told her like a child learning her letters. 'Like the alphabet it starts with A. That is A for adultery. Once adultery is established we can start to look for other crimes to qualify you to divorce a husband. If he has not committed adultery, you simply cannot proceed against him. It is the *sine qua non* of the process.'

Dorothea did not know the Latin phrase but she saw that her way to dispose of Edward was blocked unless she could catch him in adultery. She scowled at the solicitor, her black eyebrows knitted into a basilisk stare. The solicitor scoured his mind for some small gift he could offer to mollify this angry goddess.

'Oh.' He jumped, like a man startled by a bright idea. 'There is one other solution to your dilemma.'

Dorothea leant forward eager to hear his suggestion.

'Of course, I cannot guarantee it will work,' he prevaricated. The young man was rapidly losing faith in what had seemed like a good idea at the time. 'Well,' he said, 'you could always commit adultery.' He batted the air with his hand to waft his words away, like some tiresome insect.

Dorothea pursed her lips as she gave his suggestion serious consideration. If adultery was the only escape route she would take it. The solicitor saw the direction her mind was taking and panicked.

'Forget I said that. The idea is absurd.' Did the silly girl not understand? Did she know nothing of the world? He spoke forcefully in an attempt to remedy his mistake. 'Adultery by a wife is the most heinous of crimes.' With all the force of a man in terror for his professional reputation, he marshalled the facts and set about explaining them.

'If you commit adultery your husband can and most probably will, divorce you. Adultery is the only grounds that a husband needs in order to dispose of a wife. There is no troublesome alphabet of offences to prove. Your adultery alone would be enough. No matter what cruelty you have endured at his hands, in the eyes of the law and the world, you will be the guilty party. You will be cast out to survive alone in a hostile society. Your children will be kept from you and your friends and family will most likely shun you.' He stabbed a finger at her. 'You will be the guilty party.' He sat back, mopped his brow and prayed he had convinced her not to follow the advice that had slipped inadvertently from his lips.

'I see,' said Dorothea. The guilty party. She had to admit that was a fair description of her part in the marriage. She rose to leave. The solicitor was temporarily bereft of words. Her hand was on the door handle when she turned round to ask, 'Do I have to provide proof? Is my word for it enough? Of the adultery, I mean.'

The solicitor was on his feet and coaxing her back to her chair. 'Not so hasty, my dear Mrs .. er'

'My name is not important.' Dorothea had given a false name to the clerk and could not now remember it.'

'Oh! but it is. Your name, or rather your reputation, is very important. A good name is vital for a lady. Ladies who lose their good name have unhappy and lonely lives. They are scorned by respectable society.' His voice throbbed with genuine concern. 'Forgive me. I spoke ill-advisedly. Let me explain. I do not wish to be responsible for your doing something rash that you will regret.' That was exactly what Dorothea had in mind but she forced herself to listen.

'As long as a husband has not condoned a wife's adultery, we can practically guarantee that the court will grant him a divorce if he applies for one.'

'Condoned?' asked Dorothea, 'what does that mean?'

'Forgiven. The husband must not accept back the guilty wife. Cannot allow her back into his home or,' he paused, 'into his bed.' The solicitor felt the need to spell out the details to this unworldly woman. He leant forward to stress the seriousness of his next remark. 'The man in question, the...er...guilty party is named in court.'

Dorothea was sure that her host at lunch would not find that an insuperable obstacle. He might even welcome a little notoriety. A pity he was so unattractive. Her mind turned to the handsome Neville. She smiled at the thought.

The solicitor could not believe his eyes. The woman had no sense of propriety. 'You do understand what damage naming the man causes. It gives the gossips material to work on. They wait with bated breath to see if the couple marry. Even if they do, they will always be second-class citizens. There will be thresholds they can never cross. They will never be received at court or by royalty.'

The solicitor examined Dorothea to check that she was properly appalled by the fate of the guilty wife. Finding no obvious sign of dismay he prepared to play his ace. 'No gentleman would put his wife through such an ordeal. Or his children.'

Is Edward a gentleman, wondered Dorothea. He'd never insisted on his 'rights' after the twins were born. That was how gentlemen were supposed to behave. But her father had bought Edward for her. Plucked him out of the filthy slums in exchange for half his empire.

'Children. There are children of the marriage?' The solicitor tapped the blotter on his desk with his pen to get her attention.

'Oh yes. Two.'

'You see,' he explained patiently. 'Adultery on the part of the wife calls the paternity of the children into question. No man wants that for his children. And mothers most certainly don't.'

Dorothea stood up and went to the window. In an attempt to divert herself from laughing she looked down at the pavement where people were going about their everyday business. If only this lawyer knew the truth about her children's parentage. That they were begotten by a Polish cavalry officer and part-time dancing teacher called Aleksy. She pulled a handkerchief from her pocket and passed it across her face to wipe away her grin. The solicitor saw the shaking of her shoulders and misinterpreted the emotion coursing through her. He thought she wept. He allowed himself a moment of triumph. At last. She was beginning to understand the absurdity of her desire to be rid of her so far blameless husband.

Dorothea suppressed the last of the mirth from her face and returned to her chair. 'You have told me the things that won't work. Now tell me something that will?'

'Most certainly. Your husband must admit to adultery. The other woman need not be named. As I have explained the adultery is just the starting point. Then we have to prove him guilty of some other unpleasant crime. There is a long list of them. Forgive me if I do not go into details at this stage. I will say only that they are activities best confined to the beasts of the field.'

He paused to gather his breath. Now he had skipped nicely over the embarrassing part he returned to his subject with vigour. 'Cruelty is your best hope. In my experience, cruelty is the least intrusive into intimate matters. But it must be severe cruelty. There should be witnesses, or visible evidence of injury. The one great advantage is that the wife appears blameless.'

'And if there is no other woman?' demanded Dorothea.

The solicitor shrugged his shoulder and held out his hands with the palms upwards to show he was helpless; he had no more suggestions to offer. Dorothea's face collapsed with disappointment; she was used to getting what she wanted. Tears came into her eyes. Her shoulders drooped. A pang of pity went through the solicitor. Perhaps she was the victim of some vicious villain whose refined torture left no evidence. He racked his brain for some other escape route to offer her.

'There is judicial separation if your husband is very cruel to you.'

'What is that?'

'A court rules that you may live apart from your husband. That he has no control over your life. He cannot insist that you fulfil your wifely duties, but you are not free to marry elsewhere.' He shook his head sadly at the prospect.

Men, thought Dorothea, they always assume a woman wants to be married. She counted out her father's sovereigns to pay the bill. The same funds that had bought her a convenient husband were now paying for her to find the means to dispose of him.

As the train rumbled back to Atherley, she leant against the plush seat to sort out her thoughts. As husbands go Edward was not objectionable. To give him his due, he had helped her with her music, persuading her father to get the car and the chauffeur that made her lessons and performances possible. The problem was not her status as a wife but as a daughter.

All the serious opposition came from her parents with their rigid expectations, backed up by society at large, of how a married woman and a mother should behave. Such a pity there was no judicial separation from parents. Something, she decided, had to change. She looked back to her time at school and how she had bent the other girls to her will until the Truesdale girls came and fomented rebellion. Her 'mice' had helped her then. What she needed now was an ally – and another weapon or two.

'You are back early, Dorothea,' said Mrs Woodward. 'Did you buy anything nice in Manchester?'

'No,' lied Dorothea as she rushed upstairs to hide the rouge and face powder in the drawer of her dressing table. 'Sorry, mother, I can't stop to talk. I want to get to the nursery.' Mrs Woodward stood looking up the stairs with her jaw hanging open. When had Dorothea ever rushed to see her children?

It was 6 o'clock before Dorothea appeared again. She came with Nanny as she brought the twins to the drawing room for their hour of family time. Mr Woodward refrained from asking about the meeting with Mr Martelli while his grandchildren were present; he enjoyed their games and chatter too much to spoil the happy atmosphere. Edward arrived with the welcome news that the car had been repaired. The time passed peacefully until Mr Woodward kissed the twins goodnight and Nanny took them upstairs. Then his face grew dark and serious as his gaze settled on his daughter. The moment had arrived for him to tackle Dorothea about the reckless rendezvous she had kept that day in Manchester.

He didn't get the chance. She beat him to it. She stood up and addressed the room as if she were the head of the family. 'I've got some news for you all.' Her manner was positively queenly. 'I have today signed a contract and I intend to honour it. I know you both think it important to keep your word and I would like you to help me keep mine.' Her effrontery stunned them into silence. She unrolled a document and held it up.

Her mother was the first to find a voice. 'You can't sign a contract; you're a married woman. You need your husband's permission.' Mrs Woodward had married at a time when her signature was not worth the paper it was written on.

'Those days are long gone, mother.'

Mrs Woodward might have lost on a point of law, but she did not give up the fight. Her fears of social disapproval, another scandal and further tarnishing of Dorothea's reputation poured from her mouth in a steady stream.

It was left to Edward to ask, 'What exactly is the contract for?' He sat back to listen. The Woodwards followed his example.

The contract committed Dorothea to perform a series of five evening concerts in town halls around Manchester. She would appear with Neville, the tenor from Henshaw's. The audience would be the cream of local society. Lord Mayors were expected to attend and reports would be published in the local newspapers. Word of her talent would spread and offers would come from further afield. In reality Mr Martelli had his eye on Leeds, Bradford and Halifax. Dorothea knew better than to mention cities in Yorkshire.

'You can't stay away overnight on your own,' squealed Mrs Woodward. 'What would people say. Edward will have to go with you.'

Mr Woodward was quick to squash that idea. 'Edward cannot always go with her. He has work to do.'

Edward felt that he'd had a narrow escape.

'Mr Martelli has everything planned,' said Dorothea looking smug. 'As you know, Neville is blind and so is Duncan the pianist. Well he can see some things but not much. Duncan's sister acts as guide in new places for both of them. Gets them to the hall. And the lodgings. That sort of thing.'

'So there would be another woman.'

'She would chaperon me and would act as lady's maid to me. Also, it may not be necessary to stay away. We only have five firm engagements. Higgs can do those,' said Dorothea with an airy wave of her hand.

The rest of them sat silent, picturing how peaceful their lives would be without Dorothea's incessant singing and sudden rages. Dorothea took advantage of the pause to play her master stroke. 'The only problem is the twins.'

They stared at her. When had Dorothea ever worried about her children?

'I have had a big talk with Nanny about it and Nanny and I think it will be best if, in future, I have tea with them. Nanny says it is good for them to have a regular time with their mother. It will help settle them for the times I will be away.' There was nothing they could say. No-one argued with Nanny.

It had been Nanny's idea when she learned Dorothea wanted to lose weight. She'd gestured at the table, the softly boiled eggs, the thin fingers of bread, the little bowls of jelly and slices of apple. 'Small portions are they not?' asked Nanny with a sideways look at Dorothea. 'And your family will be happy to hear you want to spend time with the twins. Two birds with one stone.' She winked at Dorothea and without apology went on to ask about her fees. 'You'll be wanting your own bank account then,' she said as she offered her half a chocolate fairy cake, 'to keep your money safe. You might find it useful one day.'

Dorothea went to bed hungry and happy. Her family's opposition had proved less vociferous than she expected. She had an ally and an unexpected lever in her hands – the twins. It was time that the little wretches came in useful, was her final thought before her eyes closed.

CHAPTER 7

Jenny's visits to Cozy Corner with Mavis quickly became a regular feature of life. She happily paid Mavis's share of the bill; she could afford it. In exchange she caught a glimpse of a less rigid world where people did not concern themselves much with how things looked or what the neighbours thought. They were too busy keeping the wolf from the door, or in Mavis's case, saving up for a home of her own.

They settled themselves in the 'Ladies only' area, where they were surrounded by small tables with starched white tablecloths and women quietly exchanging confidences. As Mavis adjusted her scarves her perfume wafted across the table. 'Your scent smells nice,' said Jenny.

'Mmm. Yes, it is nice. My Mam gets it.'

'Does she get your powder as well? And the salve for your lips?' asked Jenny and watched for her reaction. She had not mentioned the make-up before. Mavis was not embarrassed. She looked straight at her friend. 'I am not ashamed. They are the tools of my trade.'

Jenny flapped and floundered, muttering sorry and I didn't mean to pry, though that was exactly what she intended.

'You must know there's no other way I could hope to make the kind of money I need to get a house. You being a finance officer and all.'

'I did wonder.'

'I'm not ashamed of it. I'm not the first girl to do a bit on the side and I won't be the last. Following in my Mam's footsteps. She's done her best but she's getting on. The rent man's telling her to her face she's not worth a whole week's rent.'

Mavis searched Jenny's face for signs of shock or distaste. She found none, just interested listening. 'There's no father to put his hand in his pocket for me.'

'I am lucky,' Jenny admitted.

The tea arrived. To assert herself Mavis took charge of the pot, fussing about with the strainer and pouring a few experimental drops to test the strength of the brew. As they sipped their tea their friendship reasserted itself.

'The way I see it, I'm not selling myself. I'm renting. While I'm young and good looking I can get a good price. That won't last. But bricks and mortar will. When I've got my house, I'll rent out rooms. But that's all I'll be renting out.' She cackled with sudden laughter, strident against the background hum and discreet murmurings of the women customers.

'How do you find them?'

'Customers you mean. I don't. They find me.'

'You mean they come up to you in the street?' Jenny managed to tone down the shock in her voice.

'Certain streets at certain times. Where professional women go.'

'No man has ever done that to me.'

'Course not. He knows that he would be wasting his time. You've got 'Unavailable' written all over you.'

Jenny looked round the 'Ladies only' section to see if anyone else had 'Unavailable' written over her. Mavis saw what she was doing. 'They are all like you, respectable women. Most are married or here with their mothers. They are all Unavailable. But it doesn't stop the men from coming and looking.'

Jenny covered her ears. 'Don't say that. My father will stop me coming. It will join that long list of places I can't go."

'Don't worry. It is respectable. Look'. Mavis waved a hand towards the fringes of the room where men were permitted. There were a few couples, a family or two but most customers were solitary men sometimes reading newspapers. 'They come to look. It's only natural. Men like to look at women. Particularly young ones. They are not coming up to you, offering 5 shillings for a quick'... Mavis's voice trailed away. She envied Jenny's ignorance of matters she had been forced to learn too soon. She knew only too well that innocence, once lost cannot be recovered.

Jenny refused to be fobbed off so easily. 'A quick what? What is it you do with them?

'It's no use, Jenny. I can't explain it. I don't have the words.' Mavis waved her hands to show helplessness. 'You'll find out one day. There's a first time for everyone. Even men.' Her face softened at the memory of one of the more rewarding aspects of her trade – the beginners. They were usually young, attractive and profoundly grateful.

Jenny felt that her investment in teacakes had been wasted until Mavis threw out a casual, 'Sometimes the excitement's too much for them and they can't, you know, manage it.'

Jenny had no real idea of what '**it**' was, but she tucked away Mavis's handy tip for dealing with the situation in case it was needed one day. 'If that happens I get them to hold my breasts,' said Mavis with a discreet gesture in the direction of that part of her anatomy. 'I find it quite pleasant and it usually does the trick. It's sort of comforting.'

That night, Jenny totted up her return for the cost of Mavis's tea. She decided that it was a worthwhile investment. She now knew for sure that Mavis was working as a prostitute, a trade that filled respectable women with horror. The fear of being mistaken for one in the street kept their skirts inconveniently long and their hair hidden under hats. They could not run, laugh, shout or be seen in the company of men without a chaperon. The conventional wisdom maintained that such behaviour led to their being solicited by men with illicit intentions. Jenny decided she need no longer concern herself about that possibility. She had 'Unavailable' stamped all over her. Or did her label read 'Property of Edward Carter'?

Dorothea was busy preparing for the concerts that Mr Martelli had booked for her. When she wasn't rehearsing or doing her vocal exercises she did anything that diverted her from feeling hungry. Nanny was proving a hard task master. She would gently tap Dorothea's hand when she stretched out for cake or a second slice of bread and butter. 'Are you sure?' she would ask and Dorothea would withdraw her hand. At Nanny's bidding Dorothea accompanied the twins on their daily walk. Clare and Isambard scampered ahead, setting a brisk pace for their mother to follow. Those extra pounds melted away.

The new figure demanded new clothes. The sober Sunday suit was condemned as fit only for Atherley. There were two new outfits for travelling to the city or to engagements. They were decorated with theatrical flourishes to distinguish their owner from the uniform of the working woman. The pale grey costume had flounces trimmed with black velvet and the blue one was bound with navy satin. When it came to evening gowns for the concerts there was no fabric in Atherley that satisfied Dorothea. Telegrams were sent to Manchester demanding samples of silk in shades of crimson, scarlet, indigo and peacock blue. None of them would do. Mr Woodward contacted his agent in London, who sent his wife to Liberty's. The samples of fabric were rushed to Euston Station, where they were entrusted to the guard on the next train to Manchester.

The Woodward mansion hummed with activity. The adult residents were busy making progress with their lives, whether it was improving their breath control, training children, running a business or paying the many bills. The children were busy learning to count, throw a ball or master the alphabet. Time softened the older Woodwards' feelings about Dorothea's behaviour; they began to see it as unconventional rather than flagrantly outrageous. They were rewarded by her spending time with their beloved grandchildren. It was true the occasions were brief, and Nanny's presence was essential, but it was definitely an improvement.

The first concert passed smoothly. The trusty Higgs drove Dorothea there and brought her back soon after midnight. The second concert was similarly uneventful. On the third occasion Higgs underestimated the distance and they arrived late. Neville, Duncan and his doughty sister, Charity, who all travelled by train, were delayed by missed connections. There was no time to test the acoustics of the hall or check the piano. Dorothea's dressing room was so cold that she demanded a hot water bottle. Only one could be found; she had to forgo its comfort to let Duncan warm his frozen fingers so that he could play the piano. Overcoming these tribulations lent their performances extra zest and passion. They ran late, the applause was long and loud, and their hosts were generous in their hospitality. It was too late for the Henshaw's contingent to return by train. Beds were found for Neville and Duncan but Dorothea refused to share with Charity the slightly grimy bed she was offered. She drank several glasses of champagne while Higgs insisted that he would drive her home. His job would be at risk if he failed to return her to her family even if it was the early hours of the morning. If he delayed until the following day his life would not be worth living. The result was that a sober Higgs delivered an inebriated Dorothea to her father's house as the sun was painting red streaks in the sky.

Mr Woodward had not slept. He had worn himself out with worry, prowling about the house, jumping at the crack of a twig or a buffet of the wind; his nerves stretched to breaking point. At the sound of the car pulling up at the house his self-control snapped completely. Dorothea, in her low-cut midnight blue dress erupted into the hallway, still manic with energy from her triumphant performance.

'I got them,' she kept saying while grabbing handfuls of air to show how she had captured the audience and bent them to her will. She waltzed through the hall and burst into the drawing room. She pirouetted round the furniture, her skirts whirling. She hammered the piano and sang loud and wild, begging for her father's applause before finally throwing herself on the sofa and passing out.

Her teetotal father who had lived a life of discipline and restraint was horrified. This was not one of Dorothea's usual tantrums; this was something different. The drumming of her heels and her shrieks of rage were familiar to him; they always had a purpose to them. Her violent attacks of rage were always calculated; they were staged to bring her something she had been denied.

This time it was different; she had set out no terms, demanded no concessions. Mr Woodward feared that she had lost her reason and gone temporarily mad. Women did that sometimes. It was a well-known fact among husbands and fathers. He fled to his wife for help. Mrs Woodward took an executive decision and went for Nanny. The uproar woke Edward. He lay back in his bed, heard the voice of Nanny and decided that he would sleep through the drama. He regularly worked a 16-hour day, so it was not difficult.

Before he went down to breakfast in the morning he took the precaution of checking on 'his wife'. He always thought of her in that role with inverted commas round the word. She was asleep. There was no point in trying to wake her. At the breakfast table an exhausted Mr Woodward was uncharacteristically silent while his wife described how she feared that one of her family had an apoplexy. Edward reassured them that Dorothea was sleeping and advised that they let her rest. In the meantime, it might be sensible if he talked to Nanny who understood Dorothea so well. Relief flooded their worn faces as the burden of their daughter shifted from their shoulders.

Edward soon returned to the breakfast table with Nanny's diagnosis and a remedy. The long journey and the late arrival had put Dorothea in a state of unrelieved tension for many hours. She was exhausted and overwrought. It was possible that hunger had contributed to her little breakdown. Perhaps in future, said Nanny, an overnight stay and a more leisurely return would avoid a recurrence of the unfortunate incident. Dorothea could have a light supper at the hotel with some warm milk to help her sleep. She understood that the arrangements made for her accommodation were perfectly proper.

Nanny's judgement was greeted with sighs of relief at the breakfast table. Edward struggled to keep back the smile that threatened to flood his face. Nanny's verdict suited him perfectly. Was he the only one to realise that Dorothea had been drunk? He saw no reason to disturb her parents with this piece of information when Nanny had withheld it. Dorothea could not be the first mother the worse for drink who Nanny had helped to bed.

Mrs Woodward remained concerned about her husband's health and summoned the doctor as a precaution. He prescribed a bottle of bitter-tasting tonic and a few days' rest. Edward took advantage of the older man's absence from the office to further his own plans. He summoned Jenny and Mr Frederick to his office.

'As you know, I like machinery and people to earn their keep.' He pointed at the telephone on his desk. 'How useful is that particular machine?' He was pleased that Mr Frederick, who had no telephone on his desk was first to answer.

'I believe that our coal mines have them, so they can contact you in case of an emergency. That must be immensely valuable. Save lives.'

Edward nodded. He turned to Jenny. 'Is it much use to you, Miss Truesdale?'

'To be honest, not really. The most use it gets is when you ring me to ask if it's time for a cup of tea. Not many of the firms we work with have telephones yet. If it's urgent we send them a telegram.'

'So, apart from tea breaks, it's not a lot of use.'

'It could be,' Mr Frederick intervened. 'Indeed, I would go so far as to say, it will be. More and more people will see its convenience. The newspapers tell me that Berlin has many more telephones than London.'

'You follow the news in Germany?' asked Edward.

'My relatives send the occasional newspaper. I like to read about Elektropolis. That's what they call Berlin now.'

'You are interested in electricity?'

'Very much so.'

'People are frightened of it,' said Jenny. 'My father was appalled when I wanted to train for the electric telegraph. And as for having electric lighting.' She flapped her hands to demonstrate irrational panic.

'Electricity is not so popular here,' queried Mr Frederick.'

'It's the mines,' Edward explained. 'There's always gas in mines. A spark can set off an explosion.' A moment of silence followed to mark their respect for those who worked and died in the mines. 'That's why we used ponies rather than electric trucks. What about having a telephone at home? Would you have one?'

Both Jenny and Mr Frederick would welcome such an instrument – if they could afford it.

'The problem is,' said Jenny, 'that I don't know anyone who I could telephone.' She frowned. 'No that's not true. There's Mrs

Mckenna in Manchester. My sister is a student. She lodges there. They have a telephone. Students come from all over the world. They can ring their families in America, I think.'

'The Council in Manchester have set up their own network. All you need is a licence from the Post Office.'

'When I worked at the Post Office they dismissed the idea of the telephone,' said Jenny. 'They said that it would never catch on. The telegram is so popular. People just don't like change,' she concluded, thinking of her father.

'Change can be for the better,' said Edward and thanked them for their help. It was clear to Jenny that he was working on a scheme of some kind.

While Mr Woodward was still shaken by his recent experience, Edward set about convincing him that installing a telephone in his home would spare him a repetition of his anxiety about Dorothea. 'It means that she will be able to telephone to tell you of any delay. You can ring her if you are anxious. Most of the hotels and the concert halls will have them.' As Mr Woodward was in a generous mood Edward went on to float a few more ideas past his father-in-law.

At first Mrs Woodward was disappointed in the new machine as there was no-one she could telephone except the office or the pit. When Dorothea went to her next concert and telephoned from Bolton her mother was ecstatic. She told everyone she met of this technical miracle. People were so taken by the novelty that they forgot to question the propriety of Dorothea sleeping away from home.

CHAPTER 8

'No.'

Dorothea opened her mouth as if to speak.

'No. I said No. A thousand times No,' said Edward. He wiped the water from his chest with a towel and started to pull on a clean shirt. 'Can't a man wash off the dirt and grime of a working day without his 'wife' taking him by surprise?

'Why not? I don't understand,' wailed Dorothea.

Edward tucked his shirt back in his trousers; he could think better with his clothes on.

'It seems…' Dorothea began.

'Be quiet. I'm thinking.'

'There's no need to snarl at me.'

'Snarl' thought Edward. Someone should have given you a good chewing over a long time ago. The 'someone' was, of course, Mr Woodward. The jumble of conflicting thoughts in Edward's mind suddenly fell into a neat pile. His answer was clear.

'The reason I will not allow you to divorce me, is that I have too much respect for your father.'

Dorothea's jaw dropped. Respect. Her father. Edward thought highly of him. To Dorothea he was merely a convenient and gullible source of funds.

'I value his opinion of me. We had a deal. I married you to protect your reputation and to be a father to your children. He rewarded me with a place in the business. That was the arrangement and I intend to stick to my side of the bargain.'

'But,' Dorothea began.

Edward held up a warning hand. 'Enough. Your father has a reputation in this town for fair dealing. That's the kind of reputation I want. If I shake hands on a contract I stick to it.' He looked at Dorothea with her face of thunder and smiled. 'It's not the adultery I mind. No man minds being thought a bit of a Jack the lad. Adultery wouldn't do my reputation lasting harm. No, it's the other things on your list that I draw the line at.'

Dorothea said nothing. Her face flushed and her eyebrows fought on her forehead.

'Remind me,' said Edward. 'What were they?

'The solicitor called it the ABC of divorce.'

'I can guess what the B stands for. As for publicly admitting to it, the answer is an emphatic no. So we are left with C. I guess that will be Cruelty. I will not let it be thought I raised my fist to a woman! There are limits, Dorothea. Anyway, why are you suddenly thinking of divorce? I've done my best to help you with your music. I haven't stood in your way. It's not me who questioned your contract with Martelli. Or the nights away.

'I'm fed up with having to keep asking for approval. It's like being a child again.'

'It's not my approval you're after. It's your father's. And his money. If you really want a divorce, you go and ask him for one. The way you asked him to buy you a husband'.

Edward watched her struggle until he was satisfied that she realised how outrageous the suggestion of a divorce was. 'We are stuck with each other, Dorothea. Better get used to the idea.'

She bit her lip and looked at the ground.

'Also, I keep out of your bedroom, Dorothea. I'd be grateful if, in future, you'd keep out of mine. No more ambushing me. I don't like these sudden surprise attacks at the end of a working day.'

She scowled and turned to the door. Suppressed rage and anger boiled inside her like a blocked fountain. As she stormed from the room a vapour trail of frustrated fury followed her. The familiar grin lit up Edward's face; he had quite enjoyed their little spat. A pleasant change for him to be in the driver's seat.

A knock at the door. 'More hot water, sir?' offered the cheery maid. She didn't wink at him, but it was clear she knew what had just passed.

'That'll be all for the moment.' He tried to sound distant, like a proper employer. 'Perhaps later.'

She dipped a curtsy and left.

A note of caution sounded in Edward's head. The servants knew everything. Could Dorothea use his pleasant encounters with the maid against him? He dismissed the idea; she'd never get the

76

evidence. The servants disliked Dorothea; they would cheerfully lie, invent alternative versions of the truth and develop a serious case of mental confusion. No lawyer would call them as witnesses.

And as for asking her chapel-going lay preacher of a father for a divorce! Not even Dorothea would do that. It would be enough to kill the old man. Dorothea would have to stew. With that happy thought he went off to the nursery to see *his* children. He had stopped putting the inverted commas round the word 'his' with regard to the twins. They had won a place in his heart.

Edward was lying on the floor by the nursery fire looking at the twins' latest drawings when the door was flung open. Nanny jumped up to defend her territory but stopped at the sight of the white face of the usually cheery maid. She had bad news. Mr Woodward had been taken suddenly ill.

'We've sent for the doctor.'

'Is he on his way?'

'Yes. But you know what he's like. By the time he's harnessed the horse….'

'I will go to collect him in the car.'

Edward drove down the hill at a furious pace, sounding the horn to clear his way. Fortunately most horses were tucked up in their stables for the night. He was enraged to discover that the doctor was still sitting comfortably inside his house, instead of standing on the door step waiting for him. In an agony of haste Edward banged on the door and rang the bell. He pushed past the maid to watch in dismay as the doctor clambered slowly into his coat and looked vaguely round for his hat.

Edward picked up the doctor's black bag and guided him, none too gently, into the car.

The doctor patted the dashboard in front of him as they roared through the town. 'Must be handy, having one of these things?'

Through gritted teeth Edward made noises of agreement. This was not the moment to ask why the doctor had not invested in either a car or telephone; they would improve considerably the chances of his patients surviving..

'Some kind of sudden seizure, I believe?' The doctor looked enquiringly at Edward.

Edward muttered something to show his ignorance of the details. The doctor did not pursue the matter but sat calmly in the passenger seat with his hands folded in his lap. The scenario was a familiar one for him; he had played it many times before but never in a car.

Shock, disbelief and an awareness of his wife's unscrupulous nature fought in Edward's mind. Surely Dorothea had not gone straight from her argument with him to ask her God-fearing father to arrange a divorce? His beloved daughter talking of adultery and divorce! No wonder Mr Woodward had been struck down by a sudden stroke; he truly believed in the ideal of holy matrimony. Edward knew how far his own marriage to Dorothea was from the blissful union it was alleged to be. His was a cynical façade designed to protect a falsehood. How different marriage to Jenny would be.

The warring factions in Edward's mind came to a sudden truce; they agreed an armistice. The marriage, designed to protect Dorothea's tattered reputation, had little consequence; its real function was to protect those two small creatures he had left playing by the nursery fire.

His childhood in the poorest quarter of the town came back to him: the pale and wasted children who were his playmates and their sudden disappearances from the scene. The boy who fell down a well, the girl fatally scalded while helping her mother with the washing and the babies dead of the summer diarrhoea. Their brief lives were tribute paid to the ramshackle sanitation, the outrageous burdens borne by their mothers, the cramped and crowded housing and the scourge of measles and scarlet fever.

The little scions of the Woodward clan were safe in their airy nursery, behind the fire guard, in the care of Nanny whose sole function was to protect their chubby bodies. Paid hands washed their clothes and cooked their meals.

Edward still wasn't sure what exactly a father should do. He was pretty sure he should not disappear into the wilderness as his own father had done. His mother had coped. She was a remarkable woman. He pictured Dorothea as a mother without a solid structure of family life to both support and restrain her. It was true that

Dorothea was remarkable in her own way. However, as a mother she was less than satisfactory.

The placid doctor came out of the patient's room. The emergency was over. Mr Woodward was recovering. His heart was functioning normally and his breathing was good. There were pills and powders to be taken. The patient was to be kept quiet. No excitement. His diagnosis complete, the doctor looked to Edward to deliver him home. Edward considered making him wait while he sent for a hansom cab from the town. The small pleasure it would afford him did not feel worth the effort. He drove the doctor home at a leisurely pace.

On his return to the house, he found Mrs Woodward pale but composed. Edward was surprised to find a tremor in his hand and a catch in his voice as he enquired after his father-in-law.

'He's all right now.' She looked round to make sure they were alone. 'He had a very nasty shock. We both did.'

Edward braced himself. He guessed what was coming. Dorothea was not noted for her patience. She had gone straight to her father to ask for a divorce as she threatened.

Mrs Woodward took a deep breath. 'Dorothea,' she began. Edward held his breath, expecting to hear the word divorce very soon. 'Well she told him – us I mean – that she wants to audition for a very special role. There will be a lot of competition. She doesn't expect to get it. Which is just as well,' Mrs Woodward leant forward confidentially to Edward and hissed, 'It's in Leeds.' She looked at Edward expecting to see her own shock and horror reflected in his face. She was disappointed. He obviously didn't understand,

'Leeds,' she said again, her eyes wide with dismay. 'That's in Yorkshire.

Edward laughed with relief. So that was why Dorothea was thinking of divorce; one less voice to oppose her plan to invade fresh territory.

For some days Mr Woodward sat by the fire with a blanket over his knees. He enjoyed playing the invalid; it was a new role for him. There were unexpected benefits; his grandchildren clambered over him, tucked themselves into the corners and crevices of the big chair, where they crooned and chuntered until they grew bored or fell asleep.

While her father convalesced, Dorothea pursued her new enterprise. She saw now that mentioning Leeds had been a mistake. Fortunately, the drama of her father's illness distracted her mother's attention from her daughter's ambitious project. Dorothea wanted to audition for the title role in *Tosca*. The opera had been first performed to great acclaim in Milan a couple of years ago, and cities all over the world were keen to put on their own productions. Signor Martelli was sure the opera would provide Dorothea with a once-in-a-lifetime opportunity. Who could be more suited to play a young Italian soprano than Dorothea? With her black hair, dramatic colouring and slimmed down figure she was perfect.

He knew better than to let her think so. Instead, he lamented his failure to persuade a theatre in Manchester, where she was known, to produce the opera. In Leeds her chances were slim, he warned her. He did not have the influence there that he enjoyed in Manchester and talented local singers would be in competition for the part. He sent her the score with strict instructions to study it. The selection process was likely to be lengthy.

While Dorothea practised her solos and worked on her moves in front of a full-length mirror, Edward had his eyes on a city more distant than Leeds. Dorothea could go to Timbuktu for all he cared. He had arrived at his office one day to find Mr Fredrick looking mournfully at the long thin limbs of a brass musical instrument in pieces on his desk. 'It was my father's,' he explained to Jenny.

'Is it broken?' Edward asked.

'Not broken,' said Mr Fredrick with his usual precision, 'but in need of repair. There is a dent in the slide.' He pointed to the offending dinge which prevented the slide moving smoothly. 'I do not know where to take it for repair.'

'That's easy,' said Edward. 'Take it to the mine.' Mr Fredrick looked horrified until Edward explained. 'There's a man there who looks after all the miners' instruments. He'll get that tapped out. It'll be as smooth as a baby's you know what.'

Mr Fredrick smiled but not for long. 'I'd better warn you,' said Edward wagging a warning finger, 'once they find out you play the trombone they'll sign you up for the colliery band.' He thought for a moment. 'That might be a very good thing. You'll get to know the men.'

As Mr Fredrick packed the trombone back in its case, Edward looked at his watch and came to a decision. 'It's nearly dinner time. Get down to the pit now. Pick up a bit of dinner then come back to the office. I want to talk to you.'

While Mr Fredrick was away on his errand Edward took the opportunity to talk to Jenny first. Or Miss Truesdale, as he had to call her in the office. He never took a serious step without her opinion.

'What d'you think of him?' he asked, flicking his head at the door Mr Fredrick had left by.

'He's clever. Works through things. Methodical. Serious.'

'Trustworthy?'

'Yes.'

'What do you know about his family?'

'Not much. I think his mother died when he was little. They lived in Czechoslovakia. His father took him to Germany as a small child, and he taught him the trombone. I get the feeling'… Jenny hesitated; she wanted to separate the facts from speculation. Edward signalled for her to go on. He trusted Jenny's feelings. 'I think they might have been Moravians.'

'What! What are Moravians when they are at home?'.

'My sister, Margaret, met some when she was a student at Owens College. They came to do Bible Studies to prepare them to preach. They go all over the world. They always preach in the local language. They play music to attract people to come and listen. Always brass instruments: they travel well.'

Jenny looked to Edward to see if she was helping or hindering Mr Fredrick's career.

'Do you think he'll decide to go off and preach?'

'No. I think that's over. His father had a disagreement of some sort with them. They are very strict.'

'Mr Fredrick speaks German?'

'Yes.' Jenny looked up at Edward and found that he was looking directly at her. Their eyes locked and they gazed at each other with

81

a perfect wordless understanding of the hunger each felt. They were alone in the office. It felt as if fate had arranged an opportunity for them. It was Jenny who had the strength to bring it to an abrupt end.

'I bet when he comes back to the office he's in the colliery band.' She said it as a joke but it was more of a warning.

And so it proved. Edward took Mr Frederick, the newest member of the colliery band, into his office where they had a long talk. Mr Fredrick's hours were re-arranged so that he could attend rehearsals with the colliery band and a couple of courses at the Mechanics' Institute that Edward wanted him to take. Could Jenny cope if he left early on two afternoons each week to give him more time to pursue his studies?

Mavis bustled into the 'Ladies only' section of Cozy Corner in her usual cloud of perfume and a whirlwind of chiffon scarves.

'Would you like a teacake? My treat,' said Jenny. Mavis, uncharacteristically quiet, mimed her delight at the prospect.

'On one condition.' Jenny wagged a finger to warn her that there was a price to pay. There was something she wanted from Mavis and it had nothing to do with teacakes.

'Which is?' Mavis knew how to bargain.

'How do men know who is available and who is unavailable?'

'Didn't they teach you that at Miss Fossil's Academy?'

'Of course not,' Jenny laughed at the thought.

'Well I knew that when they chucked me out of the National School at twelve.'

'So you can tell me.'

Mavis was bewildered. How could Jenny with her extra years of schooling and her qualifications in finance not understand something so simple? 'It's hard to explain. They just do.'

'Is it the clothes? What if I got some chiffon scarves and some perfume?'

Mavis shook her head. 'It's not what you're wearing. It's the way you wear it. Catching his eye, that sort of thing."

'Like this.' Jenny rolled her eyes at Mavis.

'No. Not like that. You look as if you swallowed a frog'. The teacakes arrived so they set about the spicy buns with gusto. Mavis thought while she chewed. 'Your school was just for girls. You never flirted with the boys at the Mechanics' Institute, did you?'

Jenny shook her head while she relished a buttery morsel. 'No. Edward was there. Not the same class, but at the same time.'

'He cramped your style even then. Think of the chances you missed. Some of those lads are doing really well for themselves. Now it's like you're dragging a deadweight behind you.' Mavis scowled to show her disapproval of Jenny wasting her time on Edward, who was indissolubly tied to another woman. An idea came that made her smile. 'It's never too late to start,' she told Jenny. 'I'll give you a lesson but you must promise never to tell anyone who the man is.'

'What man?'

'The one in the maroon waistcoat, reading his paper. 'To your left. No further.' Jenny scanned the room. 'Got him.'

Mavis nodded. 'Now forget him. You have never seen him. Promise. Cross your heart and hope to die.'

Jenny traced her forefinger over her left breast.

Mavis was satisfied. 'Well. Just between you and me. he's one of my regulars. He comes here while he waits for the bus to Tilston. It's at half past 5.'

Jenny took some seconds to recover from the shock; she had not expected to find herself in the same room as a man who went with prostitutes. A discreet glance from the corner of her eye revealed a respectably dressed man, about her father's age. The thought of such a man using a prostitute was disturbing. Not for the first time she wondered if Mavis was lying. She loved a good story more than the truth.

Mavis was busy explaining. 'His wife died about a year ago and he misses her. Occasionally he comes to bend my sympathetic ear – and another part of my anatomy.' She guffawed loudly, expecting Jenny to join in. She was disappointed but carried on with her lesson. 'Like I said. He has regular habits. You can practically set your watch by him. If he's feeling peckish and I tip him the wink, he'll come back with me to my place.' Mavis sighed. 'Trouble is he won't be a widower for long. He's good marriage material. Some Godfearing woman in Tilston will have her eye on him.' She turned to Jenny who was finding the whole business unbearably sad. 'Are you ready for your lesson? And remember.' She wagged her finger. 'You must forget the maroon waistcoat.'

Mavis gave her squawk of a laugh to start the demonstration. The man must have recognised the sound. He adjusted his newspaper slightly so he could look round the edge. Mavis grew taller in her seat. Her hands fluttered about like butterflies as she adjusted her scarves, straightened her hat and patted her hair. She fussed and fidgeted until she was sure she had his attention. Then she braced her shoulders to lift her bosom and show it off to advantage. A dreamy quality came over her face as she turned her gaze on the man in the maroon waistcoat.

She gave him a look that appeared to travel through the air. Jenny could not explain the look, or describe it, but the effect on the man was palpable. He rattled the pages of his newspaper as if they had misbehaved. Then he nodded to Mavis, stood up and called for the bill.

While he paid, Mavis collected her gloves. 'Sorry. You'll be on your own with the bill again,' she told Jenny. She stopped to pull her gloves on. The one piece of good behaviour her mother had managed to instil in her was that ladies always finished putting their gloves on before they went out into the world.

'Don't hang about for too long,' Mavis warned Jenny with a wink. 'You never know what might happen.' With that she swished her skirts and strolled to the door into the street. Jenny did not watch to see if the man followed her. She was too busy summoning the waitress and asking for the bill; her need for another female presence to reinstate her among the Unavailable ones was suddenly urgent.

That night Jenny held a candle by the bedroom mirror and practised the look that had summoned the man across a crowded room. It was not an encouraging experiment. There was definitely something missing.

CHAPTER 9

Dorothea's final concert with the musicians from Henshaw's was in the county town of Lancaster. Although not so large, so wealthy or so powerful a city as Manchester, it was satisfying to finish in the historic home of a once powerful duke. A preening Mrs Woodward made sure to remind her acquaintances regularly that the Lord Lieutenant of the County was to attend the reception after the concert. He was, in her opinion, as good as royalty.

Dorothea knew that it was to be her last jaunt with Neville, Duncan and his sister, Charity. They had rubbed along nicely during their overnight stays in modest hotels, sharing grumbles about the lack of hot water and the lumpiness of the mattresses. Neville and Duncan, accustomed to enduring discomfort patiently, regularly gave way to Dorothea's wishes. Charity, who was responsible for their comfort, justified the preferential treatment of Dorothea, by pointing out she was the prima donna of the ensemble. Without her, they did not exist.

It was one of those evenings when the multitude of ingredients that make a performance were at their best. The musicians had honed their parts to perfection, the acoustics in the venue were excellent, the piano was tuned and in good voice. The atmosphere trembled at the edge of magical, the applause was spontaneous and full-throated and the kiss Neville pressed on Dorothea's lips at the end of the love duet felt suspiciously passionate. At the reception the performers were bathed in glory, compliments and champagne.

The Lord Lieutenant was in full dress uniform with an abundance of gold braid. His spurs rattled as he clicked his heels and brushed his lips against Dorothea's hand. He reminded her of Aleksy, the Polish count, dancing teacher and cavalry officer who had taken her virginity in France. The Lord Lieutenant made no secret of his willingness to follow in Count Aleksy's riding boots and spent 40 minutes of tongue-licking lasciviousness gazing down Dorothea's cleavage until his wife came to remove him.

Lust is a virus. It can infect a whole room full of people, especially if they are young and there is alcohol. The stirrings of something she had not felt for a long time fluttered through Dorothea. She thought childbirth had cured her of that. The memory of Neville's lips on hers sent her eyes searching for him. As usual he was surrounded by women enjoying his chiselled good looks, his smile and the sparkle in his less than efficient eyes.

When the time came to leave the reception. Charity took Duncan's arm to lead the way. Dorothea laid a similarly possessive hand on Neville and enjoyed seeing the disappointment on his many admirers' faces. It gave her a kick of the pleasure that she had felt in the old days, when she took revenge on the girls at school.

She heaved up some more of the bosom that had so mesmerised the Lord Lieutenant. Neville did not respond. Then she remembered he could not see; he had been blind from birth. He perceived the world through his ears and his skin, not his eyes. Accordingly she murmured in his ear and laughed softly as she ran her hand gently down his arm and took hold of his hand. He did not respond.

At the lodgings Charity took charge. She lit the gas light on the stairs, muttering that she needed to see where she was going even if the men didn't. Duncan did have some limited vision; he could see straight ahead as if through a tunnel and found stairs difficult. At the door of the boys' room, Dorothea would usually say goodnight and take herself off to the bedroom she shared with Charity, leaving her to settle Neville and her brother. On this occasion Dorothea came into the room; she was still attached to Neville's arm.

'You've got a double bed tonight. All the singles had gone,' Charity explained. 'Washstand's at 4 o'clock to you Neville.'

'Fine,' said Neville, so that Duncan could hear his voice and place his whereabouts in the room.

Charity checked the cans of water with her fingers. 'The water's warm, but don't delay too long. Our room is two doors down to the right, if you need anything in the night,' she said and prepared to leave. Dorothea stood looking at the double bed and showed no sign of moving. Charity raised her voice. 'We'd better leave the men to get washed. That water's not going to get any warmer.' Dorothea did not take the hint.

Charity diagnosed a bad case of post-performance slump combined with too much champagne. She clicked her fingers and prodded Dorothea in the direction of the door. There, the problem that had fazed Dorothea crept to the surface of her mind and popped out into the world. 'Neville and Duncan have a double bed,' she said.

'That's right. I seem to remember you had a lot to say about NOT sharing a bed.' Charity had, earlier on the tour, endured an impassioned harangue from Dorothea to the effect that she had never shared a bed in her life and she wasn't going to start now. Charity decided that it was time to strike back.

'We didn't all grow up in mansions with seven bedrooms. The boys don't mind sharing a bed as much as you do.' To Charity her younger brother would always be a boy. By this time the women had reached the bedroom they were to share. Charity gestured at the two single beds that awaited them.

'I'm not complaining,' said Dorothea.

Which makes a pleasant change, thought Charity before a warning bell rang in her head. Suddenly serious she spoke to Dorothea, 'Probably best not to talk about the double bed too much.'

'Why?'

Sometimes Dorothea could be very unworldly. She had not noticed that while many men salivated over her beauty Neville and Duncan were unmoved by it. As a conceited prima donna she assumed it was their limited vision that left them indifferent to her allure. Charity suspected there was a different explanation though she never allowed her mind to explore fully her brother's lack of interest in the women who flocked to pay Neville attention. That he might prefer hairy thighs and muscular chests to soft breasts and smooth skin was beyond her imagining. She knew just enough to sense a possible danger to the brother she loved.

'Just best not to draw attention to that bed,' she told Dorothea. 'Some people have nasty minds. They draw conclusions and spread gossip.'

'That's true,' said Dorothea. She remembered the rumour mill about her pregnancy and marriage.

That night Charity lay in bed and considered explaining to Dorothea that men risked prison if some evil-minded person jumped to conclusions and brought them to the attention of the authorities. Could she trust Dorothea to be discreet? Dorothea discreet! Not worth the risk, she decided. After all, this was the last concert of the tour and they were leaving in the morning.

Dorothea suffered a few moments of self-doubt when she laid her head on the pillow. The sudden urge to share that double bed with Neville had taken her by surprise. Not since the birth of the twins had she been attacked by such a wild desire. To find Neville did not respond to her advances was particularly peeving. Was she losing her touch? Had all those small portions and pangs of hunger been in vain? She searched for a convincing excuse for Neville's indifference and decided it was for professional reasons. He wanted to continue to sing with her without the complication of a jealous husband. After all she was a married woman, something she cheerfully forgot most of the time. This explanation suited her vanity. As others count sheep to lull them to sleep, Dorothea counted the men who found her desirable to reassure herself that she had not lost her touch. She worked backwards, starting with that drooling Lord Lieutenant.

On Mrs Woodward's insistence her husband enjoyed a brief convalescence and a total ban on mention of anything even remotely connected with Yorkshire; she held the county responsible for his sudden illness. She even stopped buying Wensleydale cheese. Her parents greeted Dorothea with delight on her return from Lancaster and wallowed in the details of the Lord Lieutenant's reception. Mrs Woodward duly conveyed the high points to all the ladies of Atherley.

The glamour of her concert tour did not last long. Dorothea began looking for fresh worlds to conquer. Where was Signor Martelli with his talk of auditions for a big role in Leeds? There was no word from him. She grew moody and started to hammer out Wagner and Beethoven on the piano until her father called an abrupt end to his convalescence and returned to work. On that day Signor Martelli telephoned and asked to speak to Miss Dorothea.

The servants were not accustomed to phone calls from strangers to the ladies of the house. It took them so long to find Dorothea and bring her within reach of the phone that the caller had rung off. Dorothea relieved her feelings by lambasting the servants with considerable vigour. They concealed their surprise at the range of her vocabulary by looking at her with dead eyes and expressionless faces until she realised that her words were having no real effect.

Signor Martelli rang again. He was pleased that Dorothea's father was well enough to return to work. He had avoided bothering him while he was ill, but time was pressing and the Leeds opera would not wait much longer. Could he visit the next day? Dorothea agreed without even pretending to consult her father. When she told Mr Woodward on his return from work, he bowed to the inevitable but insisted on a favour in return. 'Stop playing that dreadful German stuff.'

'Oh yes,' she agreed. 'It will be Puccini from now on. You will like that. It is much more cheerful.'

The Mr Martelli who arrived the next day was not the rumpled music teacher with ambition that Mr Woodward remembered. This Mr Martelli was a successful impresario. He rolled up at top speed in a hired carriage drawn by a chestnut gelding. He was greeted with a fanfare of attention from the servants who gave the impression they were receiving an Italian nobleman. It was all bustle, fuss and shouted instructions. Water for the horse. Refreshment for the driver. A royal duke arriving at his country estate would not be greeted with more ceremony.

In Mr Woodward's study Mr Martelli was fulsome in his praise for Dorothea. The concerts had been a great success and there was already talk of further bookings. The Lord Lieutenant was not the only who passed on his compliments. Dorothea glowed with smug satisfaction; false modesty was not one of her failings.

'Now the important thing is to build on your success. The role of Tosca.' Mr Martelli turned to Dorothea. 'It is within your grasp.'

She almost fainted with joy.

'There is one tiny obstacle to fulfilling your ambition. He pinched his thumb and forefinger together to demonstrate the Lilliputian nature of the difficulty. 'I am desolate but I have not been able to persuade them to audition Neville for the part of Cavaradossi. I regret to say they have one of their own tenors in mind for the role.'

'Oh. That's a shame,' Dorothea offered breezily. 'I think Neville and I go well together. Do you have a date for my audition?'

'Yes. Thursday next. That will give you time to refresh your knowledge of the part. You have been studying the libretto?'

Dorothea mimed her emphatic agreement.

'The director is very demanding. He was an actor of considerable renown. He will test your knowledge of the work rigorously.' Mr Martelli looked at his watch. 'You should check the train times. You may have to spend the night in Leeds.'

His bombshell dropped, Mr Martelli picked up his hat and expressed his regret that he had to leave so soon; he had many other calls to make. There were musicians to audition and subscribers to cultivate. He would telephone the next day to make the arrangements.

Mr Woodward began to wish he had stayed at work. He foresaw only too clearly the problems of etiquette and propriety that his wife would agonise about in unanswerable questions. If she ever exhausted that subject she would move on to demanding a thorough explanation from Heaven of what exactly she had done to deserve such a headstrong daughter. Then Dorothea would wail, plot and scheme until she got her own way. He wondered whether to ring Edward at work. After all, he told himself, Dorothea's reputation was her husband's problem now.

Noises in the hall saved him from taking that cowardly way out. As Mr Martelli made to leave the twins could be heard returning from their walk. Above the scuffles of feet and childish murmurings a woman's voice floated clear.

'Isambard, put that down.'

Dorothea rose to her feet. 'Good. Nanny's back.'

A gloomy Mr Woodward watched as the study door closed behind Dorothea and Mr Martelli. He could not help thinking how much more satisfactory it would be if Dorothea's first thought was not of Nanny but to rush out to hug her children. On the other side of the closed door, Dorothea's joy at securing the audition, overwhelmed her. She just had to hug someone. Her arms found themselves round Signor Martelli and her lips landed on his cheek.

'Have no fear,' she told him. I will be in Leeds next Thursday if I have to crawl there on my hands and knees.'

When Dorothea arrived in the nursery Nanny sent for another small portion of shepherd's pie and settled down to listen to the children – and their mother. Isambard and Clare dealt succinctly with the events of their morning at nursery school. Sums. Milk. Football. Hopscotch. Letters. Johny Entwistle sicked up on his shoes.

The nursery regime insisted on a half hour of quiet time after lunch. While the children drew or read, Dorothea talked of the audition and the ferocity of her ambition to have the part. Routine then dictated that, weather permitting, a walk followed. The twins scampered about while Nanny quizzed Dorothea about the concert tour. 'A pity Neville and Duncan can't audition.'

'I know. They are good. I expect Mr Martelli will get them plenty of concert bookings. They'll be cheaper than me.' Dorothea smirked smugly.

'How will they manage? Not being able to see.'

Dorothea came to a sudden halt with surprise written on her face. 'Strange. I forget about that. Once you're inside working with them and they know where things are they just power along. They must have terrific concentration.'

'But travelling? That must be difficult for them.'

'Duncan's sister, Charity, looks after all that.'

'She sounds a useful sort of person. Tell me about her,' said Nanny. 'How old is she for a start? Does she organise her brother's clothes? Is she any good at it?'

Back at the house Nanny enquired whether Mrs Woodward had returned from her visits. She had. Dorothea was poised to escape to the piano to practise for her audition when Nanny laid a restraining hand on her arm.

'Remember what we said about getting people on your side. Your mother first. Then you might like to phone the office to see if Mr Carter will be home in time to have tea with the children.' Nanny gave one of her meaningful looks. Dorothea got the message and went to make the telephone call before going to face her mother.

She found her in a good mood. Mrs Woodward had been introduced to a lady new to Atherley who had not heard the full details of the Lord Lieutenant's reception. Mrs Woodward had enjoyed enlightening her.

'Well, mother, there'll be plenty more such occasions if I get my way. There must be a Lord Lieutenant for Yorkshire and if I get that part ....' Dorothea's voice trailed away as she looked misty-eyed into a glittering future where she was feted by the cream of that large and wealthy county. Mrs Woodward glimpsed the same vision. Suddenly Yorkshire did not seem so far away.

Dorothea broke the news of the overnight stay and the absence of Neville and Duncan at the audition to her mother. She forestalled the inevitable complaints of impropriety by suggesting that Charity should be her travelling companion. She had successfully guided two blind men by bus and rail to unfamiliar destinations and found them places to rest their heads at night. Not only did she deal with the travel arrangements, she also organised the singers' wardrobes. They were remarkably well turned out.

Mrs Woodward chewed the matter over before conceding that the presence of Duncan's sister would satisfy the conventions. The woman's name alone promised virtue of Biblical proportions.

'If she will come,' Dorothea warned and looked serious.

Mrs Woodward rose to the bait. She spluttered outrage. 'What silly nonsense. Of course she'll come. She'll be well paid, and she must know about all the good work that your father's done for Henshaw's'.

'Her brother might need her.'

'It's only one night for goodness sake. Somebody else can do that.' Mrs Woodward could not envisage anyone turning down an offer from the Woodwards. So it was agreed that Dorothea should spend the night in a hotel in Leeds with Charity as travelling companion, maid and chaperon. Dorothea slipped away to the nursery to run the arrangement past her husband who was busy demolishing tiny sandwiches and iced cake.

'I've never stood in the way of your musical ambitions, Dorothea,' Edward told her. 'If your mother – and father – are happy with the arrangements, then I am.' Dorothea took the hint and went to tell her father the good news. After all he would be paying for it.

CHAPTER 10

While Jenny lived in hope of extracting more information from Mavis about the exact nature of her professional activities, a much more serious problem was tormenting her friend; it was the security of her savings. As they grew, her fear of losing them increased. She tucked the bank notes and the coins behind bricks, up the chimney and under floorboards in the room she shared with her mother. Given the flimsy nature of the door lock and the unsavoury nature of the neighbourhood, Mavis decided that secrecy was her best defence. When leaving for work in the morning, she warned her mother with monotonous regularity, 'Be sure to lock up when you, go out.'

Her mother! She was another major cause for concern. Her hours of work as a seamstress were erratic. An unexpected death might involve working long hours to complete making the necessary mourning clothes, followed by days with nothing more arduous than letting out a bodice. On such days Mavis's mother sought consolation in the pub. Sometimes she came home in the afternoon with a drinker who had turned into a client. While his money was welcome the risk he presented was not. Mavis pictured a satisfied customer prowling round the room in search of the tell-tale scratches and signs of wear that would give away her hiding places, while her mother snored on the bed.

At their next rendezvous at the Cozy Corner the urge to share her problem with Jenny overwhelmed Mavis. She leant across the table, to avoid being overheard.

'I've got nearly £90,' she confided. Jenny raised her eyebrows in query. 'The money for a house,' Mavis explained.

'That is amazing.'

'I know. I counted it up last night. I could hardly believe it myself.' Mavis squeaked with triumph. Her enjoyment was brief. 'The trouble is that I'm scared. I'm scared I'll be robbed. I have to leave it when I go to work.'

'Surely you've put it in your Post Office Savings account?'

Mavis pulled a face.

'Why not? For goodness sake, Mavis, you work there. It couldn't be easier.'

Mavis looked stubborn. 'That's exactly why. I don't want people to know how much I've got.'

'It's supposed to be private.'

Mavis gave her friend a withering look. She forgave Jenny her ignorance of the ways of the world; she had led a sheltered life.

'I know it's supposed to be private but word will get out. It always does. And everybody who's a bit short on the rent will come to me for a loan. The next thing will be a man in a mask with a crowbar levering up the floorboards.'

Jenny could find no words of comfort for her friend. Only last week her father had recorded the death of an old man bludgeoned to death in his lodging for a few gold sovereigns hidden under the mattress.

When she went home she sought help in finding an answer to the problem. Her Aunt Anna was busy laying the table for tea.

'You know I still have my Post Office Savings account,' Jenny began.

'Pleased to hear it,' her aunt answered with a smile. 'Your father is still very keen on the Post Office.' They both chuckled softly.

'Is there anywhere else I could keep my savings? Apart from the blue tea caddy.'

'Well, there are banks,' Anna ventured. She felt uncomfortable talking about savings; she had determinedly kept the existence of a small inheritance a secret from John. Experience had taught her that, if humanly possible a woman should have a nest egg in case of emergencies. 'You can put your money in the bank. They will look after your savings for you,' she told Jenny.

'You mean, like Parr's Bank. Carter-Woodward use them for the business account.'

'You don't have to be a business to open an account there.'

'You mean me. I could have one.'

'Women can have their own bank accounts.' Anna felt no need to reveal the existence of hers. 'This is the twentieth century.'

'I thought Parr's was just for business.'

'And men,' Anna joked. She gazed wide-eyed at Jenny and put on a shocked face, as if in disbelief of the girl she regarded as her daughter. 'And you're supposed to be a finance officer!' She raised her voice in mock outrage.

It came to Jenny as a startling revelation that a finance officer without a bank account was about as convincing as a coal miner without a Davey lamp. Accordingly she put on her best hat and braced herself to pass through the glossy green doors of Parr's Bank. The clerks looked up from their counting at the unfamiliar sound of a woman's high heeled shoes clicking on the marble floor. Behind their metal grilles the young men exchanged excited glances. Who would be first to approach this rare and exotic visitor from the world of women?

The manager's nephew rose to his feet and was about to claim that privilege when a bark of disapproval from behind a bushy grey moustache put an end to his chivalry. His uncle, the silver-haired manager strode out to deal with the intruder.

Jenny explained she had come to open an account. The manager stroked his moustache and looked thoughtful. He did not show the enthusiasm she expected from a man who'd just been offered money. Instead he droned on about contracts, signatures, legality and formal agreements. While he talked, more customers of the trouser-wearing variety arrived. They were greeted with 'Good mornings' and whisked off into private offices to do their business.

Unlike the male customers, Jenny was kept standing on the marble floor until the moustached manager could no longer avoid asking the indelicate question of her age. On finding that she was not yet 21 he looked serious as he told her that she could not open an account in her own name. She must return with a husband, father, brother, anyone as long as he was male and prepared to be her guarantor. He gestured to the door.

As she described her experience at home that evening Jenny's cheeks burned pink with indignation. John Truesdale did not take kindly to his daughter being shown the door. He patted her arm and promised to accompany her to the bank the next day. This time she was not left to cool her heels, but ushered into a room with a table and chairs so they could sit in comfort as they dealt with the formalities. It was all deference and respect until the banker wanted proof of Jenny's age. John, well-known in the town as the Registrar of Births, Marriages and Deaths, had to admit, with some embarrassment, that he could not produce the necessary evidence. Jenny was a foundling and John had not got round to supplying her with an adoption certificate.

The banker laughed. 'The carpenter's table,' he said with a smile. John assured him he would stand as guarantor and took the opportunity to brag about Jenny's position of finance officer at Carter-Woodward. There was an immediate and subtle change in the banker's demeanour. When they rose to leave he rushed to open the door for Jenny. Safely outside Jenny asked her father what the bank manager meant about the carpenter' table. John laughed. 'It's always the carpenter's own table that wobbles. Just as it's the plumber's tap that leaks.'

At their next meeting Jenny was quick to tell Mavis that she had found an answer to her problem.

'I've put my money's in Parr's Bank. They look after the firm's money, and they would look after yours. Nothing to do with the Post Office.'

Mavis fell silent. The prospect of walking through the bank's dark green door with its polished brass fittings sent her cold with fear. Her good clothes would help her pass at first sight as a respectable young woman of the middle class. However, connoisseurs of the subject would quickly relegate her to the lower end of that wide and successful slice of humanity. When she spoke her accent would send her sliding further down the scale. 'Banks only look after posh people's money,' she declared mournfully.

I'll go with you,' said Jenny. 'They know me now.' She remembered the courage it had taken and the frostiness of her reception. 'Bring your birth certificate with you.'

Mavis wailed. 'You mean, I really have to go there. In person. To the bank.'

'Of course. You will have to take your money to them.'

'Can't you do that for me?'

'No. it's your money. They might think I've stolen it.'

'They might think **I've** stolen it,' said Mavis, her voice suddenly shrill.

Women all over the café pricked up their ears. Jenny shushed her friend. Better not to feed their curiosity. 'True', she conceded. 'We'd better have an explanation. I think your mother should be part of it. You'll want her to be able to get money out.'

'No.' Women's heads turned towards them again. The panic in Mavis's voice was unmistakeable. She beckoned for Jenny to lean closer. 'My mother's part of the problem. She likes a drink, and a bit of company in the day. She's a soft touch.'

'Don't say anything. Just nod if you agree,' said Jenny, aware that their voices might carry in a sudden lull in the hum of conversation. 'Just nod.'

Mavis did a lot of nodding as Jenny sketched out a plan. They agreed that speed was important. The fatherless Mavis was in possession of a birth certificate, an irony that did not escape Jenny. Mavis, was 21, so would not need a male guarantor. With some trepidation Jenny offered to ask her father to accompany them. The mere presence of a man always made things go more smoothly.

Jenny was surprised to find that John Truesdale needed little persuading to help 'that Mavis' open a bank account. The discovery that the girl had sufficient savings to be concerned about its safety gave him several rounds of fresh ammunition for his disapproval of Jenny leaving the Post Office to work at Carter-Woodward.

'You see, Jenny, that Mavis must have some serious savings. She has a good reliable employer – the Post Office. Not liable to slow-downs and short time when demand is low.' Jenny bit her lip. this was not the moment to start an argument.

The next day at dinner time, John Truesdale left his office to walk to the Carter-Woodward office to meet his daughter and 'that Mavis'. She arrived promptly in the white blouse and dark jacket she wore for her work at the Post Office. She carried with her, concealed about her person, all her savings and a hefty attack of nerves which was clearly visible. Mavis was convinced she would be attacked and robbed before she entered the bank. Both prospects terrified her.

Jenny came down the spiral staircase, swiftly followed by Mr Frederick, on his way to fetch a pie for Mr Carter's lunch. Introductions were made and the four chatted happily. Both John and Mavis had their reasons to be curious about the dapper Mr Frederick. John shook his hand warmly. Perhaps the smartly dressed young man would distract Jenny from her doomed infatuation with that Edward Carter. Mavis observed the secretary's polished shoes and manners and congratulated herself on not applying for the job he now held. She would have stood no chance against such competition and the promised dowry was tantalisingly close.

As they talked, the group on the pavement did not know that they were being observed from above. Hunger was making Edward Carter bad-tempered. He peered out of his office window and saw the four people on the pavement below. The sight of John Truesdale talking at length to Mr Frederick enraged him. This was the same John Truesdale who stood blocking his open front door to prevent Edward advancing beyond the foot of the steps. Now that same John Truesdale was shaking Mr Frederick's hand, smiling and talking and taking far too long to say goodbye. The temptation to lean out of the window and tell the pesky secretary to get a move on and bring his dinner was almost irresistible. Edward rested his elbows on the windowsill and screwed his hands into fists to stop himself from shouting like some irascible bully of a boss. It would not do for Jenny to hear him behave like that.

It was a relief when the group walked off.

At the bank, the moustached manager came to greet the three of them. Mavis produced her birth certificate and John stood about looking supportive. Why, he wondered, was he always standing in for absent fathers? To thank him for his generous act, Jenny whisked him off to Cozy Corner for a bite of lunch, leaving Mavis to complete the formalities at the bank.

The manager's nephew, a suave young man, ushered Mavis into a room with a large window that enabled the occupants to be observed from the central hall. Mavis had hoped for somewhere more private. The suave young man explained that for reasons of security that was not possible. She gritted her teeth, turned her back to the young man and the window, rummaged under her jacket and produced two black ribbons. She sucked in her stomach, pulled the ribbons and hauled up two packages concealed beneath her skirt. Then from the two large pockets in her skirt, she unloaded several hand sewn bags packed with coins – mainly half crowns and sovereigns. They were tightly wrapped to stop them rattling. She produced a tiny pair of scissors, slit the bags open and poured the money onto the table with a great clatter. Mavis smiled; it was such a relief to be free of the burden of keeping it all safe.

The suave young clerk, horrified by the great number of coins, promptly shouted for Perkins to come and count the money. The manager's nephew did not undertake such mundane labour if he could avoid it; money is famously dirty. He made his excuses to leave the room but insisted that Mavis stay to observe the counting; it was the custom to avoid any dispute over the final amount. A smiling Mavis agreed; she did not have to return to work as she had the afternoon off. Perkins was left to sort and count the coins. He set about it with a will, stacking them neatly in piles. He carried out the task meticulously and both were delighted to find that they agreed on the final amount. The manager returned to present Mavis with a receipt and her cheque book. He spent an inordinate amount of time warning her against writing cheques or withdrawing money she did not have. Mavis, now recovered from her fears, knew her role was to nod obediently and look as if she was listening.

The manager smiled at her and asked if she had plans for spending her money. When she said she wanted to buy a house he looked doubtful, pursed his lips and warned her she still had quite a way to go. He hinted that the bank might be able to offer her a loan, or a mortgage to make up any shortfall when the time came. The suave clerk, not wishing to be left out, arrived and talked of compound interest and debentures. Mavis put on her listening face and nodded until their egos were sufficiently plumped to allow them to take their leave.

Perkins was left to take a sample signature. He blushed as he handed her a pen and a slip of paper. All the questions Mavis had not asked the other men came bubbling up to her lips for Perkins to answer. What if her cheque book were stolen? How would the bank know it was – or wasn't – her signature?

Perkins was earnest in his reassurance. He understood her concerns; he came from the crowded smoky streets of the town where theft and forgery were not unknown and tight budgets were the norm. What if someone with the same name signed one of Mavis's cheques?

'It doesn't matter if it's the same name. If it's not your signature, it's stealing. Then it's our fault not yours.'

'You see my mother has the same name. This is not family money. I must be the only one able to withdraw money,' she insisted.

'Don't worry,' said Perkins, 'I will make a note on your account. It will be a pleasure to look out for you.' As he spoke his heart gave a great leap as the blood thundered through it and rushed up to his face. The momentous wave subsided leaving him pale and dazed. He stared sightlessly into space.

Mavis waved the pen at him. 'Specimen signature,' she said to remind him. She dipped the pen in the black ink and wrote Mavis Haslam with two very curly capital letters. She smiled at Perkins as she handed him the slip of paper with her name on it and made her way out.

The manager and the suave clerk watched her as she walked to the door. Her waist was tiny, and her skirts swung provocatively now they were free of the weight of her troublesome earnings.

'So that's what you get for half a crown,' said the manager. His lips curled with lascivious pleasure at the thought.

'More like five shillings,' said the suave nephew. 'She's very pretty and she smells nice.' They watched her leave and returned to their balance sheets.

Fortunately Perkins did not hear their conversation. He failed to hear many more important things in the course of that afternoon. In truth as an employee of Parr's bank he was useless for the rest of the day. He did not realise it but he had fallen in love.

Mavis enjoyed the rest of the afternoon away from her counter at the Post Office. She felt ridiculously happy. Freed from the burden of protecting her cash she grew positively frivolous. She might even give her mother the money to go for a drink at the pub, while she enjoyed a quiet evening with Sherlock Holmes as her only male companion.

CHAPTER 11

It took a small army to get Dorothea to her audition before the director in Leeds. Signor Martelli spoke of the man with awe. He was a famous actor of Shakespeare, who had triumphed as King Lear and now fancied trying his hand at directing opera. His insistence on perfection and his rage when it was not delivered were legendary. 'Be prepared to be rejected at least twice,' Signor Martelli had told Dorothea. She gave him a contemptuous stare and called on the many resources at her command to prove him wrong. From the voice coach to the glovemaker, they were summoned and given their orders. Charity was warned to be available to accompany Dorothea on the train to Leeds and to stay overnight if necessary.

Mr Woodward stepped in at this point. The prospect of Dorothea not sleeping safely under his roof always perturbed him. He assumed that Edward suffered from the same anxiety and suggested they sought advice from Stan Kershaw, an old business connection from his early days. Some family tragedy years ago, Mr Woodward could not remember the details, had led him to move away from Atherley. He'd set himself up in Hull where he dabbled his fingers in lots of pies: haulage, transport and finance. He even went abroad, buying and selling, wheeling and dealing. A telegram to Stan in Hull and the anxious father soon had the name of a reliable hotel in Leeds while his daughter's husband had a valuable new contact in the wider world beyond Atherley.

'Stan's a good chap,' said Mr Woodward, 'but he does like to wander. Not exactly a home bird.' Edward kept his face a careful blank; he liked the sound of Stan.

When Dorothea was satisfied that the dressmakers, launderesses, hairdressers and milliners had done their work to her satisfaction, she dismissed them. With the doughty Charity in the lead, she set off for Leeds while her father stayed behind to pay the bills. Dorothea was surprised to discover that Signor Martelli was in Leeds to greet her. He assured her that he had come to support his favourite client. She was a star in the making. He did not want her extinguished by the careless snap of some arrogant man's fingers.

The famous director proved as fearsome as his reputation. He scowled, he barked, he commanded, as he put Dorothea through her paces. Again. And again. Sweat dripped from her armpits into her linen underwear.

'Are you afraid of heights?' he demanded. Dorothea saw where he was going.

'I am not afraid of heights,' she told him. 'Or of falling,' she added to prove she knew that the character of Tosca falls to her death at the end of the opera. What might have been a smile at her answer passed across the director's face. Was she earning his grudging respect? 'How do you feel about stabbing a man?' he bellowed straight into her face. 'A pleasure', she shot back at him, her eyes flashing and her red lips curling. An electric spark passed between them. He signalled to the pianist and shouted, 'Vissi d'arte. Sing now.' As she sang the director sat in his chair examining his fingernails and swinging his legs.

'Where's Martelli gone?' he demanded when she had finished. 'Damn the man. Never there when you need him.'

Dorothea's plucked eyebrows squirmed with rage. She scowled at the director and made to leave the stage in a visibly bad temper. The director raised his hand to stop her. 'Stop now. You've got the part.' There was a sprinkling of applause from stagehands and musicians. Charity rose from her seat in the stalls and clapped.

In view of the director's reputation, Dorothea felt she was expected to act as if it was a surprise. It wasn't. She had worked for this. She had earned it. It felt that all her life, her successes and failures, her trials and tribulations were simply a preparation for this very moment. She was coming into her destiny.

Signor Martelli arrived panting. He had been working on a pretty violinist with a weakness for gin when word reached him. 'I knew it,' he told the director. 'She is perfect.' Dorothea smiled her approval at him.

'We have to talk business,' said the director beckoning Signor Martelli. He waved a hand at Charity and then at Dorothea. 'Find your mistress some tea or something,' and led Signor Martelli away to one of the boxes. 'How tightly have you got her signed up?' he asked, settling into the brocade armchair.

'Tight enough,' said Signor Martelli.

The director struck a match to light his cigar. He sucked thoughtfully on it before coming to business with the rotund Italian. Between puffs of tobacco, the director droned on, offering a rich mix of bribes and threats in exchange for the services of Dorothea Woodward in *Tosca*. It soon dawned on Signor Martelli that the director had also spotted a future star, one like Adelina Patti, who was reputed to earn £1,000 a week in London. He smiled; he knew he held the winning hand.

They agreed a fairly modest fee for *Tosca* in Leeds. In return, the director was to be praised in the press for discovering this sensational new singer, and she would be appearing in his future productions in London. He promised not to poach her from Signor Martelli. They shook hands on the deal, and Signor Martelli went to tell Dorothea that she was booked for *Tosca*. She took the news calmly; it was only to be expected.

Charity proved her worth by pointing out there was just time to catch the last train to Manchester. If Signor Martelli telegraphed the good news to Dorothea's parents they could send a car to meet them at 11.40 in Manchester.

'You're a walking timetable,' Signor Martelli told her. He calculated that it was better to return Dorothea promptly to her father and keep in his good books before the weeks of rehearsal started. He glanced at his watch. The pretty violin player might still be available.

Mr Woodward was relieved to hear that Dorothea was on her way home. Mr Martelli moved up a notch in his estimation for sending him the telegram and his daughter. Even so, a long and anxious evening awaited him until he heard the car return and saw Dorothea walk through the door. Edward had decided to keep him company in his vigil. It seemed a husbandly sort of thing to do. He planned to take advantage of the time to prepare his father-in-law for an important new project and to quiz him about Stan Kershaw. Edward settled in the armchair the other side of the fire and asked about Mr Woodward's old friend.

'Not seen him for ages. He flits about. Invaluable chap. Ask him about anything, any place. If he doesn't know the answer, he knows someone who does.' The conversation wandered on vaguely until the older man's eye lids began to droop and he fell asleep.

The arrival of Dorothea woke him. He felt his customary surprise at her beauty. She looked as groomed and glossy as she had when she left in the morning. The long train journeys and the gruelling audition had left no mark on her.

Her father congratulated her and asked about the contract. She waved a dismissive hand. 'Martelli's got it. He dealt with all that.' She urged the men to get to their beds. That's where she was going after she'd been to the nursery. Mr Woodward accepted his dismissal with pleasure. He genuinely thought that Dorothea was going to the nursery to gaze fondly at the angelic faces of her sleeping children and gently kiss their cheeks. Edward was under no such illusion.

Dorothea went quietly past the beds where her children lay and tapped gently on the door of the room where Nanny slept. She did not wait to be invited in. The moonlight through the curtains showed Nanny's night cap emerging from the bedclothes followed by Nanny herself in her long-sleeved flannel nightdress. Dorothea wrapped her arms round the woman who was an expert in comforting frightened children, and began to sob.

For some time the only words came from Nanny. 'There, there, dear girl. There, there,' as she patted Dorothea's back.

When speech returned to her all Dorothea could say was, 'I've done it, Nanny, At last. I've done it.'

CHAPTER 12

Mavis was very grateful to Jenny who, with a little help from her father, had smoothed the way to finding a safe refuge for her money. The next time they met at the Cozy Corner she insisted on paying the bill. 'Just this once,' she warned. 'I'm still saving furiously.' To Jenny's surprise Mavis was not wearing her colourful scarves and flower-trimmed hat. There was no exotic fragrance wafting from the white blouse and grey jacket she routinely wore to work behind the counter at the Post Office. Mavis might be dressed severely and saving furiously but she exuded happiness. She smiled as she spoke and even offered to order a teacake, which Jenny tactfully declined.

How can she look so happy, wondered Jenny, when she makes her money by letting strangers free with the secret bits of her anatomy. A cheery Mavis hummed as she dealt with the teapot. Jenny surreptitiously scanned the edges of the room for the man with the maroon waistcoat. She spotted him quietly reading his newspaper. She hoped he wasn't feeling peckish again. She didn't want Mavis to dash off leaving her alone with the bill again.

Mavis saw the direction of Jenny's eyes and guessed where her thoughts were going. 'No,' she snapped and raised a warning finger. 'Do not ask. You have forgotten about him completely.' It was the old Mavis, the sharp, snippy girl who could stop a wild youth in his tracks with a well-chosen word and a dagger of a look.

Jenny gulped back the question rising to her lips. Mavis leant forward to explain like a kindly teacher. 'I know you want to know about '**It**' but I can't talk about **it.** It's the rule. Tarts don't talk.' She handed Jenny a cup of tea as she explained. 'It's not fair to the other person concerned. Take my advice. When your turn comes just make sure he's the right one.' Mavis stirred sugar into her tea and smiled at the memory of a recent event. 'It helps if one of you knows what you're doing,' she added with a meaningful look.

Why is the continuance of the human race such a great mystery, Jenny wondered. **It** can't be too unpleasant a process. Babies are being born all the time.

Mavis tried to soften her friend's disappointment. 'You're in business, Jenny. You don't give away information about your customers. It's not good practice. Same for me. If a man pays me, we have a contract. Silence on my side is part of the deal.'

Jenny could see she had lost her one source of information on the subject. There was no use in asking her sister Margaret, a student of the Classics who kept to herself the juicy details of the more notorious aspects of Roman life. It seemed to Jenny she would remain in total ignorance unless – or until she got married. Given her love for Edward, it seemed most likely she would soon become that most despised cartoon character, an old maid.

To her surprise it was Mavis who returned to the subject. Most unusually she went pink and hesitated before launching herself into new territory. 'If I were to fall in love', she tittered girlishly, 'that would be a different matter. If there was no money involved, and I did it because I wanted to, because I felt attracted to the man and just couldn't stop myself. Well that is very private. I wouldn't talk about it. Just a kiss can be so very wonderful.' She gazed dreamily at the teapot for several seconds before remembering her promise and calling for the bill.

When the waitress arrived, Mavis was true to her word and paid for both of them. 'I may not be able to meet you here on our usual day next week,' she warned Jenny, but gave no explanation, leaving her friend thoroughly puzzled. Mavis kept secret the slip of paper in her pocket that had been passed across her counter at the Post Office. It asked her to meet the writer in the Market Place at 6 o'clock. It was signed Andrew Perkins.

A week later, Jenny with her customary quiet speed, came down the spiral staircase from the office. She was looking forward to meeting Mavis at Cozy Corner. As she swung open the heavy door with its grubby window of bubbled glass, she found a small boy standing outside.

'You Miss Truesdale?' he demanded. 'Lady gave me a note for you.' He held a note up in his grubby fist and put on a hard face.

108

Jenny knew how to deal with the miniature gangsters who thronged the streets. She handed him a halfpenny in exchange for the note though she guessed what it said. The boy ran off happy and Jenny read that Mavis was not coming. She gave no reason.

'Drat,' she said.

'A problem?' Mr Frederick was behind her.

'My friend's just cancelled.' Jenny waved the note as proof.

'Let me guess. You were going to have a cup of tea and a pleasant talk.'

Jenny laughed. 'Are women so predictable?'

'No. But that is exactly what I am going to do. Perhaps you would join me? I am going to Cozy Corner. I believe it is an acceptable place for a lady such as yourself.'

Jenny brightened up. She could sit with Mr Frederick, where the man in the maroon waistcoat read his newspaper as he waited for his bus; it would be interesting to look at the 'Ladies only' section from the outside.

When they arrived at the café they circled the temporarily forbidden Ladies Only section and headed to the perimeter. Mr Frederick indicated a table and looked to Jenny for her approval. She nodded Yes and settled herself on the seat that he had pulled out for her. These little courtesies were very pleasant. They could be hers on a regular basis if only she could rid herself of her love for Edward. That she knew would be an act of unimaginable violence, leaving her limp and lifeless like a rag doll robbed of its stuffing by an inquisitive child.

'Tea?' Mr Frederick was asking. 'English Breakfast?' He raised a hand with the forefinger pressed against the thumb. Jenny was pleased to see he did not, as so many men did, click his fingers. The waitress arrived when she spotted his gesture. What it is to be a man, thought Jenny. Able to go where you please with every expectation of a welcome, no asking permission or worrying that it might not be respectable. When the tea arrived, the waitress left a saucer with the bill laid on it. She set it directly in front of Mr Frederick, making it clear that the man was expected to pay. This settled a problem that had been niggling Jenny, so used to negotiating that question with Mavis. She need not offer to share the bill on this occasion.

When it came to the teapot, the waitress turned the handle towards Jenny. Pouring tea was woman's work. Once that task was completed Jenny racked her brain for a topic of conversation that did not involve work.

'How are you getting on with the colliery band?'

'Splendidly. A great set of men. They have invited me to play my trombone in one of the competitions. I get to visit other towns.' Mr Frederick came to life as he talked about his trips with the band. At first there had been difficult moments because he did not always understand their customs or their jokes, but they forgave the mistakes he made through ignorance. 'We've all got to learn,' they would say and clap him on the shoulder. As he talked Jenny looked for the man in the maroon waistcoat. Perhaps he had already gone for his bus. She glanced towards the clock to see if was already half past five, but she never found out. Something distracted her from seeing the time.

The something was Mavis, the very same Mavis who had sent a note to say she could not come to Cozy Corner. True it was not the Mavis in a cloud of pastel scarves, wafting perfume and sparkling jewellery. This was the Post Office Mavis, in her dark suit and high-necked blouse and this Mavis was not in the Ladies Only section. She was sitting at a table opposite a young gentleman in a dark suit. Jenny strained to see his face. A woman's wide-brimmed hat trimmed with osprey feathers blocked her view. There was only one explanation. Mavis had dumped her friend to accommodate a paying customer, a man that she was going to go and do **it** with while still refusing to explain to Jenny exactly what **it** was...

As Jenny planned her revenge, she was surprised by the appearance of her Aunt Anna who emerged from the Ladies Only section where she had been waiting – rather a long time - for Jenny's father. Anna explained that tea at Cozy Corner was a small treat they enjoyed when John's fees as registrar passed a certain level. Jenny gestured for the woman she regarded as her mother to join them.

'Mavis had to cancel?' Aunt Anna enquired. Jenny avoided going into detail by introducing Mr Frederick. He raised his hand like a guilty schoolboy and explained that he had taken advantage of Mavis's absence. John Truesdale arrived, another chair was found and the four sat to enjoy their tea.

'A profitable week is not always an occasion to celebrate you understand,' said John. 'In the winter influenza is the main reason why people need my services. In the summer it's weddings.' He beamed at Mr Frederick as if giving his blessing to a happy couple. Jenny glared at him until he changed the subject by asking the younger man if he still spoke German.

'I read it more than I speak. I keep up with the newspapers.'

John was a great reader of the newspaper. Now they had a topic of mutual interest the conversation flowed. Jenny found that it was pleasant to sit with her family with a man at her side. This must be how a married woman feels, she thought, no longer the child of her parents, but a grown-up with a seat at the table. She quickly dismissed the daydream. It was all a façade, a façade built on a lie, a lie that started with Mavis. She flicked a glance towards the clock and saw that Mavis had gone. Just as well. Better that her parents did not spot her as Jenny would find it difficult to explain to them exactly what 'that Mavis' was up to.

When it was time to leave John shook Mr Frederick's hand, making no attempt to disguise his approval. When it came to paying the bill he over-ruled all the younger man's offers to pay.

'Nice chap that Mr Frederick,' he said when they got home. Anna went to play the piano. She knew what John was trying to do. He still hoped to cure Jenny of Edward, but Anna knew that the attempt was doomed. If there was a cure for hopeless love, she would have found it. It was a disease that had afflicted her for many years.

Five whole days passed before Jenny's curiosity about Mavis got the better of her. Edward was in his office in deep conversation with Mr Frederick, something that happened a lot recently. They were planning something. Jenny put her head round the door and announced they were out of stamps.

'See if the penny post works for Germany while you're there,' Edward called after her. Germany wondered Jenny. Mr Frederick said nothing but looked meaningful. She would find out later; her immediate target was Mavis who owed her an explanation at least. At the Post Office, Mavis had the grace to murmur, 'Sorry,' through the metal grille. 'It's a long story,' she began 'and I'm not sure how it is going to end.'

They arranged to meet in the Market Square after work in 2 days' time. 'Not the Cozy Corner,' Mavis insisted, 'I'll need something stronger than tea.'

It was again Mavis the working woman who waited in the Market Square. No chiffon scarves, no powder or pink lip salve. She greeted Jenny with her familiar, 'All right then,' grabbed her arm, and steered her towards the Coach and Horses.

Jenny gasped, 'I can't go in there. It's pub. They sell beer.'

'Shows how much you know about pubs. A pub is full of drunks. This is an inn. Travellers stopped here in the old days to rest the horses and take refreshment. Nothing wrong with taking a little refreshment.' Somehow Jenny found herself seated at a table with an elegant glass of golden liquid in front of her.

'Sip it,' warned Mavis. 'I don't suppose you've had Madeira before.'

The wine scalded the back of Jenny's throat and rendered her speechless. Just as well, Mavis could not wait to tell her news. 'Sorry about the notes and stuff. When you get the whole story you'll understand it was all absolutely necessary.'

'Skip the flimflam. Get to the point. You've some explaining to do.' Jenny gave Mavis a commanding stare. To her horror Mavis, the child of the slums, toughened by hardship and the rough end of the stick, melted into tears. Her face crumpled and her voice strangled in her throat as she struggled to tell Jenny how happy she was.

'Happy!' Jenny shrieked in disbelief. The weeping Mavis nodded and unable to explain in words laid her left hand on the table. A ring sparkled on her third finger.

Jenny pushed her wineglass across the table to Mavis; her friend's need suddenly greater than hers. She settled herself down to listen.

'It was that trip to the bank that did it. You know that young clerk, not the snobby one, the nice one that does all the real work.' Jenny nodded. 'Well, he came to the Post Office, passed me a note. He'd like to meet me. Here in the Market Square. Brought me here for a bit of supper. Walked me home. Perfect gentleman. Same again the next week. He's not a big talker. Week 3 and I can't wait any longer. I sent my Mam to the pub, took him home and gave him something to loosen his tongue.'

Jenny knew better than to ask exactly how Mavis had persuaded the young man to talk.

'It's real love,' said Mavis, disbelief in her voice. 'The minute he saw me. The words came into his head. That's the girl I'm going to marry. Went all to pieces. Couldn't count the coins, balance the books or remember what he'd gone to the safe for. They didn't know what was the matter with him. Thought he'd caught something nasty.'

'Does he have a name?'

'Andrew. Andrew Perkins.' Just saying his name brought a tender smile to Mavis's lips.

'I remember him. He must be a clever lad to work at Parr's bank.'

'Oh yes. Not much longer though. We've got plans.'

'I'm guessing marriage is one of them,' said Jenny indicating the ring.

'It was his mother's. She died a couple of months ago.'

Just as well thought Jenny, given Mavis's recent choice of career. That was exactly the kind of information a hostile mother-in-law would ferret out.

'We are getting married.' Mavis thumped the table to show her satisfaction. 'And I will get my dowry.' Another thump on the table.

The noise attracted a glance from two men at the bar. They quickly looked away and returned to their beer.

'We must both have Unavailable stamped on us,' said Jenny. They started to laugh. Life was suddenly wonderful, or was it the

Madeira? To make sure, Mavis ordered two more glasses and insisted she really would pay this time. She had a lot more to tell Jenny and money was no longer so tight.

It was late when Jenny returned home. Anna had her suspicions but asked no questions until she had given her a sandwich and a cup of tea. Fortunately her father was out at a council meeting. 'Something to do with street lights,' her aunt explained.

'That'd get my vote,' said Jenny. She had watched nervously as Mavis disappeared into the blackness of the cramped dark streets where she lived. Even her own journey home along wider roads in a respectable neighbourhood had proved mildly alarming. She was not accustomed to being out so late on her own and was grateful for the lanterns on the occasional carriage or the headlights of an even rarer passing car.

The thought that one of the passing cars might be Edward's sent her mind reeling. It hit her with the force of an express train. He was so close, but was as unobtainable as the Man in the Moon. She boiled at the injustice. Mavis getting married, when she, Jenny, was forever condemned to watch from the side-lines the life of the man she loved. She was like a child standing with her nose pressed against the plate glass of the sweetshop window, an invisible barrier between her and Edward. Her arms ached to hold him, to feel the reality of his strong warm flesh. All she had to console and comfort her was the mirage of his presence.

Jenny put her head in her hands and wept.

Anna put her arms round her and led her to the sofa by the fire where she let her cry and listened to the jumbled protests and gulps of complaint against the rules of a society that insisted Dorothea's hastily acquired husband was condemned to stay with her for the rest of his life.

It was the first time Jenny had spoken openly of her feelings about Edward. Anna stroked her hair and let the emotions and the tears pour out. She had borne her disappointment without complaint until now. They talk about boys having a stiff upper lip, thought Anna. In reality it is women who have specialised in suffering in silence for centuries.

'You've been very brave about it,' she told Jenny. The similarities between Jenny's situation and her own flashed briefly through Anna's mind. Like Jenny she was forbidden by law to marry John, the man she loved. Jenny did not even know of their desire to wed. Anna, the grown up, resisted the temptation to confide in the girl. The child had heartbreak enough of her own. A glance at the clock told her that even a notoriously long-winded council meeting must finish soon.

'Better get to bed before your father gets home,' she told Jenny. 'We don't want him to find out you've been drinking.' She gave her a conspiratorial wink.

It took Jenny a week of serious brooding before she could face Mavis again. She suggested they meet in their lunch hour and stroll round the churchyard which provided the residents of Atherley with their only convenient green space. It seemed better to avoid both Cozy Corner and the Coach and Horses. Mavis, a sudden convert to church attendance, was keen to learn the correct etiquette from Jenny who had been taken to church every Sunday since she was a child.

'Vicar's calling the banns for the first time this Sunday.' Mavis oozed satisfaction as she told Jenny her news.

'So you are having a church wedding?'

'Of course. Andrew has come here,' she gestured at the church, blackened with soot, 'for years. He wouldn't settle for anything less. Said his mother would turn in her grave unless he did.'

'She's not been in it very long, has she?'

Mavis barked a quick laugh. 'Just as well. I've a feeling she'd be wanting to put a spanner in the works.'

'Andrew knows how you earned your money?'

'There was no need to tell. He knew. There's not many young women who open an account with half crowns and ten-shilling notes. The bankers know them all. If they don't have a shop there's only one way to earn it.'

'They never taught that in the Commercial Finance course.' Jenny laughed at the thought. 'Won't he be a bit uncomfortable? Working with people who know that about you.'

'That's partly why he gave in his notice the day he asked the vicar to call the banns.'

'Isn't that a bit rash. He must have prospects.'

'Not for Andrew. That's the other reason for quitting. It's clear that any promotion will go to the manager's nephew, the snobby one. And he's got four brothers. You know how they stick together.'

'What will your Andrew do for work?' A man not working was unthinkable to Jenny.

Mavis appeared to add a couple of inches to her height before she answered with queen-like dignity. 'He will be looking after our business. He's good with figures. He's persuaded Parrs to supply us with a mortgage.' She paused for effect. 'So he will be busy looking after the houses.'

Jenny deluged Mavis with questions. Together the happy couple had considerable resources — a legacy from Andrew's mother, a mortgage from Parrs and Mavis's savings. Enough for at least two houses. Also when they married Mavis would legitimately receive her dowry from the Post Office but would have to stop working for them.

'Just as I planned,' she crowed.

'You'll be unemployed.' Jealousy writhed in Jenny's stomach. 'So this is your famous fool-proof plan'.'

'Not exactly. This time the bridegroom's real.' Mavis beamed with delight. 'I wasn't really going to get married. But I did have a plan.' Happiness loosened her tongue. 'You know my mother has the same name as me. I was going to get her to take one of her drinking chums and apply for a marriage licence at your father's office. It's not like having the banns called when half the town hears it. They just stick the form on the wall in the waiting room.'

'So that's what you mean by fool-proof,' said Jenny. 'My father's the fool. He can't tell the difference between a woman of 21 and her mother of 40-something.'

Mavis rushed to undo the harm she had done. 'They'd never turn up for the wedding. The actual licence costs money. It was just something to tell the Post Office if they wanted to check. I'd hate

116

to make your father look bad. If he'd not gone to the bank with us, I'd never have met Andrew.'

The grim line that had settled on Jenny's jaw softened. Mavis saw she was winning her friend round. 'It was a stupid plan really. So much could go wrong. I kept worrying I'd be left with no job and no dowry. I think the fool was me.'

Jenny didn't disagree with that thought. She crossed her fingers and hoped that Andrew Perkins really had fallen in love with Mavis and wanted to marry her. Otherwise they would both be out of work. 'To be honest, Mavis, it's the Post Office that's not very sensible. Paying women for getting married and then not letting them work just because they are married. Not everyone has a baby straight away.'

'That's not going to happen me.'

Jenny wanted to ask Mavis how she planned to avoid the traditional fate, but the smile of intense happiness that suffused her friend's face stopped her. Mavis hugged herself and rocked on her heels murmuring how she'd never felt so happy. 'And soon everyone will know.' She gestured to the Church. 'You will be here on Sunday when they call out my name – and Andrew's.'

'Just don't shout 'Here'. It's not like the register at school,' Jenny warned her.

The church clock told them it was time to return to work.

Come Sunday Jenny accompanied her parents to church with a little more enthusiasm than usual. She wanted to hear the vicar call the banns for Mavis. Until then she could not believe that Andrew Perkins really wanted to marry Mavis. By all accounts he was a regular attender at church, with a respectable job and conveniently dead parents. Such an eligible young bachelor would be a prime target for every family in the neighbourhood with a daughter of marriageable age. Mavis, a girl who had never been to church, a girl with a past seemed an unlikely choice for him to make.

Most of the congregation at the Atherley Church of England were regular attenders who would bow and nod to familiar faces nearby. Many had their favourite places to sit and would take umbrage if a stranger inadvertently occupied it. When the vicar called the banns for Mavis Haslam, spinster of this parish, there was a rustle among the local matrons. The ladies' hats bobbed about as they looked round the pews for this unknown Mavis. Jenny glanced at her father to see if he had realised Mavis Haslam was 'That Mavis.' He bore the tranquil expression of a man in blissful ignorance with a whole hour of idleness ahead of him.

When the vicar named the intending bridegroom as Andrew Perkins there was subdued exhalation of breath from the matrons and girls in the pews. It was scarcely audible but Jenny and Anna both recognised it for what it was, It was a collective sigh of mourning for the loss of an eligible bachelor. This time the feather-trimmed hats all turned the same way and were directed at the back of the head of a young man in a dark suit. Jenny half expected him to jump up and deny he had any intention of marrying that Mavis; she was a tart. The moment passed without any drama, and it seemed that Andrew Perkins' fate was sealed.

In the week that followed. Jenny went to buy stamps so that she had an opportunity to congratulate Mavis. It seemed as though her marriage really was going to happen.

'I didn't see you in church,' said Jenny.

Mavis went pink. 'I got scared. My Mam got all dressed up but at the last moment I panicked. We just snuck in the back after the service started and left before everyone came out.'

'You did hear the vicar call the banns?'

Mavis beamed with happiness.

'First time's the worst,' said Jenny as if she knew what she was talking about. 'So we'll see you in church next week. You must introduce us to Andrew.'

Mavis passed the unnecessary stamp Jenny had bought across the counter to her. 'We'll see,' she muttered.

As Andrew Perkins had not leapt to his feet in church to deny his intention to marry, Jenny thought it best to make her father aware that Mavis Haslam, spinster of the parish was 'That Mavis' who worked at the Post Office and who John had helped open a bank account. He would meet her at church next Sunday.

If John was looking forward to meeting the happy couple on the second calling of the banns he was in for a disappointment. Neither the intending bride groom nor the future bride put in an appearance. If Andrew Perkins wanted to dismiss the marriage as the fantasy of a disturbed girl he had missed his chance!

Mavis had sent her mother as a representative and an observer. Jenny caught her as she was scuttling away to avoid shaking hands with the vicar. From her mother's stumbling explanation of the happy couple's absence Jenny guessed that Mavis and Andrew were enjoying a Sunday morning in bed. The mother had come as a witness on this occasion but the couple had every intention of being present for the third and final calling of the banns.

'She's done well for herself,' said John. 'Marrying a man who works for Parrs Bank.' He turned to Jenny, who kept her face carefully expressionless as she guessed what was coming. 'You see what you're missing Jenny. That Mavis will get a husband and a dowry from the Post office.'

Jenny paused, savouring the moment before she said, 'And she'll get the sack at the same time.' She grinned at her father before telling him, 'At Carter Woodward we don't have a rule against married women.' She steered him towards the vicar before he worked out how to strike back. It's good to end with a win.

In the safety of her bedroom Jenny pondered the strange rules that she was forced to live by. Carter Woodward had no need for rules for women workers. They only had one, which was Jenny herself. Women never worked in the mines; it was illegal. The cotton mills were big employers of women but the machine shop and the factory were exclusively male. The work was physically demanding and the apprenticeships lengthy; they usually passed to family members or close relatives, sons or nephews. Perhaps it was time to infiltrate some more women into the firm. They'd be sure to spruce the place up a bit. A few clean windows wouldn't go amiss, and she would gladly share her precious flushing toilet with a woman who'd clean it, a job she currently did herself. In this way, Jenny successfully diverted her mind from the troublesome subject of marriage.

CHAPTER 13

A clergyman calling the banns for a wedding can be as disturbing as the arrival of a comet. It warns a community that the settled order of things is going to change. When Jenny sat in the Atherley church and heard the banns called again for the spinster Mavis Haslam and the bachelor, Andrew Perkins, her friend's marriage began to feel like a real possibility. The dowry and the wedding were not just the fantasies of her cheerful chum. The countdown had begun for a process to transform the teenage scallywag into a respectable matron with property and a new surname. The structure of Jenny's world quivered and shook as the once familiar features of life shuffled about like the pieces of coloured glass in a kaleidoscope and re-arranged themselves into new patterns. Even the reliable world of work with its regular routines shifted on its foundations.

People say that these life-changing events always come in threes. The news that Mavis, the teenage flirt and part-time prostitute, was to marry was only the first upheaval in Jenny's life. It was swiftly followed by Edward's announcing that he planned to go to Germany to research the process of building a power station. Jenny pictured him sailing off on a stormy sea and disappearing over the horizon. He might be unobtainable, but he had always been there and the prospect of his absence made her anxious and shivery. Was she succumbing to that exclusively female complaint commonly known as 'nerves'?

The office of Carter Woodward in the week before Edward and Mr Frederick were to leave for Germany was chaotically busy. Edward toured the factories and the mines to let everyone know he was leaving on a fact-finding tour of Germany. Word spread like wildfire. The workers took the news stoically. Was it a warning of a slowdown or a chance for new markets? Many had grown familiar with Mr Frederick through the brass band so the mention of Germany did not raise their territorial hackles. After all the royal family came from there. Even so they found excuses to trickle into the office with trivial questions to check that business was continuing as usual and to sniff the air in case a storm was brewing. They kept Mr Frederick so busy that he had.no chance to brew their customary pot of tea in the afternoon. Jenny missed it and foresaw that the following week would be very short on comfort.

She would be alone in the office, except for Mr Woodward; she could not ask him to put the kettle on. Good employer though he was, Mr Woodward was not at the top of his form; he found it difficult to concentrate on business and was constantly distracted by thoughts of Dorothea and the opera which was to open next Friday. He was also afraid that Edward would not be back from the continent in time. 'He's cutting it very fine,' he would tell Jenny. A Lancastrian born and bred, he did not trust the people of Leeds to appreciate just how wonderful his Dorothea was.

On Wednesday Edward produced an office boy to make tea and run errands. After some tuition he might be allowed to answer the telephone. The 12-year-old Oliver had been scrubbed clean by his mother, the widow of a collier killed in a mining accident. He would spend the morning in the office and the afternoon in school. His eyes rolled at the mention of his half-time schooling. To accommodate children with jobs, teachers repeated the lessons of the morning in the afternoon. The tuition lost its lustre the second time around.

'The lad will be useful,' Edward confided to Jenny, 'and will distract Mr Woodward from fretting too much. It's a chance for the boy to learn about the world of work. His Dad died in a pit accident. Not one of our pits,' he added hastily. 'If he's no good send him packing. There's plenty more where he came from.'

When Jenny got home from work that day Aunt Anna brought her a cup of tea which she accepted gratefully. Oliver's tea was improving but still left a lot to be desired. She had just leant back in her chair with a sigh of contentment when she was struck by a third thunderbolt unleashed without warning from the hand of some unseen deity. It came from her blind side. John Truesdale walked in from the kitchen and put his hand on her shoulder. When he had her attention he told her that Aunt Anna had agreed to marry him.

121

Jenny said nothing as she tried to process the news. What did he mean? He was getting married! It was young people, like Mavis, who got married. While John and Anna were not exactly old, they were definitely middle-aged. They lived in the same house. They shared the responsibilities of the family. They were to all intents and purposes married. The blood rushed to Jenny's cheeks as she realised what it was that was missing from their comfortable domestic arrangements. **It** was that unique ingredient, forbidden to everyone, except couples sanctioned by a wedding ceremony of some kind... **It** was that mysterious thing that married people did in their bedrooms. And Mavis used to do with her customers.

Jenny swallowed the thought down in one gulp. It was much too embarrassing to think of **it** in connection with her father. Or rather the man who had taken on the role of father when she was abandoned as a small child by the thief who stole John's bicycle. How lucky she had been.

John explained that he had wanted to marry Anna for a long time but there was a much-disputed law, created in Parliament, that forbade a man from marrying his late wife's sister. 'Parliament has now repealed that law,' he told Jenny, 'and Anna has agreed to marry me.' His face melted into a smile. 'We shall do so as soon as the formalities can be completed.' As he spoke he held out his arms to Anna who leant in to his embrace so he could kiss her on the lips. He had never done that in the sight of Jenny before.

How she wished Edward could hold out his arms for her. She would kiss him on the lips in full view of her father. When she recovered enough to speak, all Jenny could say was how surprised she was at the announcement. John and Anna were loving parents to John's son and daughter by his late wife, as well as to Jenny the foundling. Yet somehow they had enough love left to share between them.

It was John who put her straight on that point. 'We are not issued with a fixed amount of love at birth,' he told her. 'Like bottles of milk that hold exactly one pint.' Jenny remembered she was not the only one who found her way into the family's protection. There was Margaret's friend Effie, and the stray dog, now sleeping comfortably on the hearth rug. John had even supported 'that

Mavis' to help her open a bank account, though he must have had suspicions about how she made her money. Jenny began to wonder if her love for Edward had somehow blinded her, given her a tunnel vision of the world.

Anna came from the kitchen drying her hands on a towel. There was no ring yet for her to show off. 'We shall have to let the family know.'

'They could come tomorrow. It's Saturday; the day off.'

'Will you send them telegrams, Jenny? Don't explain. Just make sure they know it is good news.'

'On my way,' shouted the fleet-footed Jenny as she closed the front door behind her.

As she flew down the hill two cheering thoughts came to her. The first was, that she would not send telegrams as agreed. She would go to her office and use the telephone. Margaret was one of the few people she knew who had access to a telephone. Mrs McKenna, her fearsome landlady had one installed at her lodging house. Jenny would ring her to show her father how useful it would be to have one in their own house. It was just one of the many conveniences that John regarded as unnecessary new-fangled inventions. The second piece of good news was the realisation that it was a change in the law that allowed John and Anna to marry. The law, it seemed, was not carved on tablets of stone; it could be crossed out, torn up and written anew. Perhaps one day the law would open an escape route for Edward to slip free of the ties that bound him to Dorothea. It's that or I'm going shopping for rat poison, thought Jenny.

At the factory Jenny roused the nightwatchman who let her in and gave her a taper to find her way up the spiral stairs. 'Not a problem, is there Miss? Only the boss came in not half an hour ago.'

'I don't think so. If it was the pit we'd hear the hooter. Must have forgotten something. It was a bit hectic today.'

Jenny found her way to the telephone on her desk and dialled Mrs McKenna's number. Although that formidable lady had been quick to buy a telephone she had no faith that it would work. She bellowed her questions loud enough to reach Jenny's ears from Manchester without troubling the telephone wires. Effie came to the phone and promised that she would bring the brother and sister to Atherley for a celebration on Saturday. That was all Jenny needed to know; to avoid questions she hung up. In the sudden silence a door clicked and a shadow fell over her desk. 'I'm sorry, Mr Woodward. I'll pay for the call. It was an important family matter.'

'I should hope so, Miss Truesdale, or as it's out of office hours can I call you, Jenny?

There was a piece of Jenny's brain that functioned in spite of the shock of hearing Edward's voice. The nightwatchman had called him, Boss. Did the workers no longer think of Mr Woodward as the Boss? How completely Edward had established his presence in the firm. He proceeded to do the same with Jenny. He insisted he drive her home. He held the taper to light her way down the stairs to where his car was parked at the back of the building.

Once there he pinched the taper out, took her in his arms and kissed her. It was only the second time that he had kissed her. The first was when he told her he was to marry Dorothea. That kiss said farewell, but this kiss felt like a greeting.

It was a mesmerised Jenny, who went to sit in the front passenger seat. As he drove out through the factory gates Edward wound down his window to tell the nightwatchman he was taking Miss Truesdale home. The man could be witness to the fact that there had been no time for what was known locally as shenanigans; Jenny would have enough to cope with at work in his absence without office gossip. While he drove she recovered her wits enough to tell him John and Anna's news.

As he drew up at the Truesdale house Edward considered going in to congratulate John but decided against it. John never exactly laid out the welcome mat for him. He tended to lean forbiddingly against the door frame and scowl down as if at an armed intruder. One day, Edward promised himself, one day he would walk into Jenny's home and her father would listen to him.

That night, Jenny wished she kept a diary. Then she could write in John and Anna's news and that Edward kissed her for the second time. She relived the sensations it aroused in her body to imprint them on her memory. Mavis's description of the man who held her breasts came into her mind. She reached up under her nightdress to feel their weight and their warm softness in her hands. It was comforting. As she drifted to sleep she felt she was beginning to understand much more about **it**.

The next day, the Truesdale family gathered together to learn that John and Anna were to be married. As Anna was the bride in waiting Jenny offered to do the cooking. It seemed only fair to let her mother-aunt wear her best dress and spend her time accepting felicitations rather than basting chicken on the kitchen range. Anna had dealt with their domestic needs for years. Today she deserved to be the centre of attention.

Margaret and Effie were discreet supporters of women's suffrage. They had little patience with Parliament and its laws, particularly those that limited women's freedom of choice. Tommy let them ramble on without comment, but when his father announced that the vicar would be calling banns on Sunday he leapt up and spoke with unexpected passion. He demanded that John stick to the conventions and move out of the house. Neighbours gossiped behind their hands and sent sly glances at any bride who shared a roof with her intended husband before the actual ceremony. Tommy was very protective of Anna, the only mother he had known. He blushed and stammered unable to specify the nature of the gossip he wanted to protect her from.

'Anticipating matrimony,' Effie supplied.

John agreed with the principle and went several doors down the hill to knock on the door of Mrs Carter, Edward's mother. She lived in a house that her son had provided for her and his many brothers. No-one knew for sure how many Carter boys there were. There was bound to be one of them away crewing a clipper or building a railway in Africa. Mrs Carter agreed to take in John Truesdale, unaware that he was the man who kept her son waiting at the bottom of the steps. Edward was not able to enjoy the irony of the situation. He had left for Hull and a ship to Hamburg.

Jenny went to bed, exhausted by her labours in the kitchen and the company of clever young people with a lot to say. They had given her much to think about. The law and what it had to do with love. She liked the expression Effie had used. Anticipating matrimony. That made you think. And was there any sense in the conventions? Once again listening to the vicar reading the banns at church the next day would be more interesting than usual. Who would be first? Her father or Mavis? It was the third time of asking for Mavis and Andrew but Jenny still had doubts about the reality of her friend's engagement. She needed further evidence. Perhaps to hear it from the lips of Andrew Perkins himself.

CHAPTER 14

On Sunday morning the Truesdales went to church, as usual. There was a discreet murmur of surprise when the vicar announced that John and Anna were to marry. If anyone had an objection he, or more likely she, kept it quiet. When the banns for Mavis and Andrew Perkins were called for the third time, Jenny felt the wave of resignation that came from the parishioners in flowery hats as they crossed Andrew Perkins off their list of eligible bachelors. The intending bridegroom sat upright in the pew with his future bride blushing beside him. Mavis had screwed her courage to the sticking point to make this very public appearance at Andrew's side.

'Damn,' said Mrs Murdoch who had four daughters. 'We should have moved quicker. That nobody has nobbled him while he was missing his mother. If she'd been alive she'd have sent the baggage packing.'

When the service was over the Truesdales were kept busy by their fellow parishioners wanting to congratulate them and in some cases interrogate them. The older happy couple provided a welcome diversion allowing Andrew Perkins and Mavis to slip away quietly. 'They'll calm down,' said John Truesdale. 'The novelty will soon wear off.'

Monday morning came and Jenny's heart sank. A whole week of work without Edward and only the new boy to act as a buffer between her and Mr Woodward. At the office Jenny took Oliver on a tour, explaining to him the telephone and the typewriter. She demonstrated how to answer the phone and to take a message, ringing him from Edward's office to give him practice. She showed him the door to her private cloakroom and forbad him to enter it on pain of death. Finally she took him to the gas ring and taught him to make tea.

Higgs arrived to tell her that Mr Woodward was on his way up the spiral staircase. 'No rush. His sciatica's troubling him.' Would a cup of tea help? It would certainly help Higgs who happily tested the boy's brew and pronounced it to be promising. While Mr

Woodward drank his tea, Jenny wondered out loud if it would be wise to take the boy to the mine and introduce him to the staff there. They would then recognise him if he had to deliver messages in an emergency.

'Like the old days,' said Mr Woodward, 'before we had phones and certified managers and all that flimflam.'

'It will reassure them to see you are here while Mr Carter is away,' said Jenny, looking innocent.

'My Dad was a miner,' said Oliver, removing the last shred of Mr Woodward's reluctance to tackle the corkscrew stairs again. The three males bustled out of the office. There was nothing like the robust company of miners to distract Mr Woodward from worrying about his daughter. The dirt, the heat and the noise took him back to the days of his prime when there were genuinely serious matters to concern him. Firedamp, explosions, roof falls and flooding, to name a few.

Jenny's plan worked beautifully for the morning. The older man thoroughly enjoyed passing on his wisdom to the wide-eyed boy who knew better than to reveal that he found the journey by car more exciting than removing coal from the ground. They returned for what was called dinnertime in the office.

'The miners call it 'bait', Mr Woodward explained to his young charge. The arrival of a telegram assured him – and Jenny – that Edward and Mr Frederick had embarked in Hull en route for Hamburg. Mr Woodward then went home for what in his house was called lunch. He planned to spend the afternoon with his grandchildren and perhaps ring Dorothea. He would leave the office in Miss Truesdale's capable hands.

The day was not progressing at all smoothly in Leeds where another thunderbolt had crashed unexpectedly from the sky. In a cold dusty rehearsal room Dorothea sat ripping her handkerchief into thin strips of linen. She watched them float down to the floor where they formed a small pile. The plinky plonk pianist, temporarily redundant, was doing a crossword puzzle. The tenor who played Cavaradossi was not available for rehearsal. He was prostrate in hospital after being hit by a motor car. *Tosca* was due to open in 5 days' time. The director rampaged about the stage, spewing hate, venom and foul-mouthed despair at the top of his considerable lungs. He had reached G for gonorrhoeic in his alphabet of abuse when Dorothea found to her surprise that she was wishing for Mr Martelli to arrive. If anyone could save *Tosca* for her, it would be him.

The director had moved on to cursing the motor car as a bloody stupid and superfluous invention in a world where both people and horses had legs, when Dorothea reached the end of her handkerchief. There was no strip wide enough to shred. Was she going to sit silent while that useless ranting director let the production of *Tosca* that was going to make her a star, drown from neglect and bad management? No she was not. She stood up, moved towards the director and spoke straight into his face. It was a technique she had learned from Nanny; it worked well on children.

'I don't know why you are making such a fuss. The solution is simple.' To Dorothea, whose father bought her a husband, most problems were simple. She willed the director to pay attention and watch her lips as she spelt out the solution in the clearest tones. 'It is simple. You get another tenor.' She said it again to be sure there was no mistake. 'You get another tenor.'

The director turned on her, roaring like an angry lion, his hands raised to her throat. Charity, thinking to save her mistress from attack, rose from her chair. Dorothea did not even flinch which enraged the director more.

'Only a god-damned amateur would have the brass neck to say that 5 days from opening, when the bloody useless tenor has contrived to break both his legs by getting tangled up with a motor car, which means he is flat on his back in effing hospital where some sodding padre is sprinkling holy water on him in expectation of his imminent demise, an event which I, for one, am devoutly praying for.'

Even actors trained in Shakespeare have to pause for breath occasionally. Dorothea took advantage of the enforced gap to enunciate with crystal clarity her previous advice.

'Get another tenor.'

'Get another tenor,' said the director in a shrill girly voice. 'Only some silly bitch with a rich father who never washed her own drawers would say that.' He clenched his teeth and mimed the action of wringing out washing. Judging by the pleasure the act gave him it was Dorothea's neck that he was wringing. When he had squeezed the last drop of satisfaction out of strangling the imaginary Dorothea he turned to the real one and asked in his famously loud theatrical voice, 'Have you any idea what you are saying. Tenors are as rare as hens' teeth round here.'

Dorothea was an experienced player in the game of power; she had practised on her family and her classmates since she was in short skirts. She knew when to circle round her target and attack from an unexpected angle. 'You always said that he was wooden, lumpish and fat. And he hasn't learned his words properly. Makes them up as he goes along. Thinks no-one will notice because they're in Italian. I notice.' Dorothea pointed at her heaving bosom. 'It pains me here to hear him. And as for acting. Have you seen him with the paintbrush? He's supposed to be an artist. Looks like a housemaid brandishing a feather duster. He never moved well even when his legs worked'.'

The director's eyes narrowed as his blood pressure dropped and the power of thought returned to him. Perhaps this silly soprano had a point. The unfortunate accident might provide him with an excuse to cancel the whole production which bid fair to be a disaster. Cancellation would save his professional reputation. Everyone would understand he couldn't do *Tosca* without a tenor. No blame could be attached to him. He rolled his eyes and looked at the ceiling, a ham actor's representation of a man who is having an idea he is reluctant to put into words.

'I've never cancelled a production before,' he began. Every nerve in Dorothea's body screamed in agony. She had gone too far. Cancellation would be fatal for her. She would never get such an opportunity again.

The door opened and Mr Martelli walked in.

'I heard about the accident,' he said. 'I came straightaway. Tell me everything.' They turned to him as to their saviour. Dorothea and the director clamoured round him, their voices loud and their feelings raw. The pianist returned to his crossword puzzle.

'This will be the first time I have ever cancelled a production,' wailed the director.

'And you're not going to now,' snapped Dorothea.

'Then what the hell am I going to do?'

'Get a better tenor.'

'And where exactly is this tenor to be found?'

Mr Martelli held up his hand. 'It just so happens that I can find you a much better tenor.' He turned to Dorothea. 'You can vouch for his talent, can't you?"

Light dawned on Dorothea. 'Of course. Neville.' Why hadn't she thought of him. She rushed to make good her mistake. 'Neville is a much better singer. I worked with him and I tell you he's good. He already knows the part because we used the arias in our act.'

'And where exactly can we find this Neville?'

'Manchester. Henshaw's Asylum for the blind to be exact.'

'Asylum,' scoffed the director. 'That's where we'll all end up.'

'No. As I said I've worked with him and Duncan the blind pianist. They really know how to work.' Dorothea pointed to the pianist. 'They don't sit about doing crossword puzzles. Their concentration is amazing. It has to be. How else do they manage to get about a whole world they cannot see. They listen, they understand, they remember. Neville will learn the moves in no time. What's a few square yards of flat wooden stage where everything and everybody is in its right place?'

Dorothea saw she was winning. She administered the coup de grace. 'You made a big mistake not giving him an audition. If you'd seen him you would have given him the part straightaway. He has the looks of a Greek god and moves with the grace of a panther. When he is still, people just watch him. They can't resist looking at him.'

The director raised his hands in surrender. 'Just one question. How do we get him here quickly?'

'Simple.' Mr Martelli stepped forward. 'He is a client of mine.' He turned to Dorothea. 'Are you happy for Charity to go for him? And her brother.'

131

Dorothea showed that she was more than happy. She felt no need to consult her father who paid Charity to be her maid and chaperon. Charity, the walking railway timetable, had only one reservation about her mission. She pointed at the clock. 'If only you'd said sooner I might have done it in the day. As it is I may not get back till tomorrow. As long as the boys are not working tonight we can be here tomorrow morning.' Charity looked enquiringly at her mistress. Would Dorothea object that she would have no chaperon for the night? Dorothea seemed unconcerned about her reputation and Charity valued her brother, his friend and their work much more than Dorothea's reputation. Only one question was left. The money for her train fare? Dorothea, accustomed to her father paying, had not thought of that. She rummaged about in her purse where she found a few shillings. Was that enough? Charity shook her head. It was not.

They turned to the director who set about fishing in his pockets in a way that told you he was determined to find nothing. It was Mr Martelli who pressed pound notes into Charity's hand. Dorothea insisted on going to the station with her so she could have the satisfaction of seeing her on to the train to Manchester.

When the women had gone, the director took his empty hand out of his pocket and tapped Mr Martelli on the arm. 'It's time we had a talk about money. Let's find somewhere private where I can have a cigar.' They found their way to the circle bar where they stretched out on the brocade seats. The director called for brandy to keep his cigar company. He made a performance of lighting it before settling down to suck it, like a baby with his bottle. Mr Martelli, with a little help from nicotine and alcohol, had transformed him from a man preparing to abandon a sinking ship to a man who foresaw possibly the greatest success of his theatrical career. His production of *Tosca* just might turn into something truly remarkable and earn him the kind of fame he had not enjoyed since his youthful portrayal of Hamlet. With luck he'd be able to return to London with his head held high. And that soprano was definitely coming with him; she was a tiger.

132

He chomped on his cigar before pointing the wet end at Mr Martelli. 'If these boys are as good as you say they are, this might just turn out well.'

Mr Martelli sat back and looked smug. 'You'll find out tomorrow.' He was confident that the money he'd invested in train fares would pay dividends.

'And Dorothea?' asked the director of Mr Martelli. There was a speculative look in his eye. 'You've got her signed up?'

Mr Martelli twisted two fingers into a knot and brandished them at the director to show how secure her contract was. As he grinned smugly at the director, a worm of doubt whispered in his ear. But is it tight enough?

While the men talked, Dorothea watched Charity start her journey to Manchester. 'You will do your best to get them to come. It's a great opportunity for them.' Charity treated her to the look she gave anyone who stated the blindingly obvious as she boarded the train. When Dorothea returned to the theatre she found the rehearsal room empty except for the pianist who had finished his crossword and was twiddling his thumbs.

'You're sacked,' Dorothea told him and swept him off the piano stool. A glance at her face told the pianist that it was not worth arguing. He slunk off. Dorothea took possession of the piano stool, raised her hands, spread her fingers and brought them down on the keys. The great clashing chord made her feel better. She wanted to ring Nanny but knew it would raise the alarm in the Woodward household. Her father would start to ask questions. It was better to avoid such complications. She would concentrate on playing the piano. It would have to be Beethoven. There was nothing like old Ludwig to settle the turbulent feelings the stormy morning had stirred up.

When she finished playing the sound of clapping alerted her to the presence of Mr Martelli sitting behind her. He had crept in as she played. As he watched and listened his desire and ambition hardened into an unshakeable resolve. She was special. And she was going to be his. It was only fair. He had found her, spotted her talent when she was simply Miss Dorothea, an ignorant school girl. He should have grabbed her then. Now there was a husband and

133

children somewhere to complicate matters. And a superannuated thespian director with an inflated reputation and an ego to match who had just begun to appreciate her talent and her attractions. Too late, thought Mr Martelli with grim pleasure. She's mine. Dorothea finished playing. He went to congratulate her and kiss her hand.

'Please, please, Miss Dorothea, can you just leave all that moody German soul-searching and come to Italy, to Roma. That is the beautiful city where *Tosca* takes place. There all is love and passion. Trust me. Neville and Duncan will be here tomorrow. In the meantime there are some steps we can take to improve our chances.'

'Such as?'

'For a start, we must alert the tailor. His services will be needed tomorrow when Neville arrives. The previous tenor, now alas injured, was of my build.' He pointed a finger at his short legs and protuberant stomach. 'Neville is…' Words failed him.

'Tall. Slender. Elegant,' the heartless Dorothea supplied.

'Yes. Exactly so. A new costume must be found for him. And while we are talking to the wardrobe department perhaps there is something we could do to improve yours. Our beloved director has very traditional views on his heroines. He thinks they are all princesses in need of a husband so he insists on virginal white.'

Dorothea's heart leapt at the chance to rid herself of the wishy-washy dishcloth the director had condemned her to wear.

'Come,' commanded Mr Martelli with a lordly gesture. 'We will show him that Tosca is an Italian woman of passion. Like yourself, my dear Miss Dorothea, she is a singer devoted to her art, a woman who is not afraid to love. She should wear scarlet. And gold.'

Before she could concentrate on her costume Dorothea had one further matter to deal with, and it was important that the director was involved. She sent a message asking him to join them. No response. Mr Martelli sent a message. The director sent word that he was having a nap. The businessmen of Leeds met at his hotel in the evening and he had been invited to join them; he would use the opportunity to publicise the opera. He refused to come to the stage as they requested, insisting that he needed time to recover from the stresses of the morning. As a result it was Mr Martelli who valiantly

134

went on his knees to write the numbers of the clockface in chalk on the boards of the stage. Left and right would not be enough for Neville. The director would be able to use the fingers of the clock to tell the blind tenor the angle and direction of his moves.

The wardrobe department declared themselves ready to make a costume for Neville in a day but could not supply anything to meet Dorothea's exacting standards. The trunks that had accompanied her to Leeds contained a few of her evening dresses. One of them might do. Perhaps Mr Martelli would advise her? He accompanied her to her hotel, where he insisted on summoning a chambermaid and keeping the door open to preserve her reputation while they settled the important question of which gown Tosca should wear.

'You should wear it to the dinner at the director's hotel tonight,' he told her. A lot of business men will be there. It is expensive and very stylish. The director will use it to spread excitement before opening night. God willing that we do indeed have an opening night'.

He looked steadily at her to see if she had understood his message. She had. A dramatic entrance to get the attention of the diners and an air of mystery to create a buzz of interest for the performance which she was confident would happen. Dorothea felt a sudden urge to hug him. She resisted. He bowed and took his leave. It was time for them to dress for dinner. He would return to escort her to the hotel. He had not been invited but was not going to let that stop him from being there. It was traditionally the time a leading lady delivered on any promises she had made in exchange for being chosen for her part. Mr Martelli thought it best to keep that piece of information to himself.

Two hours later the director watched as Dorothea made a spectacular entrance on the arm of Mr Martelli. In her crimson gown she stopped the cream of Leeds society in their tracks. Who was this new beauty? Word soon spread that she was an Italian countess. She was the mistress of the famous director. The funny little man beside her? He was the husband. An Italian count. The important thing was Friday, the first night at the Grand Theatre. The race for tickets began. Subscribers to the opera found they were suddenly popular as their acquaintances wondered out loud if their seats might be available.

The director ground his teeth in rage and cursed the opportunity missed by his after-lunch nap. That Italian agent had got there first. He was mildly cheered as businessmen bought him drinks and offered cigars in the hope of a complimentary ticket. For a day that started with a catastrophic car accident it was ending well enough. *Tosca* had not been cancelled and if Dorothea could be believed the new tenor would be an improvement. He ordered champagne. After a glass or two, Dorothea asked the musicians on the balcony to accompany her as she sang the Brindisi, a drinking song from *La Traviata*. They were happy to oblige. Someone sent for a photographer from *The Leeds Mercury*, and in the glare of a flash bulb she was immortalised with a champagne glass in her hand.

Mr Martelli ordered more champagne, secure in the knowledge that it would be charged to the director as he was the one resident in the hotel. When Dorothea returned to the table amid rapturous applause, he laid a hand possessively on her white arm and stared with cold eyes at the director, the host who had not invited him. As he had engineered Dorothea's arrival at dinner, so he arranged her departure. She did not want to leave. The applause and the champagne had gone to her head; she was not accustomed to alcohol. She protested when he whispered that it was time to leave until he crushed her complaints with the old theatrical adage about leaving the audience wanting more. '

You want them to come to the first night, don't you?' he hissed at her. 'Because with a little help from Neville that is going to happen.'

She smiled upon him. This time he did not send for the chambermaid to keep her respectable, but arranged for the night porter to bring a glass of brandy to her room. It was in chaos. The gowns that she had rejected were strewn over the beds and the floor. When the night porter arrived with the brandy he offered it to Dorothea who had thrown herself into a chair. He assured her that it would help her sleep as he paid the porter in cash to spare Mr Woodward the anguish of finding alcohol on her bill. For half an hour Dorothea relived her triumph with flamboyant gestures, snatches of song and word for word repetitions of the many compliments lavished upon her. While she relished her triumph and drank the brandy Mr Martelli tidied the room, smoothing and folding the silk dresses, the turquoise, the indigo and the gold, sliding them carefully onto the shelves in the wardrobe or back among the tissue paper in her trunk. The brandy did its work. Dorothea fell asleep.

Mr Martelli eased her out of her complicated clothing, unlacing her corset with skilled and gentle hands. There was scarcely a moment to admire her body before with her fuddled co-operation he slid her between the sheets. He looked round the orderly room with satisfaction. A glass of water on the night stand was the finishing touch. He removed his evening clothes and hung them on the back of a chair. He might wear them in the morning when he escorted Dorothea to the rehearsal. It gave him pleasure to picture the director's face when presented with such an obvious clue as to where the man he had not invited to dinner had spent the night.

Whistling *La donna è Mobile* he washed in the geranium-scented soap and slipped into bed with the sleeping Dorothea.

CHAPTER 15

Tuesday

In the morning a telegram from Edward assured the offices of Carter-Woodward that with Mr Frederick he had crossed the North Sea, arrived in Hamburg, and was preparing to catch the train for Berlin. What the telegram did not convey was the excitement he felt at the sheer size of the world as it opened up before him. As a young man, who had only recently crossed the boundary of Lancashire, it thrilled him to be putting his feet on foreign soil, where he quickly discovered, people did not speak English. Thank the Lord for Mr Frederick who had negotiated the complexities of sending the telegram and was now ascertaining the way to the railway station. Edward tried to memorise the route. He was leaving Mr Frederick in Berlin and would have to find his own way to the docks in Hamburg on his return to England.

The telegram did nothing for Mr Woodward's anxiety. 'He's cutting it fine,' he complained. 'Tuesday morning and he's just getting the train to Berlin. That could take ages.' He was determined to be pessimistic as the days counted down to Dorothea's opening night on Friday. It was his insurance policy against disappointment.

'He'll be in Berlin tonight,' said Jenny. It's not the Russian steppes he's crossing.' She went to Edward's office to look at the map on the wall. It consoled her to see the little flags he had pinned to mark the route of his journey. She traced the lines that joined them and found that it shrank the world to manageable proportions. With luck the map might have the same effect on Mr Woodward and stop his endless fretting if she could persuade him to come and look at it. She decided to use Oliver as bait.

'Come and see where this telegram started, Oliver.' Mr Woodward followed him. At first the boy thought the piece of yellow paper in Jenny's hand had literally come from Hamburg. Mr Woodward couldn't resist explaining how the message had travelled vast distances by the power of electricity and the actual writing was done in Atherley. 'Electricity. That's what we're going to make. Put that kettle on, lad, and I'll explain to you about steam. And James Watt.'

Oliver looked to Jenny. 'All right to put the kettle on?' He had worked out who really ran the office.

While Mr Woodward explained how the power of steam could be harnessed to make electricity, the early train from Manchester arrived in Leeds. Two men and a woman dismounted carefully from a second- class carriage. Unusually the woman seemed to be in charge, choosing the route and giving directions to the men. In reality Charity was not sure where to go next. She had fulfilled her mission of bringing Neville and Duncan to Leeds and there her instructions stopped. Should she take them to the theatre and risk confronting the director alone? A daunting prospect without Dorothea and Mr Martell being present. They would stand between her boys and the line of fire that might erupt from that foul-mouthed creature. She decided to go to the hotel where she shared a room with Dorothea. Surely someone must have arranged a room there for Neville and Duncan? It would give them a chance to wash off the smuts from their train journey. Neville, notoriously pernickety about his appearance, was busy brushing off his jacket specks he could not see but knew must be there.

In the entrance hall of the hotel Charity made enquiries, while Neville and Duncan sat and explored their new surroundings as only blind people can. They made mental notes as sounds echoed on tiled floors or were buried in thick curtains. They smelt subtle changes in the atmosphere and felt variations in the temperature on their skin. The receptionist promised them coffee while Charity went up to the room to see Dorothea. By the time the coffee arrived the men knew the kitchen was to the left and the wide, but shallow staircase was thickly carpeted, there was a revolving door on to the street, a wooden one with a latch to the garden on the right and a large fireplace where the remnants of yesterday's fire smouldered.

Charity did not notice her surroundings as she opened the door to the room she shared with Dorothea. All she saw was that Dorothea was still in bed. And Mr Martelli was with her. She froze in the doorway. Their bare torsos emerged from the bedclothes. There was no mistaking their identity. She felt a shriek rise in her throat and quickly bit it back. Some instinct told her that silence was her best course of action. Her own job and her brother's future employment were dependent on these two people. She turned and fled.

Minutes later she was back in the lobby, struggling to hide the shock she felt. 'A double room will be fine,' she assured the receptionist and went to tell Neville and Duncan they could be sure of a good room in this very comfortable hotel. 'When you've unpacked we'll get a bite of breakfast. We can put it on the bill.' No-one had authorised these expenses but under the circumstances Charity did not expect either Dorothea or Mr Martelli to quibble.

They were finishing breakfast when Dorothea appeared ready to accompany them to the rehearsal. She looked both composed and properly dressed, a considerable achievement under the circumstances. At the theatre the director was stalking about the stage in a fine fury while the cast lounged about the stalls. The singers with small parts or walk-on roles hung around with sullen faces unsure of their futures. The piano was closed and the stool was vacant.

'Some buckethead,' bellowed the director, 'has chalked graffiti on the stage.' He scraped the toe of his boot across the number 12 written at the back centre stage. 'Is there no respect for the sacred boards where the followers of Thespis ply their trade and deliver the immortal lines of Shakespeare?' He held out his arms in a dramatic appeal to the glum crowd of extras. They shuffled their feet and coughed.

It was the fearless Dorothea who arrived in time to answer his challenge. 'I told you to get a better tenor.' She raised her arm in triumph. 'And here he is.' Neville stepped forward.

The director forgot his manufactured rage, his failure to bed the leading lady, and the inescapable fact that the opening night was only 4 days away. All his trials and tribulations melted away as he gazed at the most beautiful man he had ever seen. Neville was tall and he was slender. His limbs were long and the features of his face might have been chiselled in Athenian marble. Golden lights gleamed in the wavy brown hair that framed his face. Neville moved forward, held out his hand and smiled shyly. He knew that he was

140

under close inspection and was aware of the full weight of expectation thrust on his shoulders.

'Welcome,' said the director. The word emerged as a croak. The famous Shakespearean voice had temporarily deserted him. The company stood around in a reverent circle and simply looked at Neville. They felt like ordinary mortals who had stumbled upon a god fallen from the skies.

The arrival of Mr Martelli brought them back to earth. He had decided that diplomacy was his best strategy and had gone to change out of his evening clothes. He beamed at the cast, like a proud father.

'Now we are together, I am confident that with your talent and hard work *Tosca* will open on Friday.'

'Hear, hear,' bellowed the director who rarely agreed with anything unless he said it first. He did not care whether Neville could sing, but with the right lighting his mere presence on stage would mesmerise the audience. The mind that had, in an emergency, mastered the part of Mercutio in a morning, moved into gear and focused its attention on the task to hand.

'This morning we will rehearse Act One,' he announced, 'so that I can concentrate on the movements of Cavaradossi.' He turned to Neville, 'This will be the most complicated part for you, my dear boy, so we'll tackle it first. After this you are taken prisoner. You just have to go where the jailers push you.'

The old hands exchanged glances. 'My dear boy already,' whispered one, 'and we don't yet know he can sing.' That mystery was soon solved. Duncan sat at the piano and Neville proved beyond doubt that he could sing. The sullen cast of the morning was transformed into a cheerful band of individuals, each convinced that *Tosca* was going to be a successful production that would raise their status in their chosen profession.

Mr Martelli came to sit next to Charity as she sat knitting in the stalls. Neville was on stage practising his moves and Duncan was busy at the piano .

'This morning,' Mr Martelli began delicately. 'It must have been a shock for you.'

Charity stared at her knitting and braced herself for the request for secrecy she was sure would come. 'I'm not going to lie about it. No use asking me.'

'Good, because that is the very opposite of what I want you to do. What I would like you to do, is to tell the truth.'

'You want me to say what I saw? You want me to tell her husband?' Shock and outrage coloured her voice. He shook his head.

'Not her father?' Her voice rose with horror at the thought of telling the Methodist Mr Woodward she had caught his daughter in adultery.

'No. Not a person. I want you to tell a piece of paper. I want you to write a record of the facts. Just the facts. The date, the time, the place. What you saw. You might like to start by saying that you left your duties here on the specific instructions of your mistress who put the success of the opera above her own personal comfort and convenience.' He stopped and gave Charity a meaningful look to emphasise that he was offering her the way to keep her job. Charity pursed her lips and looked thoughtful to show she understood.

Mr Martelli went on, 'Seal it in an envelope and give it to me. It is simply a precaution. A protection for you in case questions are asked. I will not open the envelope unless it is absolutely necessary for us all.' He described a circle with his hand; it enfolded Charity, her brother, Neville and Dorothea. He leant close and spoke quietly in her ear. 'By the twitching of my thumbs, something special this way comes. I can feel it in my water. This production of *Tosca* is going to be very, very special. We will be in demand. Everything will change. Doors will fly open. It is different for Miss Dorothea.' He stopped and laughed. 'See. I still think of her as Miss Dorothea. She was a schoolgirl when I first met her.' He shook his head in disbelief at the changes brought by time.

Charity was not keen to write an account of seeing her mistress in bed with the agent, but soon squashed her squeamishness. It was a chance to show that she was blameless – she had not neglected her duties. She would write no more than the truth; there was no harm in telling the truth.

'Try the manager's office. There's pen and paper there,' said Mr Martelli. Charity obediently set about her task. While she was away he relived the moment she had caught them asleep. He had not expected her to arrive back from Manchester so early. The scene in the bedroom that morning was not what he had hoped for. He had envisaged some serious conversation, some heart-searching and a few tears of regret as Dorothea made up her mind to leave her domestic life. Triumphant joy would follow as she embraced her inevitable destiny as an artist and a woman of the world. Instead he got shrill squeals of dismay and frantic searches through drawers for underwear. The prospect of being late for the crucial first meeting between Neville and the director panicked Dorothea. The brandy had made her oversleep and worse still, she had never in her life got dressed without the help of a maid. There was no point in trying to haul Charity back from wherever she had fled. Too embarrassing for all concerned. Accordingly Mr Martelli set about the task of dressing Dorothea himself. Fortunately he knew his way around the many complex and troublesome garments women wore.

He was fastening her corset when a second wave of terror hit Dorothea. Pregnancy. That is what had followed her encounters with Aleksy. As Mr Martelli brushed the great mane of her black hair he assured her she would definitely not be having twins again. When he had knotted it neatly into a chignon, he put his hand on his heart and swore that she need have no fears on that account. A few hairpins, her jacket eased over her shoulders, a quick pinch to her cheeks and he was pushing her towards the door to welcome Neville and Duncan and face the director. 'When there is time, Dorothea, we will talk about this, but for the moment, my dear girl, the play's the thing.'

It warmed his heart to see her chin lift and her jaw set. A real trouper. Afterwards he could not help wondering about her horror of pregnancy. Did that mean a complete absence of sex in her married life? The husband was always a shadowy figure in comparison with her father. At that moment Charity returned and handed him an envelope. He put it in his breast pocket.

'No harm in telling the truth,' she said. If she said it often enough she would come to believe it.

143

'You'll feel better now you've written it down,' he murmured. No point in telling Charity that her interpretation of events was wildly wrong. The fact that he was found naked in bed with Dorothea screamed, like a newspaper headline, that the eighth commandment had been broken. He wanted Dorothea, oh how he wanted her, but he wanted her to come to him of her own free will. He had not spent years, cultivating her talent, building her career step by careful step to risk it all by taking her when she was drunk and to all intents and purposes asleep.

Franco Martelli was not some debased creature to take advantage of a woman at such a moment. There was no risk of pregnancy from their supposed encounter because the complete sexual act simply had not taken place though both Charity and Dorothea assumed it had. As soon as an opportunity presented itself he would explain to Dorothea what had really happened – or not happened. Until then all the darling girl's thoughts and attention had to be focused on her role in *Tosca*.

CHAPTER 16

Wednesday

Dorothea, Neville and the cast in Leeds started work early. All their squabbles and petty jealousies were forgotten as they watched in awe while Neville convincingly dabbed paint on the mural of the Mary Magdalene that he could not see and sang his first big aria to perfection. His concentration was so complete and focused that the director decided to follow his example and set aside his habitual swearing and cursing.

There was no stopping for lunch as they powered on to Act Two. When she thrust the shining knife into Scarpia's back Dorothea was relieved, to find that it collapsed on contact as the stage manager promised. She placed the candles round the corpse and laid the crucifix on his chest with all the seriousness of a convinced catholic, though it did flicker through her mind to wonder what her Methodist father would think of that particular bit of stage business.

They grabbed sandwiches and mugs of tea as they moved on to Act Three when Cavaradossi is arrested. At first the men acting as jailers were wary of being rough with Neville. His blindness and the slenderness of limbs inhibited them until he began to join in enthusiastically. Between them they choreographed a convincing tussle; the slapping of their beefy thighs added some convincing sound effects. It ended with the singer's body, elegantly draped from their shoulders like a wounded Christ, being dragged across the stage. Neville, apparently unperturbed by the experience went on to sing '*E lucevan le stelle*' while his jailers stood panting in the wings as they got their breath back. His singing brought the tears to the tough men's eyes. 'Amazing chap,' they said. 'We gave him quite a hammering. You'd almost think he enjoyed it.'

In comparison with the intense concentration of the rehearsal in Leeds, life in the Carter-Woodward office was positively lethargic. The telephone seldom rang and the usual stream of visits from men in overalls with urgent queries in need of a speedy decision, dried to a trickle. Were the men keen to show Edward they could manage without him? Or were they avoiding asking Mr Woodward? He was not as up to date as he used to be. Jenny could not decide. Whatever the reason, the office was unnaturally quiet.

The morning was uneventful and so felt very long. She was relieved when it was time for Oliver to leave for school and sent up a silent prayer that Mr Woodward would get Higgs to take him home for his lunch. Her prayer was answered with the result that she spent a long, lonely afternoon in charge of a telephone that seldom rang. The only break in the monotony was the sound of the doorbell. The first time it was a telegram from Edward reporting good progress in his negotiations with AEG. As there were no witnesses Jenny was able to press the telegram to her breast as if it carried the touch of Edward's hand. She was laughing at her own foolishness when the doorbell rang again, too loud and insistent to be ignored. A glance out of the window showed Mavis pressing the bell. Next to her, hidden beneath a bowler hat was a man. Jenny guessed he must be Andrew Perkins.

'You all alone then,' bellowed Mavis as she pushed her way in and set off up the spiral stairs.

'Fortunately, yes.'

The Mavis who arrived in the office was not the Mavis from the Post Office and she was not the Mavis on the lookout for customers at Cozy Corner. This Mavis wore no make-up or frilly scarves. There were no bunches of violets on her jaunty straw boater but her white blouse was trimmed with lace flounces and a brooch decorated the lapel of her dark blue jacket. This Mavis stood in the doorway and held out her hand to Jenny.

'Say hello to Mrs Perkins.' Mavis waved her left hand. Beneath the sparkling engagement ring sat a solid gold band. 'It was Andrew's mother's ring,' she said proudly.

Jenny wished the bride happiness and congratulated the bridegroom as the book of manners advised. The firm handshake and steady gaze of Edward Perkins took her by surprise. Something had happened to the tongue-tied youth, half hidden by floppy hair, who had counted the coins at Parrs Bank. He had grown into a man.

He was taller, straighter and looked more solidly built, no longer a gangly teenager who had lost his mother. Mavis's fingerprints were all over him.

'The vicar unexpectedly had the morning free,' said Andrew, 'and Mavis's mother was available. The banns had been called for the third time. We saw no point in waiting. '

'Not now my dowry's in the bank,' crowed Mavis.

'I checked it this morning. My last task as an employee of Parr's bank'. He grinned. 'I am a free agent now and a man of business.'

Jenny was saved from her long slow afternoon. When the clock struck five they made their way to the Cozy Corner Café to celebrate the marriage. There Mavis and Andrew told Jenny of their plans to make their living from property.

'And that won't be my only source of income,' said Mavis. 'Now I can stand in for Mr Frederick first thing Monday morning, if that's all right with you. Let us have the weekend for our honeymoon.' The young couple exchanged long lingering looks as only lovers do.

'So you are finished with the Post Office?'

'More that the Post Office has finished with me, now I'm a married woman.' Mavis flashed her wedding ring. 'I should warn you that I might need a bit of practice on the old typewriter. I'm a bit rusty.' '

'Not to worry. Mr Woodward's not exactly rushing to deal with the correspondence. It'll be good to have you in the office. It's been a bit cheerless recently. Oh, I forgot to tell you. We've got a boy to make the tea. And he washes the cups up.'

Mavis clapped her hands with delight. 'You'll still have to wait till Monday. This is our honeymoon.' She turned to gaze at her new husband who smiled and discreetly stroked her hand. So this is what consummated love does for you, thought Jenny as she watched her tough friend melt into a warm puddle of pleasure.

The arrival of the bill rather spoilt the moment. The waitress set it in front of Andrew as was the custom. This time there were none of the usual arguments between the women about who should pay. The man paid. As he was sorting through his change to leave a tip, he suddenly stopped.

'What's this?' He held up a penny and inspected the coin on both sides. He set it to one side as he placed a tip in the saucer and scooped up the rest of the change to put in his pocket. 'I can't use that. It's not legal tender any more. Defacing the coinage is a criminal act. You can go to prison for that.' His face flushed with the outrage of a law-abiding citizen who discovers a crime. Jenny caught a glimpse of the pillar of society that he would become in middle age. She looked for his permission before she reached out for the coin he had rejected.

'Obviously I've heard about them,' he was saying to Mavis, 'but I didn't expect to find one here.'

Jenny examined the penny. It was dated 1903 and bore the standard image of Britannia on one side. The other side held the profile of King Edward VII. Someone had stamped the message Votes for Women over the king's face. Each letter had been individually stamped; they were placed too erratically to be done by a professional. Jenny doubted any woman had the kind of strength or skill to stamp the letters so thoroughly. However it was hard to imagine one of the tough muscular men, toiling in the deafening racket of the machine shop, who would take the opportunity to support the cause of women's suffrage by immortalising Votes for Women on a coin of the realm. She started to look for her purse. Andrew was bringing Mavis up to date with the latest developments in women's suffrage.

'They call themselves suffragettes and they don't care what they do. Sometimes they deliberately try to get arrested and sent to prison.' His new wife widened her eyes to show that she shared his shock at such unwomanly behaviour.

'Swap?' said Jenny holding up a blemish-free penny. Andrew wafted a hand to show her offer was unnecessary. Jenny added her coin to the saucer with waitress's tip and pocketed the defaced one. Her sister Margaret and her friend Effie would be interested to see it.

Her action brought the old Mavis back to life. 'Do you think it might be valuable?' she demanded of Jenny.

'No. Not valuable. Just interesting.'

'We missed a chance there,' Mavis told Andrew and shook her head in mock sorrow. 'True,' he said. 'I should have asked for tuppence.' They laughed happily together.

CHAPTER 17

Thursday

Mr Woodward woke with the sense of a black cloud hanging over the day; he had never liked Thursdays. An inexplicable dread stole the flavour from his breakfast and kept him from enjoying his newspaper. It was the day for the dress rehearsal of Dorothea's opera, an event, that he knew from his experience of the Henshaw's concert, was loaded with superstitious significance for theatre people. A piece of him wanted to leave for Leeds immediately so that he could protect his darling girl from the misfortune he was convinced lurked nearby for him or his family.

He consulted his wife. Mrs Woodward was no help; she had flatly refused to put so much as a foot in Yorkshire, the polar opposite of Southport, and saw no reason to change her mind, or for her husband to change the arrangements that had been agreed previously. The plan was for Mr Woodward to travel to Leeds on Friday in time to watch the first performance in the evening. Edward, newly arrived from Germany, would join him there and afterwards the two men would bask in the congratulations that were sure to pour in for Dorothea's performance.

It was a good plan but that morning Mr Woodward, with his gnawing sense of imminent disaster, could see only the cracks, the opportunities for it to go wrong. He was convinced that a thunderbolt was going to fall in his vicinity. 'Dear Lord, please, just don't let it strike Dorothea,' he prayed. She had put so much into that opera business. Failure for her would be catastrophic. The tantrums and tempers of the past would be as flea bites compared to the pain she would feel if this project went wrong.

He wished that Edward was there to encourage him, to smack him on the back and tell him not to be so daft; that the mine and the mills were in good hands, and it was scarcely 50 miles to Leeds. The thought of Edward reminded him of his immediate responsibilities in Atherley. At the mine and the mills he could contribute practical help. In Leeds all he was good for was signing cheques. He did as his Bible bid him and resisted temptation. He would not dash across the Pennines but stay to fulfil his responsibilities to his workforce.

At the office, Jenny tried diverting him. There was a stack of letters in need of replies, and Mavis could begin typing them when she started work on Monday. He determinedly ignored her request to look at them, scowling into the distance and gnawing at his finger nails, so she busied herself with the month end figures while Oliver brewed a pot of tea. Mr Woodward was in the mood for some masculine company so he shouted for Higgs the chauffeur, who was always ready for a brew to come up and join them. He could divert them by talking about car engines. Oliver loved hearing about the different models and their designs. Higgs was well aware of the boy's desperate desire to ride in the car and constantly looked for excuses to make it happen. He had to tread carefully though; Mr Woodward, his employer, the man who paid his wages, regarded the feeble combustion engine driven by petrol as a pale shadow of the mighty machines driven by coal and steam. Higgs suspected this prejudice was the result of Mr Woodward's inability to master the skill of driving a car, but diplomatically avoided saying so..

The phone rang. Oliver leapt to answer it. 'It's for you, Mr Woodward. Mr Lawson at pit.' He held out the receiver. A horror-struck Mr Woodward, convinced that Jove had launched his thunderbolt and it had landed on his pit, sprang to his feet and lunged for the receiver. In his haste and panic he toppled sideways, bounced off the desk and sent Oliver crashing to the floor. Higgs went to help Mr Woodward to his feet. First he had to untangle the telephone wires that wrapped themselves around him. In the process he discovered the shards of black plastic that had once been the receiver. Oliver was scrabbling to his feet. 'All right, lad?' asked the kindly Higgs. He turned to check his employer was not injured.

Mr Woodward was clambering back onto his feet. 'We must go to the pit,' he shouted. 'Come on now.' His head was full of horrific images: the broken bodies of miners, the flames devouring the limited air supply and the flash and roar of firedamp exploding. He ran to the top of the stairs, shouting for the others to follow him. With the help of the handrail, he sped down the spiral staircase three

151

steps at a time. Higgs was at his heels and Oliver in hot pursuit. The boy saw his chance for a ride in the motor car.

'Hop in, lad,' said Higgs.

Mr Woodward took the boy by the scruff of his neck and pulled him into the car. 'It's all hands to the pumps.' he shouted. 'You can take messages. That old doctor still hasn't got a phone'…. His voice trailed away at the prospect of the casualties reaching the point of needing the old doctor's services.

While they drove to the pit in an agony of expectation Jenny had found the wreckage of the shattered phone, abandoned it, and used the phone in Edward's office to ring the pit manager, Mr Lawson.

He sounded very relaxed and unconcerned. 'No. There's no problem here at the pit. I rang to tell Mr Woodward the new Schiele fan has arrived. It's an absolute monster of a thing. Thought he might like to come and check it out. Oh. And Mr Carter's just rung. Very pleased to hear the fan's arrived. He wasn't satisfied that the Parson's fan was working as well as it should.'

Jenny could not stop herself smiling at the thought of Edward as she went to inspect the results of the banging and shouting from Mr Woodward's office. The legs of chairs pointed skywards, the desk was at an angle and the telephone in pieces on the floor. There was no sign of the two men or the boy, but she could hear the car engine roaring in the yard. She opened the window to shout reassurance to Mr Woodward in her loudest voice. It was no use. They were on a mission to deal with a disaster.

A hundred yards from the pithead, Mr Woodward realised that he had made a mistake. The hooter was not blasting the air with the dreadful sound that roused miners from their sleep. There was no clatter of boots on cobbled streets as they rushed down to the pit to rescue their fellow workers. There were no explosions, no flames flickering round the winding gear. All was tranquil. The only movement was a group of men who were finishing unloading a huge fan bought to ventilate the mine.

Mr Martelli let the dress rehearsal run for a couple of hours before he made an appearance; such affairs were notoriously long-winded and ill-tempered. He spent a leisurely morning moving himself into a pleasant spacious room in Dorothea's hotel. It was, as he expected, expensive. After all Dorothea's father had chosen the hotel for her. Nothing but the best for Miss Dorothea when he was paying the bill. Mr Martelli wrote the room off as an investment now that Charity had returned to the room she shared with Dorothea. Neville and Duncan were also staying there and he wanted to keep close to all his clients. He felt supremely confident that the opening night would be a stunning success and the air would be thick with offers for their services.

The musical director stole a strategic advantage on the theatrical director by insisting that the musicians had no need for further rehearsals. They knew their parts and the timings had all been thoroughly worked out. They should work with the pianist alone; it was better for the soloists to rest their voices to preserve them for the opening night. They should wear their costumes and do the appropriate gestures in the right places, but they should not sing – except for the newly arrived Neville. Both directors wanted to be sure he could sing Cavaradossi. The other singers had been thoroughly rehearsed. Even the children's choir brought in from school for the 'Te Deum' at the end of Act One moved and sang with the precision of a miniature army.

This left the singers free to get familiar with their costumes and lounge about in the stalls watching the performance take shape and colour as the director experimented with the lighting and grumbled at the scene changers. For the first time they saw what the audience would see and had to admit that the director had his uses. Dorothea had protested at the costume he had chosen for Act One when Tosca tries to persuade Cavaradossi to return to their cottage with her. She felt the dress and jacket in pale green did little for her complexion.

'Wait till the stage lights are on,' the director told her, 'you'll look as fresh and innocent as a daisy. Don't forget Tosca is jealous. Jealousy is green.' Most of the time he concentrated his attention on Neville, his costumes and his stage directions. The longer and narrower artist's smock the wardrobe department had hurriedly provided was pronounced too stiff. It did not move with the singer, and made him look like a fieldhand rather than an artist. Two women took it away and scrubbed the starch out of it. They spent 2 hours treading it in hot water, pummelling it with their bare feet until it reached a texture that satisfied the director.

'We wouldn't do that for everyone,' they said as they tested the finished result on Neville. 'It's what they do in France, to the grapes. But for you, sweetheart, nothing is too much trouble.' They ogled his good looks, patted him gently and wished him good luck as the officers came to arrest him. 'Be very careful with him,' warned the director as the jailers rattled their chains. 'I don't want any more tenors with broken legs.'

The director mopped his brow with relief when the first run through was over. His energy was running low and he was beginning to think longingly of his nap. When Dorothea appeared in her crimson gown for the stabbing of Scarpia he made no objection to her abandoning the white costume he had decreed. His only comment was, 'I suppose it won't show the bloodstains.'

'Exactly, said Dorothea.

Two cups of coffee and a swig of whisky later and the director was arranging for dawn to rise over Castel San Angelo and coaching Neville for his difficult death scene.

'You see, dear boy, you believe Tosca has arranged a fake execution for you. So you have to pretend to pretend to die but really you have to die. Got that? Pretend to pretend but really do die.'

Neville nodded patiently. The director had not finished. 'The bullets come from your right. At 8 o'clock.' Dorothea's clock face chalked on the stage had proved useful. 'Simple really, my dear boy.' The director put a reassuring hand on his shoulder. 'Don't worry. It's just sound effects and few flashes. Best if you sort of rear up with shock and take some seconds to collapse forward. You are tied to the post so you won't hit the floor.' The director squeezed his arm as Neville put on his brave soldier face. 'Piece of cake, dear boy, piece of cake.'

Mr Martelli watched Dorothea as she waited for some equally detailed direction for her own death scene; she had to leap suicidally from the battlements into a dark space offstage. Nothing happened.

The director ignored her. Mr Martelli knew he was responsible for the director's pettiness; it was Dorothea's punishment for leaving the hotel dinner on his arm, making it clear to all that the director would not be claiming his traditional reward for casting her as the leading lady.

'Curtain calls,' said the director and took the cast through the order of their appearance. While they were lined up on stage, he addressed them in his fine Shakespearean voice.

'Some people think a smooth dress rehearsal is a recipe for a disastrous opening night. Fortunately I am not one of those people. We showed today that we all know our lines, our places and our tasks.' He broke off to smile at Neville and Duncan. 'Even those who only arrived here on Tuesday. Go home, rest and I am confident the opening night will be amazing. What you have seen on the stage today is the skeleton, the bare bones of *Tosca*. Tomorrow the music will fill these empty veins and pump the life blood through its heart. *Tosca* will come alive.'

He took a bow and left to warm applause.

Charity came fussing up. She wanted to give her boys time to rest at their hotel. People forgot the heavy price they paid for the dedication they brought to their work. Neville was pale with exhaustion and beginning to feel the bruises that resulted from his manhandling. Duncan was holding a page of music against his face and sliding it down to catch a phrase he was not sure of in the narrow tunnel of vision in his right eye. He had played the piano non-stop and stood in for trumpets, drums and the children's choir. His wrists throbbed with pain but he wanted to be prepared for the professional musicians' arrival the next day.

'I thought your father was coming tonight,' said Charity making it clear that Dorothea should behave like a dutiful daughter and accompany her and her boys to the hotel.

'No. Tomorrow.'

Mr Martelli stepped in. 'I will escort Miss Dorothea to the hotel. First there are some details of her leap from the battlements that I want to go over with her.'

Dorothea shot him a look of gratitude and followed him onto the stage where he helped her pace out the moves for her leap into the dark. There was a mattress for her to land on backstage.

'Should I scream as I jump?'

'Oh yes. You have lost your love and your life. You are in despair. Your cry should fade as your descend through space down the lofty walls of the citadel.'

Dorothea jumped twice but refrained from screaming. It was not a thing she could practise in the empty theatre; it would be too spine-chilling. There are some things you only do once, she thought, like losing your virginity.

'Perhaps a couple of feather pillows from the hotel?' Mr Martelli suggested. 'This mattress is very firm. The stage manager probably expected a soprano of the traditional build; they are often quite substantial ladies.' His appreciative eyes slid down her slender figure, making her grateful for Nanny's stern management of her diet. He offered her his arm to walk to her hotel. 'I have taken a room here myself. After all, three of my clients are under its roof. I want to be handy for them. Any questions or problems, here I am. Room 16 in case you should need me.' He set off to the stairs but turned back on the first step. 'Perhaps you would join me in the dining room for supper. Just a light meal. Nothing too heavy?'

Faced with prospect of 2 hours in her room under the disapproving eyes of Charity, Dorothea thought that was a very good idea. Two hours later, after a light supper carefully curated by Mr Martelli, Dorothea was sitting in the dining room with a small glass of red wine, a sliver of cheese and a large glass of water. Mr Martelli had forbidden her to have coffee as it would disturb her sleep. He urged her to swallow her father's principles along with the red wine. It would help keep her calm.

'We cannot live by other people's beliefs, not even our fathers' most cherished principles,' he told her gently wagging a finger as if at a naughty child. She chewed the cheese slowly to extract the many layers of flavour from it and sipped the wine to delay the moment when she had to put her head on the pillow and try to sleep. The fears and doubts she had kept at bay by working, practising and rehearsing were still in existence. They waited, gathering their forces

156

and building up their power to come and torment her in the hours of darkness.

'Your father will be here tomorrow, Miss Dorothea?' She nodded. Mr Martelli leant back in his chair and folded his napkin. 'It is fortunate that you are no longer, Miss Dorothea.' He stressed the word Miss.

'Why?'

'Because I would be knocking on his door, paying him my respects and asking for your hand in marriage.' He sat back and chortled as if that was a completely ludicrous idea. Dorothea compressed her lips and puckered her eyebrows to show that she was not amused by his finding the idea of marrying her to be some kind of joke. Surely it was the other way around. Dorothea Woodward (she forgot she was technically Mrs Carter) marrying a tubby theatrical agent who lived in grubby hotels while her father owned a mansion as well as a coal mine, several cotton mills and a large slice of the town of Atherley. Now that was a joke. She smiled once she had successfully worked it out. The softening of her lips encouraged Mr Martelli to go on to explain.

'It is fortunate those years have passed. I am older and wiser. I know that conventional marriage is not for me.' He leant towards her, his brown eyes earnest. He tapped the table with his finger to emphasise each word he spoke next. 'Correct me if I am wrong. I don't think it is for you either, Dorothea.'

Shock showed on her face. No man had ever spoken like that to her before. He had overturned the values engrained by years of training and the heavy expectations of society with a single sentence. She sipped her wine as she thought about his words.

Martelli leant forward. 'You, Miss Dorothea, are more than a wife and mother. You were born to sing. Music is the lifeblood in your veins. You are like Tosca who lived for love and for her art. '*Vissi d'arte, vissi d'amore.*' They were the words of the aria that Dorothea would sing the following night. 'Tosca lived for art and for love. But for you Dorothea, from your cradle the world has dripped its poison in your ear. Forget singing. Forget music. Your job is to be a wife. Run a house. Get a husband. Children. Family. That is a woman's role in this world.'

He sat back and waited. His preparations had been long, slow and careful, but now the time had come to roll the dice. He watched Dorothea. Would the years of training and the conventions of society win?

Dorothea licked her lips. Her words did not come easily. 'You are right. At this moment I care more about singing *Tosca* than anything else in this world.'

A promising start but he had to press further. 'Your husband?' he asked and tried to remember the man's name. She never talked about him.

Dorothea tossed him aside. 'You mean Edward? My father bought him to make me respectable.' It was clear to Mr Martelli that the husband was not an immovable obstacle.'

'Your children? Is *Tosca* more important?'

Even Dorothea had to pause for thought before dismissing her children. 'I want them to grow up well and, to be honest, the family and Nanny are doing a much better job than I could.

'So if I ask you to throw in your lot with me, and we will go where the music takes us, and believe me, Dorothea, this opera is going to take us to places we have not dreamt of, there is no one thing and no one person that would stop you coming with me?'

She had to think. Her voice shook when she said, 'My father.'

'Ah.' The generous Mr Woodward with the deep pockets and the Methodist principles. Mr Martelli bowed his head in what he hoped would be a temporary defeat. An indulgent father could not be rubbed out in a day. He rose from his seat and offered Dorothea his arm. At the door of her room he knocked and stood back respectfully as Charity opened it and fixed him with the stare of a basilisk while Dorothea went in.

'Sleep well, Miss Dorothea. It is an important day tomorrow.' Charity closed the door and Mr Martelli set off along the corridor his room.

While Dorothea was sailing through her dress rehearsal without incident, her father floundered and flapped about in a cloud of gloom, convinced that disaster was about to strike. When the pit manager rang he had panicked so completely he broke the telephone and knocked the tea boy over. His chauffeur's breakneck speed through the town would be the subject of raised eyebrows and shocked remarks for weeks. It might even make the local newspaper unless he had a word with the editor.

When he got out of the car at the pithead, Mr Woodward saw that all was calm and orderly. Apart from the arrival of a huge fan it was business as usual. There was no disaster. He forced himself to put his silly misjudgement out of his mind; after all no actual harm had been done. Lawson, the manager was admiring the new arrival from Germany.

'Ah yes, the Schiele fan.' Mr Woodward turned to Oliver in an effort to restore his image as an unflappable engineer with detailed information at his fingertips. 'It's a new design. In the event of fire you can make it switch direction and it will blow the flames away. Fire is a terrible thing in a pit.' A strange look came over the boy's face, he sighed deeply and cupped his left elbow with his other hand,

'This is Oliver.' Mr Woodward put his hand on the boy's shoulder as he introduced him to the manager. 'He's working in the office while Mr Carter and Mr Frederick are in Germany. Getting a feel for mining. It'll stand him in good stead in the future.'

'That reminds me. When Mr Carter rang about the fan this morning he asked me to warn you that he might be a little late for the opera tomorrow. Ferry timings have changed.'

'I hope he's not too late. It's Dorothea's opening night. I'm on my way to Leeds tomorrow. Wouldn't miss it for the world.' Mr Woodward automatically broke into a smile at the mention of his daughter. As it spread across his face an icy hand grabbed his heart and the familiar dread of disaster striking Dorothea sent his muscles into a spasm, twisting his grip on Oliver's shoulder tighter and tighter while he struggled to keep his composure.

With a sharp cry Oliver, sagged at the knees and crumpled to the ground. He lay unconscious, his face deathly pale. A distraught Mr Woodward looked at the motionless body and felt like a murderer as the boy lay skewed at his feet.

It was the mine manager, Lawson, who worked it out. 'Look at his arm. I see too many fractured limbs in my line of work not to know a broken arm when I see it.. We'd better get him to a doctor.' He looked to his boss.

'We'll take him in the car.'

The men who had unloaded the mighty piece of engineering turned their attention to the boy, gently easing him on to a stretcher and sliding him on to the backseat of the car, where Mr Woodward sat looking anxiously at his smooth young face and remembered the boys who had been briefly his. He told Higgs to drive straight to the old doctor who refused to have a telephone.

'If he won't have a phone, he can't grumble when people come knocking on his door,' said a defiant Mr Woodward

The doctor pronounced Oliver to have a broken humerus and strapped it in a sling. 'There's no bruising yet. There will be,' he told Oliver who was no stranger to livid marks on arms and legs. The boys at school regularly compared the size and colour of their bruises.

'How did it happen?' enquired the doctor with a routine suspicion in his voice. In his experience a common cause of a child with a broken limb was an angry adult.

It was Higgs who explained. 'It was the telephone. We thought it was an emergency at pit. Grabbed at it. Knocked it over. And the lad fell. Must have happened then. He didn't cry out, and we was so busy rushing off to do our bit we didn't think to check. He said nowt.' He looked at Oliver's pale face. 'Brave lad.'

'You see now why I won't have one of those infernal telephones,' said the doctor. 'All that rushing about in a panic when it's not necessary.'

Mr Woodward chose to ignore him. He patted Oliver on the head and lamented, 'I wish you'd told me you were hurt. It must be very painful.'

'I didn't want to miss a ride in a car,' said Oliver, 'It must be wonderful being able to drive it.'

Mr Woodward paid the doctor who assured him that young bones healed quickly. Higgs suggested that as a reward for his bravery Oliver should sit next to him in the front as they drove to school to explain his absence to the headmaster. The injured boy waved his good arm at his school friends who lined up at the

160

window to enjoy the unusual sight of a motor car at the school gate. His next appearance was in the street of terraced houses where he lived. The residents poured out of their homes as if he was royalty. They had never seen such a magnificent vehicle in their road before.

As Oliver's mother was still at work a reassuring message was left with a neighbour and the boy was taken into the care of Mrs Woodward and Nanny. Mr Woodward was firmly of the opinion that the care of the sick and injured was women's work. Oliver was smothered in motherly attention and gazed at with wonder by the Carter twins who did not know you had bones and that they could break. They understood about his mother being out at work. That's where their mother was.

There was one final task left for Higgs before he could hang up his driving gloves for the day – reuniting Oliver with his mother. On his return he reported to Mr Woodward, 'All's well that ends well. His mam was mighty relieved to see him. She lost her husband to pit. Not our pit. Somewhere further north.'

Mr Woodward had not properly registered the fact that Oliver's father had died in a pit accident. He knew the boy's surname and it was not one of those killed in his pit. The names of the few who died in his pit were engraved on his heart.

Higgs ploughed on with his mission. 'Lad's really keen on the car. If it's all right with you I'll let him do a few jobs, a bit of polishing, clean the headlights, when Miss Truesdale doesn't need him in the office. He says he'll be back on Monday and making the tea. He's right-handed, so he can do the kettle.'

Mr Woodward clicked his tongue in annoyance. 'I forgot about Miss Truesdale.'

'Don't worry about her,' said Higgs. 'She'd rung the pit to check and passed the good news to Mrs Woodward. She didn't want her getting anxious.'

If Mr Woodward had been a mediaeval monk in one of the sterner orders he would have lashed his bare back with his leather whip that night. As he was a 20th century Methodist he said his prayers and examined his conscience severely before he went to bed. He played the parts of both the prisoner in the dock and the prosecutor in chief. His first offence of the day was giving way to

161

an irrational and superstitious belief in fate, rather than trusting the Lord. He saw how his excessive concern for his daughter had given him tunnel-vision and blinded him to the welfare of others. How else to explain his failure to see that his clumsiness had injured Oliver, a boy whose father had been killed in the pit. Yet he had tactlessly persisted in painting the boy's future as a miner as if there was no possibility of choice. There was no need for the jury to retire to decide the verdict. He found himself guilty on all counts. It remained only for the sentence to be pronounced. That was a task he left to a higher authority.

CHAPTER 18

Friday

In the small hours of the morning a distraught Dorothea knocked on the door of room 16. She could not sleep. Mr Martelli took her in, wrapped his arms round her and listened as she complained about Charity's snoring, the whirling thoughts in her head and her absolute terror of failure. He took her to his warm bed and murmured reassurance in her ear, listing her beauty, the power of her voice, the thoroughness of her preparations. Like a comforted child she fell asleep.

When the hotel stirred into life, he crept out of bed, dressed and quietly padded off to make arrangements. He commandeered a hotel maid and sent her to wake Charity.

Through the gap as she opened the bedroom door, he told her, 'Dorothea is perfectly safe. She is sleeping which is the best thing for her.' He killed the question coming to Charity's lips with a flash of his eyes and a brief order disguised as a question. 'Her clothes for today?' he barked. Charity set about collecting them. He gestured to show that they were to be given to the hotel maid. She was to deliver them to his room without disturbing Dorothea. Any doubts that Charity had as to Dorothea's whereabouts were resolved.

As Charity was again a witness, Mr Martelli set about sealing her lips tighter. He pointed a finger at her and spelt out emphatically, 'No word of this is to leak out. Keep away from Mr Woodward. I will look after him. If you are asked you say Miss Dorothea had a late breakfast in her room where she later took a bath. She is spending the day quietly to prepare for the opening tonight.' Charity swallowed some air ready to protest. He cut her off. 'You will make sure that your brother and Neville follow a similar pattern of behaviour. It is just possible that the director will summon Neville for some extra coaching given how recently he joined the company. If he is not needed for rehearsal, you may take him and Duncan for a stroll in the afternoon. Do not let Mr Woodward near his daughter. It is to the advantage of us all to keep her tranquil. I plan to meet his train and will invite him for lunch in the hotel here. Leave him to me. *Capisce.*' He tapped the breast pocket of his jacket where he kept the document she had written. Charity wondered if he planned to be the one to tell Mr Woodward about Dorothea's scandalous goings on. She felt a strange kick of pleasure at the prospect and hoped for a ringside seat so she could watch the fireworks.

After the painful examination of his conscience Mr Woodward awoke with a list of tasks he wanted to complete on Friday morning before going to Leeds for the opening night. Mrs Woodward had enjoyed spoiling the injured Oliver and put in a bid for the services of Higgs and the car. She thought she might go to the boy's home with a few treats for him and his mother. The answer was No. Though caring for the injured was the work of women, the task of easing his conscience was one that Mr Woodward had to undertake himself. He was happy to have his wife rustle up some suitable gifts but he insisted on delivering them in person.

A gift of food and a bunch of flowers was soon ready. As he looked at them he thought of Edward who would have delivered them with style. That reminded him that he should visit Miss Truesdale in the office to bring her up to date. It was strange how when he thought of Edward he thought of her.

When he arrived at the office, Jenny offered him a cup of tea. It felt odd to put the kettle on. She had quickly grown used to Oliver doing that task. Mr Woodward shouted down for Higgs to come up and join them. 'The lad says he'll be back on Monday. He'll have to wear a sling.

'Monday will be quite a day. Mr Carter back. And Mavis,' Jenny stopped and put her hand across her lips. 'I should call her Mrs Perkins now. She will be joining us on Monday. Only Mr Frederick will be missing.'

Mr Woodward smiled at the prospect of Edward's return. 'Until then, Miss Truesdale, you will have to hold the fort on your own.' He had many more words of advice and much urging of telegrams in the event of an emergency before Jenny could wave him on his way to the railway station and Leeds.

When she was alone she pulled the familiar shutter down in her mind to stop herself from thinking about events in Leeds. She vowed to bury herself in domesticity over the weekend, brushing her skirts and sponging off any stains on her clothes. She would overhaul her wardrobe and not think about Edward until he came to work on Monday morning. Mavis would be there to cheer up the office and nag Mr Woodward until he settled down to deal with that pile of letters he had been successfully ignoring for so long. Until then there was just a long, lonely Friday afternoon to endure.

'Don't fret, Mr Woodward,' said Higgs as he helped him board the train. 'Oliver will be as good as new in no time. I'll telegraph Miss Dorothea with the time of your arrival. I hope the show goes well.' He tucked a blanket from the car round his employer's knees; the man's need of support and encouragement was pathetically clear to his chauffeur.

Mr Martelli sat in the lobby with the hotel copy of the *Leeds Mercury* newspaper, a cup of coffee and a telegram addressed to Mrs Carter which he had intercepted and opened. Dorothea was upstairs in his room, finishing breakfast and anticipating a leisurely bath. Mr Martelli slipped the telegram in his pocket. Now that he knew the time of her father's arrival there was no point in bothering her with the information. He glanced quickly through the newspaper and flinched at one of the photographs. After staring into space for a few minutes he rolled up the newspaper, tucked it under his arm and set off to climb the stairs to his room. There he peeped round the door and heard Dorothea humming in the bath. As quietly as a thief he crossed the room, slid the paper into the wastepaper basket and left, shutting the door gently behind him.

At the station, he welcomed Mr Woodward and gave him Dorothea's apologies for not coming to meet him. It was imperative that she took the day of the performance very quietly. Perhaps they could meet for lunch, though she had to be very careful about food. Nothing heavy. In the meantime Mr Woodward might like to take a stroll round the elegant arcades of Leeds.

Inspiration struck Mr Martelli. Would Mr Woodward like to see the theatre where his daughter would sing that evening? Indeed he would. Very much so. The two men studied the exterior of the

Grand Theatre where a board proclaimed that night's performance of *Tosca* was sold out, a piece of information Mr Woodward found very gratifying. After admiring the splendid architecture of the city Mr Martelli ran out of delaying tactics. There was no choice but to return to the hotel where it would be difficult to keep Dorothea from her father. As they walked into the lobby a man sitting at the table rose to his feet and came to greet Mr Woodward, calling him Ken and slapping him on the back. It was Stan Earnshaw, a long-lost friend from his childhood.

Mr Martelli sent a quick thank you to heaven for this *deus ex machina*, who would divert Mr Woodward from quizzing his daughter too closely. This was not the time for confessions and emotional upheavals. *Tosca* was so much more important.

"Some information for you, Ken.' Stan Earnshaw was waving a telegram at Mr Woodward. 'Thought I'd bring it myself, as I was close. It's been too long since we met. Pity I missed you in Manchester.'

'I've still not managed to set foot in that Midland Hotel,' grumbled Mr Woodward. 'I'm tired of people telling me how wonderful it is.' He looked round the lobby with its elegant furniture and glistening chandeliers. 'Mind you, this place is nice. You recommended it to me for Dorothea.'

'Your daughter. The singer?'

'Yes. I wanted somewhere respectable and nice for her. A girl. You worry.'

'That's one worry I'd be glad to have.'

'Of course. Sorry, Stan. You had a little girl?'

'Not for long. She was just 2 years old. You never forget.'

'We lost two boys. Didn't make their first birthdays.'

The men gazed stony-faced into the distance for a moment. Stan was first to return to business, holding out the telegram. 'This came from your Mr Carter. He's been using my agent in Hull for travel arrangements. That's a sharp lad you've got there.'

'My son-in-law. On his way home from Germany, coming to see his wife sing.'

'Well, I'm sorry to be the one to break it to you, he doesn't think he's going to make it in time.' He handed over the telegram for inspection.

Mr Woodward was in such a state of nervous tension that he wanted to weep with disappointment. The incident with Oliver and the recent reminders of the sons he had lost, brought home to him how much he valued his relationship with Edward.

Mr Martelli felt a similar dismay. For him Edward's non-attendance at the performance was a calamity to be avoided at all costs. His seat, next to Mr Woodward's, in the front row of the dress circle, was the most conspicuous place in the theatre. Opera goers spent as much time looking at the rest of the audience as they did at the stage. They would as a matter of routine train their opera glasses mercilessly on the occupants of the dress circle, and an empty seat there would be as jarring and as ugly as a missing front tooth.

Thanks to the sensation caused by Dorothea's impromptu performance at the hotel dinner – and her low-cut dress – the first night was sold out, a fact that had been heavily advertised. To preserve the magic of the publicity the empty seat in the front row of the dress circle must be occupied. Mr Martelli himself could not sit there without leaving a gap in the front stalls which would be only slightly less deplorable. He needed a respectable looking candidate who would agree to sit next to Mr Woodward and be prepared to give up the seat when, or if, Edward arrived. He looked at Mr Earnshaw who appeared to be a jolly chap and wondered out loud if he'd consider lending them a helping hand. Stan thought it a most amusing idea. Did he have to wear a white tie and tails? Mr Martelli was sure the correct clothing would help. Mr Woodward laughed, clapped his old friend on the shoulder and suggested they set off to acquire the necessary disguise for the enterprise.

Mr Martelli watched them go and heaved a sigh of relief before taking the opportunity to make sure that Charity was busy with her boys and keeping her lips sealed about Dorothea's sociable sleeping habits. He found the three of them tucked into a warm corner of the garden playing chess. Charity was busy moving the pieces as Neville and Duncan directed. An admiring audience had gathered;

many were impressed by the mental power required to play chess when you could not see the board, and others were impressed by Neville's astonishing good looks.

Mr Martelli's next task was to check Dorothea was neither hungry, thirsty or in need of entertainment. He mopped his face with his handkerchief. So many little pots coming to the boil and they all needed careful handling. He had every expectation that they would all reach boiling point at the same time. There would be at some point a major explosion, but not yet. Not yet. Dear Lord, please don't let it be tonight. Nothing, but nothing must be allowed to spoil the first night of *Tosca*.

All was calm as dusk settled over the town and it was time for the musicians and singers to make their way to the Grand Theatre. Mr Martelli, the tubby impresario, could feel his all his schemes and dealings of the past years coming to a climax.

'I shall smuggle you into the theatre,' he told Dorothea. 'There will be opera afficionados waiting for a glimpse of you. Well, they must wait a little longer. A bit of mystery is good.' He could not relax until she was safely in her dressing room. At the theatre he could keep the door closed against her father. And her husband if he arrived. At the hotel he could not.'

It took the overture for the audience to settle down, adjust their clothing and check their neighbours. From the moment the curtain rose they were enthralled. The interior of an Italian catholic church richly decorated and elaborately carved was a revelation compared to the austere monochrome of the chapels they were accustomed to. Even Mr Woodward did not take offence at the large mural of Mary Magdalene, as it was only half completed. Neville was thoughtfully adding strokes of paint in a realistic way. The painter's smock swung and floated through the air in response to his graceful movements and long strides.

Mr Woodward nudged Stan Earnshaw and whispered, 'He's totally blind.'

'You'd never guess.'

The audience fell silent as other characters appeared and there was some business with a key. Mr Woodward was disappointed that Dorothea was not the first woman on stage. When she did appear he was pleased to see that she was demurely dressed and behaved as a woman should to the man, he assumed, was her husband, rather than her lover. He looked at his watch and feared Edward was not going to arrive in time to see Dorothea perform. Then a procession of singing children flooded on stage behind an elaborately dressed priest swinging a censer. The smell of incense rose through the air and the first act came to an end.

Stan clapped Mr Woodward on the shoulder. 'I know you don't indulge but I think we should go to the bar. See what the word is among the champagne and sherry drinkers.' He grinned, lifted his glass of whisky and wandered casually among the ball gowns and black tail coats. Mr Woodward, with no glass in his hand, stood about feeling uncomfortable until he saw a ripple of surprise spread through the crowd. A man in a dark business suit and a heavy overcoat was making his way towards him. It was Edward. Delight lit up his face as they exchanged greetings. There was no time for news as Stan Earnshaw popped up between them.

'This way,' he told Edward, pointing with his whisky glass to the cloakroom. There they swapped shirts and jackets. Stan fastened the white tie while he briefed Edward who was polishing off the whisky. 'Your missus has been on once. No bad comments. All very taken with the artist bloke. Word has got out he's blind.' A final tug at the tie and the shoulders of the jacket. 'Once you're in your seat people only see your top half,' he assured Edward.

Stan took back ownership of the empty whisky glass and started to put on the clothes Edward had discarded. 'I'll go upstairs and see what the poor people think.' He clapped Edward on the back and pushed him to the door. 'Did you get a deal with Berlin?'

Edward gave him a thumbs up and went out just as the bell was ringing to warn them to return to their seats. He gave a sigh of relief as he took Stan's place next to Mr Woodward. The older man patted his arm.

'Bit of a rush was it? I'm glad you made it. It means a lot to me.' He stopped abruptly; the curtain was going up. He'd wanted to call Edward, son. 'Been a bit of a bother to get here?' he asked. Edward gave a wry smile at the memory of the missed connections and the frantic changes of plan required for him to fill this empty seat and sit and watch people sing, an activity he was not particularly keen on.

He changed his mind when Dorothea came on in a low-cut scarlet ball gown; she was riveting. A hushed concentration fell upon the audience who listened with rapt attention and watched her trick Scarpia into writing the safe conduct. Then she moved with regal authority as she stabbed him in the back. Although no-one understood the meaning of her words the audience sensed her contempt for the now powerless Scarpia before whom all Rome used to tremble.

In the interval, the buzz in the bar was about Dorothea.

'Perhaps a little medicinal brandy,' suggested Edward. His father-in-law was white-faced with shock. The stabbing, the candles. the crucifix and the sheer power of his daughter on stage had overwhelmed him. Edward took silence for consent and supplied a couple of fortifying drinks; there was another whole act to get through. Mr Woodward remained tranquil as Cavaradossi was executed. He thought the worst was over and relaxed his guard. Dorothea expressing Tosca's despair at losing her lover reminded him of his teenage daughter's tantrums over the colour of her dress or a falling out with another other girl. She'd scream and drum her heels, he'd buy her a new dress or invite the enemy to tea. She'd get over it.

However, Tosca was not the teenage Dorothea. She was a woman who had lost her lover, who had committed murder and was now surround by armed guards. Suddenly death looked a better prospect than life. She pushed past a guard, rushed to the parapet and with a deathly scream threw herself into the dark void. A shout of dismay came from her father's lips. He was not alone in thinking she had jumped to her death; other members of the audience gasped with shock. An intense silence followed. It was broken by shouts of 'brava' which came from members of the orchestra, genuinely impressed by her performance. Then the applause started. It thundered round the theatre, a deep rolling sound, punctuated by gasps and squeals from people, stirred by some deep and unfamiliar emotion they were unable to express in any other way.

The director, never one to miss an opportunity to publicise himself, decided to appear in front of the curtain to say a few words before the curtain calls. The audience soon shouted him down. They wanted the singers, greeting them with roars of approval. Mr Woodward had to wait as Dorothea was the last to appear. Neville held up his arm for her to take his hand. The audience erupted into a roar of delight. Her father mopped his brow as he saw her curtsy, smile and wave. The leap from the battlements had been so convincing he feared that, like Oliver, her bones would be broken.

Eventually people began to leave their seats. Stan arrived, wending his way down from the balcony. He reported a most favourable reaction from the cheaper seats. 'Standing room only. People said they'd come 'cos they'd read about it in the *Leeds Mercury*.' He plucked at the lapel of the jacket of Edward's that he was wearing. 'I'm going back to the hotel. I'll make sure this gets returned to you.' Edward thanked Stan Earnshaw for taking part in a harmless bit of play-acting to fill the seats.

Suddenly conscious of the bizarre mixture of clothing he was wearing, and his exhaustion from his journey, Edward suggested that they keep the visit to Dorothea's dressing room brief. 'Just show our faces. She will be knee deep in fans and admirers. And then I expect there'll be a bit of a party somewhere for the cast.'

It was the name of Mr Martelli that brought them to the front of the queue of people waiting to congratulate, invite, employ or criticise the singing sensation of the evening. He was at the door of her dressing room to greet them.

'Ah! Mr Woodward. Was she not wonderful.' He shouted into the dressing room, 'Miss Dorothea, your father, your husband are here to congratulate you.'

As they arrived in the dressing room, Neville rose gracefully to his feet with a glass of champagne in his hand. Dorothea, still in costume offered them her cheek to kiss and after a few pleasantries declared she wanted to change her clothes. The director had arranged a little celebration for the cast at his hotel. She was not going to wear scarlet again and pointed to a peacock blue gown that awaited her.

Mr Martelli was quick to offer his services. 'I will escort her there, Mr Woodward and will make sure she returns safely.'

Suddenly redundant, husband and father returned to their hotel. Mr Woodward advised Edward to book a room for himself. 'Charity is sharing with Dorothea,' he explained. While Edward spoke to the night porter Mr Woodward went to sit at the table in the lobby. His eye was drawn to the newspaper on the table. It always diverted him to read a newspaper. He shook the pages open. He was met with a photograph of a woman on the balcony of a huge room occupied by well-dressed people with tables laid for dinner. They were raising their glasses to the woman as she leaned over the balcony in her low- cut dress. Behind her were men with the bows of their violins poised ready to play. In her hand she held a champagne glass.

The caption gave her name as Dorothea Woodward. It referred to her as a relatively unknown singer who was to sing the title role in *Tosca* later in the week. She was rumoured to be married to an Italian count. Mr Woodward groaned aloud and thumped the newspaper on the table, his worst fears confirmed. Dorothea had been led astray into drinking alcohol. Edward came to investigate the problem. He found soothing words for his father-in-law. The glass was just a prop, like the huge knife that she had wielded on stage. She did not really stab the villain. She probably did not drink the champagne, just waved an empty glass about.

Mr Woodward was not comforted. 'I was 12 when I signed the pledge never to let alcohol past my lips. My mother wanted me to do it before I left to go down the mine. Would you believe Stan Earnshaw took it at the same time?'

'He's changed his mind since then,' said Edward, and thought gratefully of the glass of whisky they'd shared as they swapped clothes. 'The pledge,' Edward went on with apparent confidence, as if he knew what he was talking about, 'allows alcohol for medicinal purposes. In the case of shock, injury or intense distress. On very rare occasions I have known a strict teetotaller drink a small amount of medicinal brandy. A man who has refrained from alcohol for years. It has to be a very remarkable occasion, you understand. The marriage of a beloved daughter for example, or the birth of two

172

grandchildren.' He gave his disarming grin. They smiled at the shared memory. 'Tonight Mr Woodward, your daughter has stabbed a man with a very large knife and leapt off a cliff to her death. I think that qualifies you for a glass of brandy.'

When the brandy arrived Edward made sure that it was charged to his room. They sipped the golden liquid and Mr Woodward's breathing settled down.

'When did Dorothea sign the pledge?' asked Edward. 'I don't remember her talking about it.' As if she ever talked to him about anything except her musical ambitions.

A significant silence followed. Mr Woodward tried to remember but had to admit, 'I don't believe she actually put her hand on the Bible and swore the oath or signed anything. Things have changed. I just assumed she'd follow my example.'

'I know you are a man who likes to keep his word.' Edward continued with his train of thought. 'So Dorothea has not taken a solemn oath to abstain from alcohol. In that case she cannot be accused of breaking her word.' The breaking of vows was much on his mind at this time. He left the thought hanging in the air; he was sure it was a topic that would demand their attention in the future.

Abruptly he changed the subject. 'What are your plans for tomorrow? For myself I should like to head home as soon as possible. Have Sunday at home. See Izzy and Clare.' He knew that he'd have to wait until Monday before seeing Jenny, the person he most wanted to see.

Mr Woodward cheered up at the thought of returning to Manchester. He had booked a first-class compartment leaving soon after 11 o'clock. He assumed that Dorothea would travel with them, but he had not yet told her the time of the train. Edward suggested they went to her room where they could leave a message with Charity. They found the room empty. They reasoned that Charity would have taken Neville and Duncan to the director's party and would stay to bring them back. They left a note of the time the train departed.

'Clare and Issy will be looking forward to seeing her,' said Mr Woodward. The thought of his grandchildren cheered him up. He went off to his room, his mood much improved. Edward went down to reception and ordered another brandy. He had not signed a pledge. He chatted to the man behind the counter and asked if they always had the *Leeds Mercury* in the lobby for guests. They did indeed, although sometimes thoughtless guests took it away to their rooms. He gestured to the paper on the round table and grumbled that Mr Earnshaw had asked specially for it when he came in not half an hour ago. They had to rummage it out of the waste paper.

And Mr Earnshaw left it on the table for Mr Woodward to find, thought Edward. He wondered if there was malice in the manoeuvre. There was definitely history between those two. One day he would ferret it out. He looked up at the clock. Midnight. Hard to believe that he had started Friday 18 hours ago in a different country.

CHAPTER 19

Saturday

In the very small hours of Saturday morning, voices echoed in the revolving door that brought people into the hotel from the street. Two men stumbled out propping each other up. 'This way my dear boy,' said a voice, more suited to a large theatre than the lobby of a respectable hotel in the hours of darkness. The director had a guiding arm round Neville, whose evening dress was looking distinctly rumpled. They were followed by a more sedate pair, Charity, leading her brother, Duncan. She shouted, 'Shush,' to the director who was whistling as he wandered past Edward to demand that whisky be sent to his room.

'But you don't have a room here, sir,' countered the night porter.

'This gentleman does,' said the director pointing at Neville. 'What's your room number, dear boy?'

Neville frowned and pointed in the direction of the stairs. 'Fourteen steps, a right turn at the eighth then corridor straight ahead, three doors along, left hand side.'

'Room 12,' said the porter and Charity at the same moment.

'Is Mr Woodward paying the bill for room 12?' asked Edward.

'Indeed he is,' said the porter.

'Then better pay cash or you will lose a good friend. Mr Woodward doesn't hold with alcohol.' He looked significantly at Charity, Neville and Duncan who had benefitted most from Mr Woodward's support. The director set about fishing in his pockets as he had when asked for Charity's train fare. On this occasion he found some coins and went to pay. The porter set off up the stairs with glasses and a bottle on a tray as the revolving door cranked into action once more.

Dorothea, swiftly followed by Mr Martelli, popped out of its jaws and into the lobby. Edward rose to his feet and went to greet them. He could feel the hair on the back of his neck stand up. He ignored Martelli and spoke to Dorothea.

'There's a message for you in your room. Your father would like you to travel home with us tomorrow morning. It's not an early start but best get some rest, as you must be exhausted. I was here in time for Act Two, by the way. You were magnificent.' There was a general murmur of agreement.

For all the notice she took of him Edward felt that he might as well have been talking to a tree. Even the appreciation of her performance failed to register with Dorothea. She said nothing but set off up the stairs. Charity, guiding her brother and Neville, followed. The director joined them in pursuit of the bottle he had paid for. Mr Martelli remained in the lobby and turned to face Edward who had returned to his chair. The porter came back and settled himself in the chair behind the desk in the hope of catching some sleep. He was not accustomed to being busy at this hour; it was not that kind of hotel.

An unsmiling Edward gestured for Mr Martelli to sit at the round table. It was time for some serious talking. He slid the copy of the *Leeds Mercury* towards him.

'Ah. I thought I'd managed to dispose of that particular edition. I am aware of Mr Woodward's objection to alcohol. Has he seen the photograph of Miss Dorothea? I had hoped to spare him distress.'

'Unfortunately it was brought to his attention. And he recognised a champagne glass when he saw it. By the way, she is Dorothea Carter, not Dorothea Woodward as it says in the caption.' Edward looked severely at the man who was not merely Dorothea's agent but who was making a bid for the role of husband, father or, most likely, lover.

Mr Martelli set about lighting a cigar. 'I take your point. In return I ask you to acknowledge that the photograph filled the seats of the Grand Theatre to capacity and your wife had the opportunity to prove herself a star. The next performance on Tuesday is booked solid. There are people coming from London to see the production, and there is talk of transferring there. Meanwhile I am knee-deep in requests from wealthy people who claim they would pay the price of a champion race horse for one recital by Miss Dorothea in their drawing room. If I can arrange for Neville to join her they will be my slaves for life.'

'You're saying that she has a future as a singer.'

'I am saying that she has a future as a singer with me as her manager.' He pointed at the starched front of his white shirt so that there could be no misunderstanding.

Edward was silent as his mind raced. 'She has worked hard, practising and studying.'

'Hard work is not always enough. Miss Dorothea knows that she could not have done it without her father's financial support. She is well aware of that, and his good opinion is of great importance to her.' Edward saw that his own opinion counted for little.

Mr Martelli waved his cigar at Edward. 'You have not stood in her way. Many husbands would.' To his surprise Edward was beginning to feel respect for the funny little Italian.

Mr Martelli pointed to his own chest and declared, 'It is me who has guided her.' He slipped into Italian for emphasis. 'Io. Io solo. Apart from that unfortunate gap when she went to France, I built her up step by careful step until she was ready to seize this opportunity that I found for her. It took courage. She has plenty of that.' Mr Martelli put his hand to his heart. 'I swear it has been successful, beyond my wildest dreams. Her fees will enable her to live independently of you, her father and your dirty coal business.'

Edward flinched at the description of his business as dirty. To be fair it was dirty. Very dirty. He had to admit that Martelli had played a part in transforming Dorothea from a demanding daughter, a reluctant mother and an indifferent wife into a woman who had found a purpose in her life. She'd had to work against the grain of the society she lived in. She deserved her success, the praise the applause, the competition for her talent. She could not have done it without her father's money, or his own refusal to play the heavy-handed husband, and it would not have happened without Martelli. However, it didn't change his opinion of her as a self-centred person with no consideration for feelings other than her own.

'Is that what Dorothea wants? To pursue her musical career,' asked Edward. The words felt strange in his mouth. No-one ever talked of women having careers.

'That is for her to decide. I, myself, think it is a little too soon to answer that question. It has all been very sudden. I will wait for the offers to come in writing.'

Edward gave Mr Martelli full marks for fair dealing. There were not many men who would sit in front of you and discuss calmly taking your wife. Husbands were supposed to resort to blows. But then he was no more a husband than Dorothea was a wife.

'There are many things to consider.' Mr Martelli leaned forward and counted them off on his fingers. 'You have children. She may not wish to throw in her lot with me. The fear of scandal. Other women can be very hard on those who decide not to live up to their marriage vows. The world of the theatre is not so judgemental as society in general, but there are those who would not allow her in their homes. Non-conformists do so like people to conform' He looked up and smiled sheepishly at his joke. He took a breath as he came to the real sticking point. 'Then there is her father. His opinion weighs heavy on her.'

'I can't help noticing that I don't appear on the list of obstacles. She really is Dorothea Woodward. Not Mrs Carter.'

'It's not as if you love each other,' said Mr Martelli with brutal honesty. 'I am not asking to marry her. I long ago decided marriage was not for me. I do want to be Dorothea's companion and manager, her guide and her teacher, and I will not deny that I want to be her lover. You can play the complaisant husband if you choose that role, but I cannot imagine you enjoying it.'

As he finished speaking he took an envelope out of his breast pocket and passed it to Edward. Without a further word, he set off up the stairs to room 16 where he hoped that Dorothea would be warming his bed. She had drunk the odd glass of champagne but the sizzling energy required for her performance on stage would soon burn off the alcohol. Tonight she might be ready to commit herself to him. He could wait if necessary. The important thing was to get her on the train in good order in the morning. He knew only too well that Mr Woodward was the greatest obstacle in his path.

178

Edward opened the envelope Martelli had given him and read the careful account that Charity had written of finding Dorothea in bed with her agent. His whoop of delight woke the sleeping porter who wondered what the clientele was coming to. Edward pressed the letter to his chest. It was a blunt instrument capable of causing massive damage. He would keep it safe and muttered a word of thanks to Mr Martelli for handing him the means of fulfilling his heart's desire.

When she went to wake her boys in the morning Charity had a shock. The room smelt of liquor and male sweat. She soon found the source. Piled on the bed was a jumble of hairy thighs, muscular arms and rounded buttocks. From it emerged various whistles, snores and sudden snorts, the unmistakeable sounds of men sleeping. Modesty prevented her investigating the naked men too closely but she was sure that Neville and Duncan had company. A leg twitched, a torso turned and a head emerged. Charity recognised the iron-grey mane of the theatre director. The whisky bottle lay empty on the floor, witness to the celebration of his unexpected theatrical success.

Charity tiptoed out and returned to the room she was supposed to share with Dorothea. Once there, she was unsure what to do next. There was no point in waking the boys, as they were not catching the train to Manchester with Mr Woodward. But Dorothea was, so it would be sensible to pack her trunks. At 10 o'clock she took Dorothea's travelling outfit round to Mr Martelli's room and tapped on the door. She accepted without comment the fact that they had been in bed together. Working with Mr Martelli and his clients was, Charity decided, going to be full of surprises. Very different from Henshaw's.

Mr Martelli took her to one side and thanked her for her forethought in dealing with Dorothea's clothes. He assured her that Mr Woodward would pay the hotel bill before he left. After that Charity and her boys would have to pay their expenses from their fees, so they might like to look for somewhere cheaper. He already had bookings for them in the coming week and he would sort out the details with them later in the day. They would not starve.

Having dealt with Charity, Mr Martelli turned his attention to his next task. Getting Dorothea breakfasted, dressed, thoroughly briefed and to the station on time. He accomplished it with minutes to spare. Mr Woodward found it gratifying to board the train with his beautiful and well-groomed daughter and his handsome son-in-law for their journey home.

'Are you happy to be coming home?' he asked Dorothea.

'Of course. I'm looking forward to seeing... She stopped abruptly and after a pause and said, 'the children.' She had been going to say Nanny before she remembered Franco's advice. Keep mentioning the children, he had urged her. She had practised saying their names, Izzy and Clare, until they slipped easily from her lips.

In the comfort and privacy of their first-class compartment Dorothea went over Franco's words of advice. 'Your father will find it easier to forgive a faithless wife than a bad mother.' The words 'father' and 'forgive' in the same sentence comforted her. She fell asleep.

Seeing his daughter so peaceful Mr Woodward began to relax against the back of his upholstered seat. Safe inside a moving train, watching the scenery pass by, he laid down the burden of worrying about her. While she slept he was safe from the sudden shocks that she was liable to spring on him. He would enjoy a few minutes of talking with Edward, a companionable exchange of information after their separation. The trip to Germany? Interesting and productive. He was more convinced than ever that he had done the right thing in exploring the German manufacturers. When they got back to the office they would go over the figures. Edward was confident they would agree.

Mention of the office reminded Mr Woodward of Oliver and Edward of Jenny, though he could not say so. An embarrassed Mr Woodward told Edward of his panic-stricken assumption of an accident at the pit that had caused Oliver's injury, which he had failed to notice immediately.

'You were unlucky,' Edward told him. 'Lads that age usually bounce.'

'He says he'll be back on Monday and boiling the kettle. Has to keep his arm in the sling.'

'Sounds like we owe him,' said Edward.

'I took some him sweets and stuff. What he'd really like is a chance to work with motor cars.'

'Too young. Let him finish school. Do his exams. Then if he comes and says he still wants to be a chauffeur or a car mechanic he'll be first in the queue. We could help to pay for his training.'

'I knew that his father had been killed in the mine and I still assumed he'd want to work there one day. Simply because that's what I did.'

'We can't assume that our children want to follow in our footsteps.' Edward laughed to find himself so philosophical. 'Remind me I said that when I'm pulling my hair out because Izzy wants to be a ballet dancer or a lion tamer.'

'Or an opera singer.' Both men laughed. It was not often that Mr Woodward felt able to share a joke about his daughter.

When she arrived home Dorothea had to take the edge off her mother's appetite for news before she could go up to the nursery allegedly to see her children. She found that Edward had beaten her to it. As it was time for the children's walk, he volunteered to go with them, which suited Dorothea. It was Nanny who she wanted to see. She told her all about Neville's last-minute inclusion in the cast, the fickleness of the director and the nerve-wracking last week with its very real fear of failure. 'I need not have worried, Nanny. It was an absolute triumph. Everybody says so, and Mr Martelli says the offers of work are pouring in.'

'And will you accept them?' asked Nanny who always came straight to the point.

'Of course. Why ever not?'

Nanny could think of several reasons. There were two small ones who would be back from their walk soon and make their presence felt. Better to let Dorothea find the problems herself. She confined herself to warning, 'People can aways find reasons to stop you from doing what you want. Sometimes it helps to anticipate them.'

'That's what Franco says.'

'Franco? Franco who?'

'Mr Martelli. He's my agent.'

181

'He sounds like a sensible man.

Edward strolled in with Izzy and Clare, putting an end to their conversation. He stayed while they played trains, drew fairies and drank imaginary potions out of doll-sized cups until it was time for the children's tea — a meal that Dorothea shared with them as part of her regime to control her weight. Edward left them. It was only fair to allow her time on her own with the children.

Dorothea enjoyed the tiny egg sandwiches and the dainty jellies. She would miss them when she was back in Leeds, or London or wherever the music took her. It pleased her to think that wherever she was, at this time of day her children would be sitting down to eat and Nanny would be at the table with them. It always soothed her to be with Nanny. She drifted off into a serene warm place with Nanny in it. When she came to, Nanny was speaking.

'Now I think we've all had enough chocolate cake. Time to wash hands and faces before we go down to the drawing room to see the grown-ups.'

Damn. There were things that Dorothea had intended to ask Nanny.

In spite of her nursery tea, Dorothea joined the family at dinner. It was all part of her model daughter act. It did not last long.

'I told you half portions,' she snapped at the maid who gave her two roast potatoes. Her mother scowled. Did Dorothea not know how difficult it was to get maids?

'It's that Yorkshire food. It's put pounds on me,' Dorothea explained.

'Well that's all over with now. You'll be back on home cooking,' said her mother complacently.

'Oh no. I've to be back for the performance on Tuesday. The rest of the week is booked solid already.' She looked round the table amazed at her parents' naivety. Surely they knew that successful shows ran for as long as they could sell tickets. The music hall filled the nights in between when the opera soloists were saving their voices.

The clamour of dismay round the table told her that they had not thought beyond the opening night. Her previous concerts had been one-off events, never to be repeated. All their nerves and

182

apprehension had been fixed on the opening, and it was a project so beyond their experience they had not thought of afterwards, like flying to the moon with no thought of the return journey.

'You can't stay that long in Leeds. People will think…'. Words jumbled about in Mrs Woodward's head. Run away. Deserted. Adultery. Fallen woman. Living in sin. These horrors scrambled about in her brain but her tongue could not name them.

Mr Woodward, the business man, asked if there were agreements in writing. Dorothea quoted several telegrams from Mr Martelli, confirming the Grand Theatre and two other bookings at fees that made his eyes pop. He went very quiet. He saw that money, which had solved all his problems with her in the past would not be such a powerful weapon in the future. As though Dorothea had read his mind, she told him how Adelina Patti was rumoured to be paid £1000 a week.

'Of course I won't get that yet,' she added modestly, 'but I stand to earn a substantial amount.'

'You'll need it,' offered Mr Woodward. 'The bill for the hotel in Leeds made me flinch. To be fair to your Mr Martelli, he paid his own way and there was no alcohol among the extras.' He stopped there. Fond though he was of money this argument wasn't about money. It was about more important matters - marriage, children, family.

Mentioning Adelina Patti, as famous for her financial acumen as for her singing, set Dorothea off into a starry-eyed daydream in the course of which she absent-mindedly announced, 'I'll probably have to go and live in London.'

Her mother shrieked at the prospect and promptly fell into hysterics. The cheery maid arrived to loosen her stays, administer smelling salts and help her to her room. When the kerfuffle was over, Edward chose the moment to ask, 'What about the children? London's a long way from here.'

Dorothea kicked herself. That was the question she'd forgotten to ask Nanny and she had no answer ready. It was Edward who broke the awkward silence.

'It's late. Hard to believe it was only yesterday I woke up in Germany. We are all tired, and it's Sunday tomorrow. What better

183

day for dealing with these serious matters? I suggest that we all go to our beds.'

CHAPTER 20

Sunday

It was the custom for the Woodward family and servants to go to chapel on Sunday. Dorothea, following Franco's advice to be on her best behaviour, went to the morning service. Only Mrs Woodward failed to put in an appearance. She had taken to her bed and had no intention of leaving it. Nanny volunteered to stay behind to care for her mistress. She entrusted Clare and Izzy to a nursery maid and gave them a special task to fulfil on their journey home. Her preparations done, she went to knock on Mrs Woodward's bedroom door. She found Mrs Woodward sitting up in bed, her face blotchy, her eyes swollen and a pile of damp handkerchiefs on the nightstand.

'What have I done to deserve such a daughter?' she wailed.

Nanny let her run through the familiar complaints enlivened only by two pieces of news. Dorothea might be away for months and that foreigner was staying in the same hotel. Her reputation, and therefore, by the logic of gossip, her mother's also would be in shreds. They would be cast out of respectable society. Invitations would stop and doors would be closed against them.

'That's not what I've heard.' Nanny's voice came loud and clear. Shock cut short Mrs Woodward's hiccupping sobs. Nanny patted her hand and went on. 'The talk among the servants is that soon you'll be able to pass round newspaper cuttings about your daughter's wonderful voice. Titled people are competing for her presence at their soirees and entertainments. Lady Clifford is sulking because a duchess of somewhere has beaten her to it. When Miss Dorothea visits, and she will visit, she will be able to give you all the details of their drawing rooms, their china, the wallpaper in their bedrooms.'

There was something about the titles that distracted Mrs Woodward briefly, but she soon returned to her problem like a dog to its bone. 'And now there's that Martelli man in the same hotel,' she complained. 'People don't forget. They still whisper about Edward. You know'

Nanny did know. There wasn't much that Nanny didn't know. 'Well,' she said briskly, 'I think that's her husband's problem. Not yours.' She took the silver-backed brush from the dressing table and started to brush her mistress's hair. Mrs Woodward felt her shoulders relax as if a great weight had been lifted from her. Was the brushing or was it the realisation of the truth of Nanny's words? Dorothea was Edward's problem now. There was something about Edward that told her he would cope. As Mrs Woodward looked ahead to a landscape swept clean of the problem of her daughter there rose a bigger and more important question.

'What about Clare and Izzy?' wailed Mrs Woodward

Nanny was reassuring. 'We've managed very nicely so far haven't we? We should just keep on going as we are.'

There was a knock on the door. As if on cue Clare and Izzy bundled in.

'Oh granny are you better? We don't like you being poorly. We brought you flowers. We picked them on the way home from chapel. And look this one's got a ladybird on it.' Nanny left the children to work their magic. She found Mr Woodward hovering on the landing.

'Should I send for the doctor?

Nanny shook her head. 'There is nothing physically wrong with Mrs Woodward.' She pointed down the hill in the direction of the doctor who refused to have either telephone or a car. 'That doctor usually prescribes laudanum for this sort of upset in a lady and that's not always helpful.' She looked her employer in the eye to be sure he recalled the nervous prostration fed by laudanum that his wife suffered until the twins arrived to cure her.'

He smiled with relief, signalled his agreement and made to move. Nanny held up her forefinger. He stopped, obedient as a well-trained dog. '

'I hesitate to suggest it as I know your feelings about alcohol.' He signalled for her to go on. 'One of my previous employers was a lady of a nervous disposition. Her doctor prescribed a small glass of port after dinner every night. It certainly helped her, and I think it might help Mrs Woodward cope when things are difficult.'

He pursed his lips and looked at the ceiling, the very picture of a man addressing his conscience. Nanny took advantage of his silence. 'Why else did the Good Lord change water into wine?

'The wedding at Cana.' Mr Woodward had the details at his teetotal Bible-studying fingertips.

'Alcohol has its uses, whether it is port to fortify you for the problems of family life or brandy to help you recover from a shock.' She flicked a glance at him to check that he had not taken alarm at her knowing of his occasional medicinal brandy, dropped him a bit of a curtsy and made to set off.

'Thank you, Nanny, I will think about what you have said. There has never been alcohol in this house apart from some medicinal brandy. I took a vow when I was 12 before I went into the pit. Before my mother and God I swore to avoid alcohol.' His voice shook.

'Would you have a 12-year-old boy in your pit now, Mr Woodward? I know it used to happen, but not now.'

Of course he wouldn't. An image of the unconscious Oliver's pale face as he lay crumpled on the floor, flashed into his mind. The boy so young, the injury he inflicted so unforgiveable. He turned to Nanny in a desperate appeal.

'What happens to people who do harm?'

Nanny looked him in the face. 'They are forgiven. Certainly where our Lord is concerned. He is quick to forgive, and mothers are even quicker.' She left a moment for that to sink in. 'We cannot live by other people's rules. We have to make our own,' she added with authority. Her answer seemed to satisfy him so she left to go about her business.

The Sunday roast was the most important meal of the week in the Woodward household. It was served at lunch time so the servants could have the afternoon off to visit friends or family or simply walk about the park. So strong was the tradition that Mrs Woodward turned a blind eye to her ban on all things coming from the neighbouring county and allowed Yorkshire pudding to be served with the beef.

The result was so tasty that Edward was glad he'd made it home from Germany in time to enjoy it. When the meal was finished it was an effort to heave himself to his feet and follow his children upstairs to the nursery for the quiet time that followed their main meal of the day. It was his turn to talk to Nanny.

While the children did a jigsaw he stretched himself out on the floor. Nanny sat in a straight-backed chair and did something mysterious with wool.

'Are they all right?' he asked indicating Clare and Izzy. 'Does it affect them that they see so little of their mother?' Nanny knew this was just an opening gambit. She made an encouraging murmur and kept on knitting. He went on, 'You see I never really had a father so I'm not sure how to do it. But I do have a mother and she was a constant presence.' Honesty compelled him to add,' Except when she was working.'

'And you haven't come to any harm,' said Nanny, putting down her knitting. 'And that just about sums up your children's situation. Miss Dorothea.' She stopped to correct herself. 'Mother.' The children pricked their ears up at the word and returned to the jigsaw when Nanny started to speak again. 'Mother comes to tea with them when she is not working.'

'I know. That's why I'm bothering you now. Thought I'd leave the field clear for her later.'

'Very considerate of you.' Nanny looked with approval at his blond good looks. 'I know your mother was on her own. Don't forget your children also have grandparents who love them and servants who have grown fond of them. They enjoy the security that money can buy: a house to call home, warmth in the winter, regular meals, clean clothes, medicine....'

'Stop.' Edward waved a hand at her and completed the list. 'And you, Nanny. They have you.' They both laughed. The twins joined in. They didn't understand the joke but never refused a chance for some fun.

When they settled down, Nanny returned to her knitting and addressed Edward. 'You may feel a little adrift at times, as your circumstances are not easy. But as fathers go, you have made an excellent start.'

Praise from Nanny! Edward felt a lump come into his throat. 'I try. I owe it to Mr Woodward.'

'The father you did not have.'

'I suppose so.'

'His daughter is doing her best.' Edward looked up in surprise. Nanny continued, 'She is not your conventional woman. Her work, her music is the most important thing in her life. You know she comes to tea when she can; it's a sort of tradition we're building. She confines all her appointments to the morning and does not waste her afternoons on social calls as many women do. In some ways she is the easiest mother I have ever worked with. She never interferes but leaves the rest of us to get on with the job of raising her children.'

She rolled up her knitting, clapped her hands and said, 'Quiet time is over. It's time for your walk. Do I have a volunteer to accompany the small people?'

Edward got to his feet. He would take his children for their walk.

As Nanny had predicted Dorothea arrived for nursery tea. 'You had Sunday lunch, Dorothea,' said Nanny and moved the cakes to the far side of the table out of temptation's way. Clare delighted her mother by giving a fairly accurate imitation of her singing a scale. 'I sometimes hear you do that in the morning,' the child confided. Izzy put his hands over his ears and stuck his tongue out for good measure.

Nanny frowned, offered him a sandwich and the offending tongue was withdrawn. While the children turned their attention to food Nanny turned to Dorothea and asked with apparent innocence, 'Have you made plans for the coming week?'

Dorothea knew exactly how her week would start. She would go to Leeds on Monday, perform *Tosca* on Tuesday and see what offers had come in.

'Franco looks after all that sort of thing. He deals with the music."

'And your husband and parents look after everything here.'

'And you, Nanny. I couldn't manage without you.'

'Hmm.' Nanny never had a problem sorting out priorities. The welfare of the children in her charge came first. Life was more complicated for other people. Sometimes you just had to watch and wait while they sorted theirs out.

By the end of Sunday the main characters in the family drama had, with the help of a religious service, a respite from work, a roast dinner and conversations with Nanny, given thought to their circumstances, their futures and the possibility of change in their lives. No decisions had been made, but the sense that a resolution was coming hovered in the air. They slept easier in their beds.

CHAPTER 21

At the start of the working week Dorothea came to say goodbye to Nanny before she left for Leeds. She kissed her cheerful children; there were no wails of dismay at her departure and they quickly settled down to their morning lessons. Nanny said very little but Dorothea had tears in her eyes as she, most unusually, hugged her.

While Dorothea set off for Leeds, most of the inhabitants of Atherley faced 5 days of unremitting toil. Jenny, however looked forward to the work with a happy heart. Seven whole days had passed since she had last seen Edward. She had never gone so long before without some kind of contact with him. It brought home how important he was to her. As if she had any doubt. When he walked into the office, she just stood and looked at him. Her joy and her love for him shone out in her face. He returned her gaze and both their hearts melted. What had been officially secret was now written all over them for anyone who cared to look. Mavis, who already knew Jenny's feelings for Edward, now saw that her love was returned. Mr Woodward and Higgs, the other possible witnesses, were skilled inspectors of machinery, not people. What little interest they had in them was at that moment concentrated on Oliver. True to his word he had come to work, with his arm in a sling.

'It works by gravity,' he was telling them. 'I don't have to have it plastered. Gravity will set my arm straight.' Mr Woodward launched into a brief history of Sir Isaac Newton. The distraction gave Jenny time to recover her wits and she set about introducing the new member of staff.

'This is'.. she began, intending to say Mrs Perkins.

Mavis stepped forward. 'Mavis,' she said firmly. 'Officially I am Mrs Perkins, but that's a bit of a mouthful.' She offered her right hand to Mr Woodward who shook it.

'Mavis,' he said.

'Yes. I am here to help with the correspondence while your Mr Frederick is away.' She gestured to the typewriter. 'What a splendid machine. You'll be pleased to know I am a fully qualified typist.' She smiled at Mr Woodward. 'Shall we get started?' He opened the door of his office and waved her in. The letters were piled up on his desk.

'I'm only here in the morning,' she warned him. 'In the afternoon I help my husband with his business.'

'What is it your husband does... er, Mavis?' It took an effort for him to say her first name.

'Property. He's in property.'

'Didn't take her long to get him on a piece of string,' was Higgs' verdict as he wandered off to make the tea. Oliver was outside polishing the car. Mr Woodward thought a boy with a broken arm should not be in charge of a kettle full of boiling water.

Jenny and Edward were left alone, still in their state of silent enchantment. They both sensed that something had change; the earth had moved, a boulder had shifted. It was Edward who spoke first.

'I am pleased to be back, Miss Truesdale. Or can I call you Jenny?'

'Not yet, Mr Carter. Not yet.'

That evening Jenny told her parents how Mavis had shaken her boss's hand, an activity usually confined to men, and insisted that he call her by her given name. John Truesdale chuckled.

'That Mavis. She's a one. She'll brighten up work for you, Jenny. Be a good thing while it lasts.'

Jenny knew that he was thinking of the almost inevitable baby that followed marriage. Given Mavis's previous career, Jenny doubted that would happen with the customary speed. Marriage had, however, produced one immediate effect. Mavis Haslam was pushy and boisterous, but would she have offered her new boss a handshake and insisted that he use her first name? Jenny doubted it. But Mrs Mavis Perkins had the confidence to do so. Jenny wondered where the magic came from. The ring? The title? Doing *it?*

The next day they were Mr Carter and Miss Truesdale again. Their seething emotions suppressed beneath a business-like surface. Higgs took to sitting on Mr Frederick's chair and reading the newspaper while he listened to Mavis chivvying his boss to complete the pile of neglected correspondence.

Edward was busy going through the figures for his great electricity generating project. He called Jenny in for her opinion. She noticed that he carefully propped the door open, so they could be observed. Together they went over the figures,

'You'll have to do a fair bit of borrowing,' she said.

'I know. It's my neck on the block. My reputation at stake.' His voice throbbed with emotion.

'You can do it,' she told him. He glanced through the door to be sure Higgs still had his nose in the newspaper and gently cupped his hand over hers as it rested on the plans on the desk.

It felt like a contract.

On Thursday Edward did not come to the office, and Mr Woodward neither arrived nor sent a message. When Jenny rang the house the servants had no explanation to offer her and refused point blank to disturb their master and mistress. In desperation she rang the pit, which was always their first priority. The manager assured her that there had been no deaths, no accidents. Mr Carter had been called away by urgent business.

A grey-faced Mr Woodward arrived as the morning drew to a close. Higgs helped him up the staircase as if he was an invalid, and Oliver delivered him a cup of tea. The older man looked wistfully at the boy's youthful face and patted his uninjured arm. He volunteered no explanation of Edward's unexpected absence and no-one dared ask for one. Even Mavis restrained her tongue, so palpable was the man's misery. At dinner time Higgs took him home for his lunch and Jenny declared the morning's work over. Oliver went to school. Mavis put on her hat and apparently left for home and Mr Perkins. In truth she dashed off on some detective work. She returned panting from running – and from excitement.

A visit to the Post Office where she so recently worked had produced a juicy nugget of information. Telegrams to the Woodward mansion were not rare, but two telegrams had been delivered in the early hours of the morning: one to Mr Woodward and one to Mr Carter. The curious thing was that they were both despatched late on Wednesday night and they both came from the same place, Leeds. Not even Mavis had been able to squeeze more details from the telegraph office, but as she said with Dorothea in Leeds there was one thing you could be sure of. Trouble.

Edward leant back and let the rhythm of the train's movement lull him until his eyelids dropped, giving him a blessed half hour of relaxation before he had to tackle the problems the night had brought him. Problems? He asked himself if that was that the right word for the events of Wednesday night. Those problems might just provide him with the opportunity he hoped for. His hand went to his breast pocket where he had kept Charity's account of finding Dorothea and Mr Martelli in bed together. Something in his stomach lurched when his fingers failed to feel the paper. Then he remembered that he had locked the letter in the desk drawer in Mr Woodward's study, along with the telegrams that had set him off on this unexpected journey that might turn out to be a wild goose chase.

It had been the early hours of the morning when the boy had shouted, 'Two telegrams,' through the letterbox to be sure they would answer the door. It was still dark and the boy was panting from struggling up the hill.

'Two!' cried a male voice.

'That's what I said. Two telegrams.'

There was the sound of grumbling and bolts being drawn. The boy listened in the hope of hearing coins clinking. He didn't give much for his chances of getting a tip if the man was in his nightshirt.

Mr Woodward was in his nightshirt and the candle in his hand shook as he held it up to inspect the boy and the envelopes he held out. 'Spectacles,' he muttered. 'Can't see a damned thing.'

Edward arrived in his dressing gown. He knew that Mr Woodward would be stricken by his customary panic as Dorothea was in Leeds, far from his watchful eye. 'Not necessarily bad news,' he told Mr Woodward. 'But at this hour it must be urgent.'

'You want to send a reply?' asked the boy.

'No,' said Edward and went to his bedroom to search for a tip for the boy. 'If I need to I'll come down the office myself.'

All right for some, thought the boy enviously. Him having a car and all. He cheered up as he remembered his own return journey by bicycle was downhill.

Mr Woodward stood in the hall, white-faced and helpless without his spectacles. He kept telling himself that the second performance of *Tosca* was safely over. Dorothea had rung just before bedtime to tell him it had been another triumph. So why these telegrams at this hour of the morning? He shuffled the buff envelopes in his hands. Edward bustled him into the warm study but the old man quivered and shook as if in a winter's gale. A tartan rug draped round his shoulders helped, but not as much as his son-in-law's youthful eyes.

'There are two telegrams,' Edward told Mr Woodward who twitched with irritation but did not point out he already knew that. 'One is addressed to you, and one to me.'

'Open mine and read it to me. The suspense is agonising.'

Edward tore open the envelope and unfolded the flimsy paper. 'It is from Dorothea.

Mr Woodward let out the breath he had been holding. 'Oh, the dear child. I pray she is well. That is all that matters.'

Edward had read the rest of the telegram. He was not so sure. 'Should I read it aloud?'

Mr Woodward smiled and nodded. Edward gave a little cough, a sort of warning to the fond father that all might not be quite as he expected. 'It says, "Wedding vows broken. Please forgive me."'

It took time for the meaning of the brief message to penetrate Mr Woodward's mind. Edward used the opportunity to rouse Mrs Woodward and find the medicinal brandy before the full horror of his daughter's news hit her father.

Mrs Woodward was summoned. There were tears and loud lamentations. The parents, true to their upbringing and their beliefs, blamed themselves. They wondered where they had gone wrong and generally clothed themselves in sackcloth and ashes. Should they send a reply? What to say? Where to send it? It would have to go to the hotel that Mr Woodward, with the help of Stan

Earnshaw, had so carefully chosen to protect Dorothea's virtue and her reputation. Realisation dawned on the mother and father. Their beloved Dorothea was in the very hotel that they had chosen, in bed, with a man who was not her husband. They could not let their imaginations travel further.

They fell silent as they contemplated the moral wreckage of their daughter's life. A youthful folly, when she was in a foreign country, away from their tender care was one thing. The arrival of their grandchildren helped them get over that fall from grace. Wilfully abandoning her husband and children was another matter entirely. It was wickedness beyond the Woodwards' comprehension. Crushed and crumpled they crept back to their beds and hoped for oblivion in sleep.

Edward poured himself a medicinal brandy and looked at the telegram with his name on it. His first thought was to set fire to it with the candle, but curiosity got the better of him. What could she say to him that she had not said to her parents?

He tore it open and grinned. She had certainly thrown down the gauntlet. The narrow strip of white paper gummed to the buff form read, 'SET ME FREE. YOU HAVE GROUNDS.

He suspected that Mr Martelli had sent the telegrams. At precisely six words in each they qualified for the cheapest rate, an economy unlikely to have crossed Dorothea's mind. He pictured Mr Martelli rising from their warm bed and trotting off to send the telegrams before Dorothea changed her mind. A flash of joy swept through him as he glimpsed a possible future. He'd better go and see if she really meant it. This was a deal it would be best to tie up quickly. He went to put his telegram with the letter from Charity and felt a flash of gratitude to the Italian who was so scrupulously helping him free of his mockery of a marriage.

During breakfast a note arrived for him from Dorothea. It confirmed that she was in the same hotel and it named Mr Martelli. She requested a parley with Edward alone; she could not at this stage face her parents. As a plan it suited him and would help to protect her parents' feelings. He cared more for their welfare than he did for Dorothea's, but above all he cared for his children. Their needs took precedence.

He folded the note carefully and took it to join last night's telegram and Charity's letter in the top drawer of the desk. As good as a loaded pistol, he thought as he turned the key. He put the key in his jacket pocket. He did not want Mrs Woodward to come across its contents while searching for a stamp. She held Southport the town of her birth as the arbiter of good taste and proper behaviour. He was sure that the word 'divorce' was never heard in society there but it was possible that poor Mrs Woodward was soon going to find it spoken in her own drawing room.

As the journey to Leeds progressed Edward considered how to play the cards he had been dealt. His original agreement with Dorothea's father was for half his business in exchange for marriage to his daughter. Edward was a man of his word so it had to be Dorothea who sought to break the bond of matrimony, flimsy though it was. He conveniently forgot his encounters with the cheery maid.

A telegram from Manchester had given the time of his arrival and requested a meeting in the hotel lobby. In this way he hoped to avoid the smirks of the staff as he asked for his 'wife' and they went to room 16 and knocked for Mr Martelli.

Edward had endured pitying stares from men who whispered behind their hands when he had married the pregnant Dorothea. Their scorn turned to envy when they realised the size of his reward. Half a business empire is not to be sniffed at. He had survived that embarrassment and would, no doubt, survive the traditional mockery dished out to the cuckold; it was a small price to pay for the chance to marry the woman he loved. A flicker of alarm warned him to keep quiet about his love for Jenny. Dorothea's spiteful nature might compel her to weep tears of regret and beg her father to forgive her, just to stop another woman having the husband she did not want.

Dorothea was sitting at the table in the lobby where Mr Woodward had come across the photograph of her with a champagne glass in the *Leeds Mercury*. It made Edward think of Stan Earnshaw. Had he left the newspaper for his old friend to see out of malice? Or was he trying to open his eyes to a reality he was deliberately avoiding?

Dorothea was dressed to her usual high standard and looked remarkably composed for a woman who had just ripped the fabric of her life into tattered shreds and thrown them to the four winds. Edward commented on her calm.

'What did you expect?'

'A little remorse wouldn't go amiss. Your parents are very distressed.'

A woman in a purple hat brought four daughters of various ages and heights into the hotel. They came through the revolving door from the street and settled themselves at a table. The mother ordered lemonade from the waiter and bowed in polite acknowledgement of the presence of Edward and Dorothea.

Edward returned to his grilling of Dorothea. 'Your father will take this very hard.'

'I know,' said Dorothea. 'He persists in thinking I'm a properly brought up woman, happy to play house all my days. But I'm not. Music and the performing of it is my life. It is the heart and soul of me.' She beat her fist against her chest to show the passion she felt.

'They do not deserve such treatment.' Edward paused and lowered his voice to avoid shocking the family at the other table. 'Telegrams in the night to announce you are with another man!'

'It had to be something drastic. Something so dreadful that there could be no going back to pretending to be a wife and a mother while I was going mad inside.' The woman with four girls looked uneasily across at Dorothea. She sensed stormy rebellion in the air.

'Was it so bad? Most women would envy you. Living at the top of the hill. Daughter of the most powerful man in the town. Wealth and position. What more could a woman want?' Edward did not include himself on this list of enviable advantages, though he could think of a few women who would happily step into Dorothea's shoes.

'Living in Atherley was unbearable to me. I woke up every morning, clawing at the walls. Let's face it, as a daughter I am a complete failure. I have no idea of how to be a mother. I only know enough to let others get on with the job. As a wife I am little more than an empty space.' She looked to him for corroboration. He gave her a wry smile.

'When I started to get singing engagements, I felt the cage door open a crack and I knew I had to keep on with music. It's the only thing that I am good at. It's not some footling hobby. I demand perfection from myself. I am a professional, an artist.' Dorothea raised her hands, palms open, and let them fall gracefully to her sides. Edward had seen her perform the self-same gesture on stage as her song came to its end and she waited for the applause.

He did not applaud but delivered a swingeing sideswipe. 'I believe that Mr Martelli is in a position to advance your career.' Most women would be outraged by the remark but Dorothea was not in the least embarrassed.

'Very much so. He is my career. I couldn't do it without him. It was time to choose. I want to be free to take the opportunities he finds for me. There is no other way. My career has to be first. I'm tired of asking permission, of living under the rules of Queen Victoria, of wondering what the neighbours will think.'

'You are determined to follow your career, no matter what pain it causes others.'

'It's not that I haven't thought about other people, especially my father. He will be very disappointed. He likes people to stick to their word.'

'I know,' said Edward who was waiting to hear her say the one word that would enable him to stick to his.

'My mother will soon cheer up when she sees I've been singing for someone with a title and starts reading about me in the newspapers. And it's going to happen. Franco is absolutely confident of that. The offers are flooding in.'

So he's Franco now, thought Edward and asked, 'Is your Mr Martelli in a position to marry you?'

Dorothea shrugged. 'He says he's not the marrying kind.'

'I just wondered,' explained Edward smoothly, 'if there already is a Mrs Martelli. Or several of them? Will your Mr Martelli pay your bills the way your father does? Will he feed and clothe your children?' He stressed the word 'your'.

Dorothea was cool in her response. 'I have every hope of being able to support myself by my own earnings. Franco will be my manager, not my husband.'

Edward's heart sank. 'So why all the telegrams? All the drama in the small hours of the morning. There was no need to announce your adultery to your parents. You could have kept it secret.' Edward thought he had said the word 'adultery' very quietly, but everyone in the lobby appeared to have heard.

The waiter tidying up the bar dropped a glass. The woman in an apron who was supposed to be mopping the floor froze in mid swipe. The lady in the purple hat felt suddenly cold. She looked at the revolving glass door to see who had brought in a rush of icy air from the street. No-one had. She started to chivvy her daughters to finish their drinks.

'You see it has to be dramatic. I learned that from *Tosca*. There can be no going back. My parents have to understand that. Then in time they may learn to live with my choices. After all,' she said smugly, 'I have provided them with two grandchildren who delight their hearts more than I ever did.'

'So why did you summon me?'

'I want you to divorce me.' At last the word that Edward had waited for dropped from Dorothea's lips. He had difficulty stopping himself blubbering with delight and gratitude. The word 'divorce' had a life of its own. It travelled straight to the lady in the purple hat. She rose to her feet with a gasp of shock, and set about gathering up her daughters, feeding them one by one into the safety of the revolving door and out into the street.

'You do understand what you are doing?' Edward asked Dorothea.

'Mm, I think so. I did consult a lawyer in Manchester once. He made it clear there was no way for me to divorce you. Now the boot is on the other foot and I am asking you to divorce me. Adultery is all you need.'

Edward nodded towards the revolving door and the hasty departure of the woman in the purple hat. 'You do see what your life will be. The doors of society will be closed to you. Respectable women will not let you enter their homes for fear you will contaminate their children.'

'To be honest I'm not too bothered about respectable society. I've had enough of it. I just want to be Dorothea Woodward again and make my own decisions without worrying what respectable society thinks. Things are very different in theatrical circles.'

'That is all very well,' said Edward, 'but I had an agreement with your father. Like him I am a man of my word. Do you think he will take my word for it that you are asking me to divorce you?'

She shook her head. 'No. He will think it is just one of my fancies and that when *Tosca* finishes, I'll come home and cry until you take me back and he decides to forgive me.'

'Are you sure that won't happen?

'Yes. For a start I don't think you'll take me back, and I don't want to spend my life as a failure in my father's eyes. I want to be a success. A successful singer.' She finished with one of the grand gestures she used on stage and gazed mistily into the future looking extraordinarily beautiful as if waiting for the music to end and the stage lights to dim.

There was a glint in Edward's eye. The prison door was open a crack, his mind raced as he looked for a way to stop it slamming shut. 'In that case, I suggest that you write to your parents a letter – no more telegrams – explaining that you want me to divorce you. They will not believe it until they see it in your own handwriting. Wait a week to show that you have thought the matter over, and please give them a return address if you move from here.' He looked round the well-appointed lobby with fresh flowers on the table. 'I know it's expensive.'

'That sounds like a good plan.' She was suddenly brisk and business-like.

'If that is what you want I will not stand in your way.' Edward held out his hand for her to shake. 'Do you want your manager to come and witness the deal? He set it up very shrewdly. I believe I have all the evidence I need.'

201

She smiled. 'The letter from Charity. The telegrams. The hotel staff to back it up.' It was clear that Mr Martelli had kept her informed every step of the way.

Edward waved his hand at the waiter in the bar with a tea towel hanging motionless on his arm and the woman in a pinafore leaning on her mop. They stood like statues, making no effort to conceal their fascinated eavesdropping. 'That's right,' he said loudly, 'the hotel staff will back me up.' The waiter started to polish the glasses and the woman to work her mop.

'You are sure, Dorothea, that divorce is what you want?' asked Edward. He felt obliged to check that it was her choice, that Mr Martelli had not coerced her into doing his bidding.

'Yes. I want you to set me free. I know the future is uncertain and risky, and that is exactly how I want to live. Anything is better than the chains of the past.' A fierce joy ran through her. Soon Edward would hold the weapons necessary to cut the ties that bound her. She would make sure he used them.

'The show's over,' Edward shouted and clapped his hands to galvanise the waiter into action. 'I need coffee and bacon and eggs.'

While he ate they talked of the children. 'You do know that if we divorce Clare and Izzy will be my children. You will be labelled as the guilty wife so the court will give me full control of the children.' He dropped his voice, 'The children who are in truth your children only. There is a wonderful irony there, Dorothea.'

She looked a little bleak but nodded. 'I know you won't be unreasonable. You'll let me visit when I can. I hope they can continue to live with my parents. And Nanny.' Tears came into her eyes.

'Of course. The lawyers will probably be involved but I can see no reason to change the present arrangements. It will be a safe haven for the children as you take a leap into the future. That reminds me. Charity and her boys. They're still with you?'.

'Yes. They're in lodgings nearby. All three will be coming with us when we move on. Keep that note Charity wrote safe.' Dorothea gave him a conspiratorial grin.

202

When the last morsel of bacon was gone, Edward threw his napkin on the plate and told Dorothea, 'I will go to your parents and explain that you want a divorce. I have to admire your courage, Dorothea. It is a brave thing you are doing.'

'Not as brave as telling my father face-to-face that I've confessed to adultery and want a divorce,' said Dorothea as she pictured the scene when Edward returned to Atherley. 'I don't envy you that task.'

She rose and set off to climb the stairs to room 16 where Mr Martelli lurked, an unseen presence, pulling the strings of the actors in the drama and directing their moves. At the corner of the stairs Dorothea stopped and raised a hand to Edward; it was a gesture of farewell.

Edward paid for his breakfast and as a final precaution took a note of the names of the waiter at the bar and the woman with the mop and tipped them generously. While the train sped to Manchester he tried to find a kind way to break the news to the Woodwards that their daughter had indeed broken the eighth commandment and was not prepared to wait till death parted her from her husband.

It was confirmation of the news that had shaken them to the core. Mrs Woodward would be horrified by the scandal and disgrace that accompanied the word 'divorce'. It would undermine her position as the righteous queen of Methodist society, and again open up that dark tunnel of despair that she had fallen into when Dorothea's unexpected pregnancy became known. This time there would be no adorable babies to lighten the end of the darkness. Seven-month babies were common in Atherley, but divorce was not. Edward racked his brain to recall a single one and failed. Well, he decided, there's a first time for everything.

As for Mr Woodward, he would take it very hard. Edward flinched at the thought of the blow he was going to deliver. As the train chugged along more cheerful matters crept into his mind. With the evidence that Dorothea and Mr Martelli had provided divorce was more than a possibility. The words, 'When I marry Jenny' came into his mind. He quickly choked them off for fear of tempting fate.

As he drove up to the Woodwards' mansion, Clare and Izzy were returning from their walk. They spotted him and broke free from their nurse to run to greet him. Their enthusiasm melted his heart. 'Daddy, Daddy,' they cried and embraced his knees. As it was time for their tea he went with them up to the nursery. It would delay the task of breaking of the news to the Woodwards. Who better to confide in than Nanny? Shrimp paste sandwiches, raspberry jelly and fairy cakes were the perfect consolation for a man whose last meal was a late breakfast eaten on the other side of the country.

After the nurse took the children away to wash their hands and get their toys, Nanny poured more tea, and looked enquiringly at Edward. 'You have bad news for them.'

'Yes. I don't know the best way to break it.'

'Fast and clean.' Nanny was crisply decisive. 'They have confided in me a little. They dread what is coming, but they still have hope.'

Nanny stirred the sugar into his tea. 'Miss Dorothea,' she began. 'Interesting isn't it the way we servants still refer to her as Miss Dorothea? As if your marriage never happened, was not quite real. We've never got the habit of calling her Mrs Carter have we? As if that role is reserved for someone else.'

Edward shivered at the uncanny accuracy of her description. Sometimes he thought Nanny was a witch.

She took advantage of his silence to sketch out a plan. 'It will soon be time for Clare and Izzy to go down to the drawing room to see their grandparents. That always cheers them. You cannot break the news to them over dinner with the servants bobbing in and out. When you are settled on the sofas by the fire and the tea has been served would be the best time.'

Edward was glad of the delay; it would give him time to arrange his face which tended to break into a beaming smile, totally unfitted for the delivery of bad news. Nanny held up a warning finger.

'Mr Woodward is prone to believing that sending for the doctor is an instant cure for emotional upset. It has been agreed that Mrs Woodward have a glass of port wine in the evening

204

after dinner. It will help to fortify her. What if I give you half an hour and then deliver the port? I will be able to reassure you that medical advice is not necessary.' She let the information sink in before adding, 'I will also arrange for hot water and brandy. No need to tell me. I know where it is hidden.'

Edward welcomed her plan.

'Did you enjoy your nursery tea?' she asked him.

'Very much so.'

'You will be welcome any time,' she told him, 'except on those days when Miss Dorothea is not working. That is her time with her children.'

The senior Woodwards were slumped in chairs by the fire like broken dolls. The arrival of their grandchildren brought faint smiles to their faces. For half an hour there was the appearance of normality as the children played and chatted. When Nanny led them away to their beds the adults sat through a desultory dinner. At last they were free of servants and could turn their haggard faces to Edward for the news they dreaded. Mr Woodward appealed to him with suspiciously damp eyes.

'Please tell me this is just one of her silly fancies. She's just trying to get more attention.' It was a technique that Dorothea had used on him all her life.

Edward offered him the only crumb of comfort he had available. 'Dorothea is in good health and is still in the same hotel in Leeds.'

'Please tell me that she has not broken her marriage vows.'

'I am afraid it is too late for that. She has used the word 'divorce'.'

They reacted characteristically. Mrs Woodward gave a shrill shriek and scrabbled to get her handkerchief ready for the tears that were sure to come. Mr Woodward went very white, groaned and pressed his hand against his chest, where he thought his heart was. Their grief was the more painful to see for being so bravely borne. They did not complain loudly, utter curses at their errant daughter or claim their fate was unjust. They blamed themselves. Mr Woodward felt it most keenly. By buying his daughter a husband, to save her reputation and keep her respectable he had made a mockery of marriage. No wonder she treated its sacred vows with contempt. It was all his fault.

It disturbed Edward to tell them he had given her a week as a cooling off period. He was feeding them false hope and risking his chance of freedom, but it had to be done; he was a man of his word.

Nanny arrived with alcohol and soothing words. Her presence helped Edward stick to the role he had chosen. Not for him the anger of the outraged husband; he was the consoling friend of the family. He talked soothingly of Dorothea's remarkable talent and how she deserved to be heard by a much wider audience. Her parents heard the words but their minds were in too much turmoil to process them. When Nanny gently manoeuvred them toward going to their beds they could not find the strength to protest. Mr Woodward refused her suggestion of taking a nip of brandy. He was determined to endure the garment of sackcloth and ashes that he had woven for himself without recourse to chemical help. Nanny laid a gentle hand on his arm as he made his way to the door.

'Sufficient unto the day,' she said in an attempt to console him. He finished the saying for her, 'Is the evil thereof.'

CHAPTER 22

When they met at breakfast in the morning, sleep had restored the Woodwards a little, though they still had a pinched and haggard look. Nothing more serious than asking for the marmalade was said at the table. The rule of 'not in front of the servants' was strictly obeyed as two maids bustled about with tea, coffee, and bacon and eggs.

When the family had finished eating Mr Woodward left for his study, where he looked at the mail. It was the custom for Edward to join him there to plan the work for the day ahead. The servants knew to leave them alone except in the case of a dire emergency. As he tapped on the door of the study they shared, Edward felt a flicker of annoyance at having to ask the older man's permission to enter. It reminded him that asking permission was one of Dorothea's many grievances with the way the world was organised.

'I've come for the paperwork for the power plant project,' he told Mr Woodward 'I am hoping to go through the finance with Miss Truesdale this afternoon.' Mr Woodward was looking gloomily at the single envelope that had arrived in the morning post. He had not bothered to open it; obviously it was not the letter from Dorothea which they anticipated in their different ways. One with dread and one with hope.

'I'll come in after lunch,' Mr Woodward offered. 'I feel the need for a quiet morning here.' He swept his hand across the smooth leather of his desk, the place where he did his calculations, where things were manageable, where there were no women to make matters complicated and demand difficult decisions.

Edward left him with his thoughts. A stroll across the paddock took him to the garage where he kept his car. Once out of earshot of the house he could not resist whistling cheerfully. He was on his way to work and Jenny would be there.

Tension tinged his cheerful mood as he approached the Carter-Woodward factory. Should he tell Jenny the news? Was it too soon? There were so many hazards to avoid, pitfalls to step over.

However, all doubts and questions were swept aside when he was confronted by a small tornado called Mavis demanding to know why he had gone missing yesterday and was Mr Woodward coming in today. There was a pile of letters she'd typed for him to sign.

'Steady on, Mavis. Let me get my coat off.' He looked towards Jenny. 'And a good morning to you, Miss Truesdale.'

'Miss Truesdale,' Mavis shrieked. 'She's Jenny. When there's just the three of us in the office.'

Edward laughed. Her forthright confidence drove away his anxiety. 'Well, Mavis. That's fine by me.' He looked across to the woman he loved. 'Hope that's all right with you, Jenny.' The simple act of saying her name out loud in the presence of another person brought a lump to his throat. He felt his face working as emotion clawed at the muscles and tears started to well. He had to turn away.

Mavis decided that she would use her own judgement for the urgent letters and settled down to her typewriter which soon produced a sound like steady gunfire, punctuated by the ping of the bell and a whizzing sound as she slid the carriage back. It gave Edward a legitimate excuse to beckon Jenny closer so she could hear him over the clattering machine.

'Did they ring from the house to tell you why I didn't come in yesterday?' She shook her head.

'No. I guessed it was urgent but the servants wouldn't say. I checked that the pit was all right.'

'It was urgent. I had to go to Leeds.' She nodded but saw no point in telling him that she already knew.

'When does Mavis leave?' he whispered to Jenny..

'Oh. She's not that bad,' said Jenny. 'She's a bit nervous, being new. She's calming down.'

Edward waved his palms to show she had misunderstood. 'I have to go out.' I don't want to leave you alone in the office.'

'I'll be perfectly safe.'

Not from me, thought Edward and asked what time Mavis finished work.

'She leaves at one.'

'Fine. I'll go now and I'll be back before she leaves. Have a look at these figures for me while I'm gone.' He reached for his hat, and left. Jenny sat looking puzzled. There was a list of matters in need of his attention but he hadn't even glance at it. He did not tell her where he was going as he set off to the solicitor's office.

Oliver was brewing tea when Edward got back to the office. Mavis, showing unexpected tact, took a long break in the ladies cloakroom. Edward and Jenny sat with their tea cups at Mr Frederick's desk with the typewriter between them. She asked him what the problem was.

'There's not a problem.'

'You are acting very strangely.'

'I know. And I probably will for a bit longer. As soon as I can, I will tell you. In the meantime, trust me, Jenny.' They looked at each other until they had to stop for fear their arms would of their own volition travel the same path as their eyes and they should find themselves in a passionate embrace.

Mavis appeared smelling of lavender soap, thinking how lovely it was to come to work and be free of those awful chamber pots and dank dark privies.

'When Andrew starts work on our house a flushing toilet will be the first thing to be built,' she told her small audience. It broke the tension. They all laughed and Jenny remembered the list of jobs that awaited Edward's attention, and he remembered the electricity project.

Dinner time arrived and Mavis put her hat on ready to leave. Oliver didn't set off with her as usual. 'No school. Afternoon teacher off sick,' was his explanation, and his mum was at work. Jenny took him with her to the park where she ate her sandwich, bought him a meat pie and asked about the missing teacher. 'She's no loss,' Oliver replied mournfully. 'Much rather go in the morning with Mr Jamieson.'

When they finished eating Jenny scattered the crumbs for the sparrows, screwed up the greaseproof paper wrapper and handed it to Oliver who dropped it in the wastepaper bin. They set off back to work together. When a gaunt-looking Mr Woodward arrived she let Oliver explain his presence and waited until Mr Woodward suggested that he swap from working in the morning to the afternoon. After all they had Mavis in the morning now. Guilt over Oliver's broken arm meant that Mr Woodward could not do enough for the boy and his mother. A brilliant idea struck him. He could do more than simply changing the boy's hours of work. He consulted Jenny who gave her approval to his idea. Edward was summoned for his opinion and agreed with an enthusiasm that seemed excessive to Jenny. She did not know how important he thought the presence of a third party was in preserving her reputation. The lad was enough for the moment but having his mother present would be better help in surviving the thunderbolt that would fall when, or if, divorce proceedings were announced.

Higgs was summoned and promptly delighted Oliver by asking him to accompany him in the car to bring his mother to the office. As she worked in one of Mr Woodward's mills they did not anticipate any problem in seeing her during working hours. They offered Oliver's mother, Mrs Penrose, work in the office in the afternoons, an opportunity she welcomed with enthusiasm, even suggesting she take an evening course on Office Practice. She was, she explained, too cack-handed to do well as a millworker. Jenny pointed out that Mrs Penrose would be a great help answering the telephone at busy times, and Mrs Penrose clinched the deal by glancing at the filthy windows and saying she was not above doing a bit of cleaning.. The end result was that Oliver and his mother, would work in the office in the afternoon until Oliver left to take up his place at the grammar school where Edward had started his meteoric rise.

'There'll be no skiving off school once you've started there,' Edward told him and sent him out to buy everyone a vanilla custard. Tea was brewed and cakes eaten with a mild air of celebration. Mr Woodward was busy planning a scholarship to help fund Oliver's time at grammar school, and pleased to have eased his burden of guilt.

'That,' said Edward, 'was a good hour's work.'

It's all very well, thought Jenny, swanning about doing good, but what about the costings for the electricity project and that list of jobs from last week. All of them urgent and important, yet he had totally ignored them to find a new tea lady. There was, she decided, definitely something up with Edward.

The Woodwards' dinner table was not as glum as might be expected that evening. The satisfaction resulting from the improvement in Oliver's life helped to lift the atmosphere and distracted them from their errant daughter and the letter that would eventually be arriving to them.

Mr Martelli didn't have an office. He carried all the information he needed in his memory, a small black notebook and scraps of paper in his pockets. He met his clients in pubs, cafes and hotel lobbies. It wasn't very private; any passer-by could hear what was said, but it was warm and refreshments were available. He took a regretful look at the elegant surroundings of the hotel in Leeds. He had been impressed by Mr Woodward's choice and ferreted about until he discovered that it had been Stan Earnshaw's suggestion. A useful man to know, he decided, wrote his phone number in his little black book and planned to make his acquaintance.

Charity, Neville and Duncan arrived through the revolving glass door and settled themselves round the table, which carried the latest edition of the *Leeds Mercury*. Mr Martelli did not wait for Dorothea but started talking to them the minute they were settled.

'This is the last time we shall meet here,' he said, gesturing at the plush surroundings. 'Our time in Leeds is coming to an end. Our only problem is where to go next.' He ran through the possibilities with them, but really his mind was made up. He told them of invitations from Bradford and Glasgow and then announced, 'Our dearly beloved and foul-mouthed director who nursed us to such earth-shaking success here in Leeds has negotiated a most generous offer to transfer *Tosca* lock, stock and barrel to London.' They cheered. 'Our irascible Shakespearean will be in charge of *Tosca*.' They groaned. 'Afterwards we will have an opportunity to start work on his next production – when he's decided what it will be.' They laughed and beat the table with their fists to show their pleasure.

'These Shakespearean hams have their uses,' Mr Martelli told them. 'His contacts and his reputation got us the booking which is on excellent terms'. With mock solemnity he announced, ' I am sorry to say that the local baritone's injured legs are slow to heal and he is still confined to his bed. He will not be coming to London with us. It is one of the risks of our notoriously unpredictable profession. I am pleased to say that our Neville will come with us and will sing Cavaradossi.' More applause.

There was a moment of silent sympathy for their injured colleague before they settled down to listen as their agent rattled through their engagements for the days ahead when they were not performing *Tosca*. Neville and Duncan quickly memorised the details and their eyes gleamed as they totted up their fees. A quick solo in the music hall would more than cover their share of the rent.

'Travel arrangements,' Mr Martelli announced. Charity got out her notebook. 'You'll be pleased to know that Lady Clifford is sending her car for you again, Neville.'

Mr Martelli waited as Duncan whistled through his teeth and leered in the direction of his friend. 'There's a few more details I want to go over with Charity. They don't involve you boys.'

Charity could take a hint. 'How about chess in the garden?' she suggested. 'There won't be many more chances and today the sun is shining.' She took her boys into the garden, found the chessboard and left them setting out the pieces.

When she returned Mr Martelli beckoned her close and spoke softly. 'I have a special task for you this afternoon. You can leave your charges here. I will arrange lunch for them.'

Charity was immediately suspicious. The impresario, as he liked to be called, seldom bothered his head with such mundane details, or took the trouble to lower his voice. 'It involves Dorothea,' he added.

Charity felt alarm bells ring. Anything involving Dorothea meant trouble. Mr Martelli went on. 'She is finishing dressing and will be down soon. We have talked it through and she has agreed that it is an unpleasant but necessary task that lies ahead for her. Here is the address of a doctor. You must accompany Miss Dorothea there and…', he grew suddenly emphatic, 'stay with her through the whole business.' He fixed his eyes on her and said it again to be sure.

Suspicion turned to horror. 'I can't have anything to do with this. It's a criminal offence.'

'What? What do you think we're doing here?' Mr Martelli bellowed.

'An abortion.' Charity mouthed the word. She did not want the sound of it to pass her lips.

Mr Martelli, roared with laughter and slapped his leg, all pretence at discretion forgotten.

'You silly madam. We are doing the very opposite. Dorothea is terrified of having another baby. You know she had twins.'

Charity did not know, but there was something so awesome about having two children at the same time, that she could sympathise with the desire to avoid going through childbirth again.

'She is going to the trouble of getting divorced from her husband. Let's make it worth her while,' said Mr Martelli with a leer. He had no illusion that she would be faithful to him.

I've come a long way from Henshaw's, thought Charity as she considered the task in front of her. Dorothea wanted to avoid having a baby but still wanted to do the thing people got so excited about that tended to result in pregnancy. And Mr Martelli was aiding and abetting her. Who'd have thought it! She wondered what her mother would think and decided that she didn't care. As guide and helper to her brother and his friend, she was doing interesting and useful work. As maid to Dorothea she was well paid and by the sound of it would be well travelled. They were going to London. Life was going to be interesting.

A tap on her shoulder brought her out of her reverie. It was Mr Martelli, wanting her attention. 'All I want you to do is stay with her. It's all paid for. Watch and learn. You are an attractive woman on your way to London. You might find it useful one day.'

Dorothea swept in. She glared at Charity. 'Let's get this over with.'

When Dorothea returned tight-lipped and grim-faced Mr Martelli reminded her of her promise to write to her father. She did not labour over it very long.

The letter winged its way across the Pennines and landed on the breakfast table in the Woodward household. The master of the house went white, scooped it up and took it to his study. Edward made a rapid departure to work. If the contents of the letter were as he hoped, he did not wish to be within earshot when Mrs Woodward learned the news.

At the office, the only way he could control the wild impulse to reveal everything to Jenny, was to go over the calculations for the electricity generating plant. When they came out the same a third time he transferred his attention to checking the plans Mr Frederick had sent from Germany.

'No Mr Woodward today?,' asked Mavis as she put on her hat to leave at lunchtime.

'No. An urgent piece of business at home.' Edward avoided Jenny's glance. She guessed that the cause was Dorothea.

Jenny drank the tea that Oliver's mother made and listened while she answered the phone. Oliver had taught her exactly how to perform both these tasks, a fact that impressed Edward. Oliver and his mother had benefitted from a broken arm and what he hoped would be his broken marriage. The boy would have an education and his mother an income and an opportunity. The presence of Mrs Penrose in the office eliminated one of his major concerns but he could not hide his mental turmoil from Jenny. He was not looking forward to the end of the working day and returning to the place he could no longer think of as his home.

To delay that moment he stopped his car at his mother's house. She carried on cooking supper for his brothers while he looked out of the front window in the hope of seeing Jenny climb the hill on her way home. He considered asking his mother if she had a bed spare but thought better of it and went to kiss the back of her neck while she peeled a great mound of potatoes.

There was no time for him to have a private word with Nanny who was on her way to the drawing room with Clare and Izzy. She gave him an encouraging look in passing, as did the cheery maid when she brought his hot water. Time with the children and dinner in the dining room followed their usual course. Mrs Woodward said few words. Her swollen eyes and pale face spoke for her. When dinner ended, Mr Woodward sent for Nanny to keep his wife company in the drawing room while he discussed business with Edward in the study.

As Mr Woodward settled behind his desk Edward strolled round the study enjoying the walnut furniture, the Indian carpet and the soft clear light from the brass oil lamps. One day, he thought, I will have a study like this but I will have electric light.

'Have a seat,' said Mr Woodward to show who was in charge. As a protest Edward took a couple more turns round the room and stopped to look at the flowers on the mantelpiece. He wanted the older man to show his hand first. For all he knew Dorothea might have gone back on her word and written an abject letter of apology to her indulgent father.

Mr Woodward cleared his throat, picked up the piece of paper on his desk and waved it backwards and forwards. 'We had a deal, Edward. Half of my business if you married Dorothea.' His face contorted as he said the name of his daughter.

'Indeed,' said Edward, determined to be non-committal. He leant casually against the mantelpiece as if to admire the view through the window.

'I regret to say that Dorothea has not kept her side of the bargain.' The words were squeezed out of Mr Woodward like sludge oozing from a blocked drain. It was clearly a heart-wrenching moment for the older man.

Edward took the chair set out for him and stretched his arm across the desk in a sign of sympathy. 'Does she still want me to divorce her?' The word 'divorce' made Mr Woodward wince. It had never been spoken in his house before.

'Yes,' he confirmed.

'The rest of our agreement still stands?'

'Yes.'

Edward felt the breath he had been holding stream out through his mouth. Success. He had pulled it off. Common decency prevented him from showing his secret delight; he kept his face serious and calm for the sake of the older man.

'We might have to make some adjustments, a few changes, but I do not see why life cannot continue much as it does now.' Edward rose to his feet and held out his hand for Mr Woodward to shake. He suggested a medicinal brandy and set about finding glasses to seal the deal.

Now that the worst was over both men relaxed a little. Edward told of his visit to Simmonds the solicitor who thought that the evidence he had suppled would be enough to prove his case when presented to the Matrimonial Causes court in London. If satisfied, the court would grant a decree nisi. 'That's Latin for a 'divorce unless,' Edward explained. 'Six months later unless the court finds either of us have misbehaved in some way, a final decree will be granted which will free us both from the bonds of marriage.'

'You will be able to marry again?'

'Yes. So will Dorothea.' Mr Woodward looked up to heaven. Edward could not tell whether it was dismay at the casual cutting of a sacred bond or gratitude for a second chance for Dorothea to redeem herself by becoming a good wife and mother. This was not the moment to point out that Mr Martelli was not the marrying kind. He gave himself a pat on the back for managing to pass on to Mr Woodward all the information from the solicitor without once using the word 'adultery' or mentioning Mr Martelli by name.

A cautious calm settled on both men as Edward warned of one thing that would have to change in the near future. 'Mr Simmonds is emphatic that I must avoid any appearance of what he calls the three Cs of divorce. They are conniving, condoning and colluding. Being found to have done any of those things would cause the case to collapse. I must not let Dorothea back into my house.' Out of deference to her father he did not mention his bed, though she had not warmed it for years.

It took some seconds for the full horror of the statement to dawn on Mr Woodward. 'You mean, she could not come here, to... her home.' His voice cracked on the word home. He stared aghast at Edward. She had disappointed him, betrayed his dearest principles, contrived to bring scandal and disgrace to his name, but she was still his darling girl.

'Not while I live here. This is your home – and Dorothea's. I think it best if I move out.'

'Could Dorothea come here then?'

'Yes. This is not my house. It is your house.' Edward watched as Mr Woodward's mind inched its way to the subject dearest to his heart. His sudden expression of alarm showed that he foresaw the risk to his relationship with his grandchildren. His face collapsed. Edward could not let him suffer further.

'I think it best if I move out. With your permission Clare and Izzy could continue to live here. When she is not working Dorothea could visit them. Have tea in the nursery with them and Nanny. It is a sort of tradition and it would be a shame for it to stop.'

'Nanny,' muttered Mr Woodward and immediately felt better. She had sat through the worst of his wife's hysterics and with luck and a glass of port would have her sleeping like the proverbial baby. 'My wife,' he ventured, 'is very concerned about scandal and publicity.'

'Once it reaches court and the judge gives his ruling the facts are a matter of public record. They can be reported in the newspapers,' said Edward. 'I doubt they will be interested as no dukes or duchesses are involved.' He looked to Mr Woodward. 'The local paper?'

'I'll deal with them.' After a moment he asked, 'Where will you go? Your mother's?'

'I'd best go there when Dorothea visits. To show the distance between us. The rest of the time I thought I'd try the room over the garage. That land is in my name, so that should be all right and I'll still be close to the children.' He glanced at Mr Woodward. 'They will be my children, you understand.' There was no need to justify the statement by pointing out that Dorothea, as the guilty

217

party stood no chance of getting custody of them. Mr Woodward, a child of Queen Victoria's time, accepted without question that where children were concerned the husband's word was law.

As they sat with their strictly medicinal alcohol, the room filled with light as the full moon rose in a clear sky. Cool white light flooded over the garden.

'Have you taken a vow about tobacco?' Edward asked.

'No.' Mr Woodward accepted the cigar that Edward handed him and with one mind they headed to the French windows and out into the garden, matches flaring yellow and orange as they walked across the lawns to the paddock.

'I miss the horses,' said Mr Woodward. 'It was pleasant to come out here and stroke their noses. Sort of soothing.'

'Have you any plans for the land?' Mr Woodward shook his head.

'I'd like to buy the whole paddock.' Mr Woodward turned to him with a question in his face.

'One day I'd like to build a house here. I'm facing 6 uncomfortable months of sleeping over a garage. There's a cold-water tap and nothing else.'

'You can come to the house for your meals. Oh we can get the gas in.'

'I'd prefer electricity.'

'I forgot. You are going to electrify the whole town.'

I need my own place. I am sure Dorothea will come to visit you and the children. Better if I'm not living here then. But I do want to be near the children.'

Hope sprang in Mr Woodward's battered heart. 'My fault, son,' he said. 'I spoilt her.'

Edward didn't dispute that but tried to share out the blame. 'Your average woman's life doesn't suit Dorothea. To be fair we should have realised when she started doing those concerts and saw how happy it made her.'

The two men looked at the ground and considered how they had missed the warnings signs. Edward spoke, 'For all we know, this mess might be the making of her. She wasn't happy.'

'Perhaps not. But I work on the principle that bad behaviour should not be rewarded.'

'You might like to think about breaking that principle. Dorothea is promised high fees but she has no real grasp of the price of anything. I cannot pay her an allowance. That would definitely be one of the three Cs. I don't like to think of her being totally dependent on Mr Martelli. Would you consider giving her a small allowance?'

'You can have the paddock for a shilling,' said Mr Woodward and sucked on his cigar, his brain whirring. An allowance. Nothing generous as she had behaved so badly, but it would give him a way of keeping in touch with her. Not a penny more than £20 a year. That would hardly keep the girl in underwear. He'd raised it to 50 by the time they got back to the house.

Old habits die hard.

CHAPTER 23

When the cheery maid brought him hot water in the morning, Edward sat her on the bed to have what he called a little talk with her.

'Don't bother yourself.' She flicked her fingers in his face. 'I know that I'm getting the shove. And I know why. You've got to be a very good boy for the next 6 months.'

'Is nothing private in this house?'

'Not if you want hot water delivering to your room and your breakfast cooking.'

'When I have my own house I shall have hot water coming out of the tap.'

'How?'

'It's called electricity and it's coming here soon.'

'Good. Cause I'm not humping hot water across the paddock of a morning.'

Edward bent down and kissed the top of her head in a fatherly manner. 'You've been wonderful, Tabby, but it's over.' He slid a £5 banknote into the pocket of her pinafore. 'I expect you've got a replacement lined up.'

'Well there's a new chauffeur over at the Larches who looks quite promising. I'll miss you though.' She sniffed and used a forefinger to wipe a tear from her eye. She went to the door and looked back at him. 'Don't worry. I know the rules.' She held up her right hand. 'I do solemnly swear by Almighty God that it never happened.'

Edward spent the whole week at work thinking that he would burst from the pressure of keeping the news from the person who meant most to him – Jenny. How can a man propose marriage to a young woman while he still has a wife? This was the knotty problem occupying his mind as he strolled round the paddock, imagining where his house would be. With his stick he thrashed at the nettles threatening to encroach on the unruly grass.

Thwack. Could he ask her at work? He pictured calling Miss Truesdale into his office. They still tried to observe the formalities when Mr Woodward was there. It did not fool Mavis but appearances have to be kept up. When Miss Truesdale arrived with her files and figures and contracts, should he sit her down and ask her to marry him? Should he kneel? He was the boss; it did not feel right to go on one knee in his office. Not with Mr Woodward there. And then either Mavis or Mrs Penrose would be there. He crossed the office off his list of suitable places to propose.

Thwack. Lunch at the Midland? Too much like a seduction, with its air of sophisticated wealth and those glamorous bedrooms available at the top of a flight of stairs. Jenny might misunderstand and take offence.

Thwack. Now that he travelled so much by motor car they had fewer casual encounters on their way home from work. Their different churches had arranged the times of their services so that their congregations never mingled. There were no more exams for them to sit at the Mechanics' Institute. He racked his brains but could not think of a public place that would do.

Thwack. The convention was that a man asked a girl's father first. He looked at his stick and wondered if John Truesdale was similarly equipped. A notoriously married man asks John, a careful father, for his daughter's hand. It could quickly come to blows. Edward shrugged. If it did, he would have to grin and bear it. Jenny was the prize and she was worth it.

Accordingly, Edward presented himself at the door of the Truesdale house on Sunday evening. The Lord's Day seemed the most propitious time for such an errand. Jenny answered the door. Her eyes popped when she saw him on the doorstep with his hat in his hand.

'What are you doing here?' she hissed and started to push him out.

He held up a hand to stop her. 'I am here to see your father. And Mrs Truesdale. She stands in the place of your mother.'

Jenny, with a premonition of disaster, turned on her heel and fled. In the sitting room the recently married John and Anna sat in a contentment too complete to be disturbed even by the arrival of

221

Edward Carter in his overcoat. John waved him to a seat, but Edward thought it better to stand. Words failed him. He coughed and looked in his hat for inspiration. He read the maker's name 'Rathbone' twice. The necessary words would not rise to his lips. John looked over the top of his spectacles at Edward Carter, successful and respected business man, standing silent like a nervous schoolboy.

'Well,' he asked. 'What can we do for you?'

'I've come to ask your permission to court your daughter with the hope of persuading her to marry me.'

John's first thoughts were of horsewhips and showing him the door. Then it dawned on him that the request was so ridiculous that he wanted to laugh. 'That's all very well,' he said with a smile, 'but if my memory serves me right you are already married.'

'That is true, sir. You performed the ceremony yourself.'

'I know. I've seen some nervous bridegrooms in my time. But you …' Words failed him. He shook his head at the memory. The lad had been so young that the question of his father's consent had arisen while Mr Woodward glowered impatiently at him and the bride.

John collected his wits. 'That's all very well but unless there's been a change in the law to make bigamy legal in this country, I can't see what you are doing here with such a tomfool question.'

A change in the law. The words struck a nerve in Anna. The law did change, as she well knew; it now allowed her to be married to John although for years their love had been forbidden by a statute of Parliament. She rose from her chair and with a curled forefinger brought Jenny from the corner of the room where she had been lurking.

'What are you thinking of Jenny? Take his hat and his coat.'

When Edward was free of his outdoor clothes the Truesdales sat round him in a circle. Anna put on her listening face.

Never one for long explanations, Edward went straight to the heart of the matter. 'I know I am married, but not for much

222

longer. My lawyer warns that it will take 6 months but after that I shall be a single man again and free to marry. I want to marry Jenny.'

Jenny gasped. Edward turned to her and for a long magical moment they held each other's gaze. John and Anna, so recently united, recognised love when they saw it written clearly on their young faces.

It was some time before Edward returned to the thread of his story. 'Dorothea has left her home and her children. Her parents are heart-broken but she is determined to follow a career in music.'

'Singing! She wants to go singing!' The words exploded from John in disbelief. In John's view mothers did not desert their children, certainly not for something as frivolous as singing; it had taken death's icy hand to part his first wife, Florence from her children.

Anna was quicker to understand; she knew the burden of being a parent better than anyone. Of her own free will, she had taken its weight upon her shoulders. Jenny, who knew the darker side of Dorothea's nature from their schooldays, was not surprised to find her able to reject her children without a second thought.

Edward waited for the first shock to settle. 'Dorothea has given me grounds to divorce her. Adultery.' The word jarred in that comfortable room where the Truesdale family spent many hours together. 'I know I can trust you to keep that detail to yourselves for the moment. You can imagine the pain it is causing her parents who are God-fearing people. When the matter comes to court the grounds of my claim for divorce will be a matter of public record. I wanted you to hear the facts from my lips first. There will inevitably be gossip.

He felt no need to ask them further for their discretion and pressed on. 'There are the children to consider. I shall have responsibility for them. For the sake of the children and Dorothea's parents, I am hoping to keep the scandal to a minimum.'

'I have read about such things in the newspaper,' said John. 'Usually there's a duke or an earl involved.'

'I hope not to feature in the newspapers. Not having a title will help.'

'I doubt the local paper will make a meal of it,' said John. Edward managed a grin. They both knew that Mr Woodward wielded considerable power over the editor.

'I am not asking either Jenny or you for an answer now. I just want you both to know that when I am free to do so, it is Jenny I want to marry. I have wanted to do so for a long time. As you pointed out, sir, I was young when I married Dorothea and I followed my ambition, not my heart. People will judge us and the gossips will have a field day.' Anna and Jenny could picture the satisfied grins on ladies' faces when they learned that Mrs Woodward had got her comeuppance.

Edward took a breath and ploughed on. 'The solicitor has warned that it will not be pleasant, especially if a further marriage follows soon after the divorce.' Edward paused and looked at Jenny. 'As I hope it will.' He looked round to see how the Truesdales, sensible reasonable people, reacted to the prospect of their daughter marrying a divorced man. Mrs Woodward would have fainted but the new Mrs Truesdale was made of stronger stuff.

'Tell me how this divorce business works,' commanded John. 'I've not had any divorced customers during the course of my work. The townsfolk of Atherley prefer bigamy to divorce. It's quicker, cheaper and, if you move 30 miles away from the town of any previous marriage, you are not likely to be caught.'

Edward explained about the decree nisi and the 6 months wait until it was possible to marry again.

'Six months is a prison sentence,' Jenny exploded, echoing Edward's first reaction to the news. She thought that it was time to make her feelings clear to all of them. 'In my heart I've been married to Edward for years. As he is to me.' She looked to Edward for confirmation.

'That is exactly how I feel,' he said.

'That is all very well, but you must observe the formalities,' said John.

'Damn the formalities,' said Jenny, forgetting that her father had never before heard a swear word pass her lips. Instant regret swept over her as she saw the effect on him.

John's lips were working but no sound was coming out. He struck his hand on his chest to find his voice. 'Damn the formalities! It is a formality that makes you a man's wife. Not some harlot he acquired for the night and will put back on the street in the morning. It is a formality that allows your children to look the world in the face, to inherit their father's property and bear his name.' He stopped; he had not meant to roar so. Silence and stricken faces surrounded him. After a breath he spoke more calmly.

'Do not forget. I am the formalities.'

'Indeed you are, sir,' cried Edward. 'You had the power to make the marriage. I ask you, if you were granted the power to undo it, would you do so?'

Perhaps it was the 'sir' that did it. The heat went out of John's indignation. It was followed by a chilling, distant formality. He looked haughtily at Jenny as if he had only just met her and didn't like the look of her.

'Jenny is 21 now. She does not need my consent.'

'I know. But I would like your approval,' said Jenny. For all the effect they had on her father, her words fell like stones into deep water where they sank without trace.

'It would mean a lot to me,' said Edward and looked earnestly at the older man.

John shuffled uncomfortably in his chair. 'Well I'm sorry I cannot give it to you at this moment. Perhaps one day when you really are a free man and there's none of this nisi business, and as long as you behave yourself, perhaps then I will think differently. Until then I simply cannot give my approval for my daughter to be courted by a married man. Perhaps when that time comes, but not before. I never thought I'd lead my daughter up the aisle to find a married man waiting at the altar.'

It was Anna who smoothed the stormy water. She took Edward's hand. 'I always remember you looking after Tommy at school.' John's stony face told her that there was no point in her continuing with that theme so she asked Jenny to see Edward out.

When they had left the room, she turned to John. 'It's not so outrageous when you think about it. They are just acting ahead of the law.' She paused to look intently at him. 'You may recall that we did exactly that for some years. Many would regard us as sinning in secret. Now Jenny is condemned to the same ordeal we endured. Hiding our true feelings from the world. As we well know, the law is not on the same timetable as love.' John tutted and looked peevish. Anna knew to give him time.

In the privacy of the hallway the young couple embraced. Edward felt tears on his face and Jenny felt kisses on hers, consoling them for the hurt that her father's words had caused both of them.

'You will have to call me Miss Truesdale in the office. Except when just Mavis is there. And I shall call you Mr Carter.' She laid her head on his chest. There was something solid and reliable about a man's chest she discovered.

'Do you think your father will come round?'

'I hope so. I do not want to marry against his wishes. Or Anna's. I think she is not as shocked as he is. She'll work on him.' Her confidence in Anna was immense. Memories of night-time noises swirled in her mind and came to the surface. Muffled moans, the patter of footsteps and the splash of water. It all made sense now that the world knew her father and Anna were a loving couple.

'The law changed to let them love each other. One day the law will let us be married.' Happiness made them light-headed. 'It seems that holy wedlock is no longer holy deadlock,' said Jenny.

Edward was quick to point out that his wasn't a holy marriage. 'It was more of a business deal. God wasn't involved. As you know your father conducted it.'

Jenny hesitated. 'You do know he's not officially my father?'

'Yes. All the more reason to consider his feelings. He saved you from the orphanage.' His arm grasped her closer at the thought of that chilly institution. 'I've not forgotten that you're Spinning Jenny, the bicycle girl.'

There were several days of armed truce and awkward silence in the Truesdale household before Anna exploded one evening at the dinner table.

'For goodness sake you two. Let's get this sorted out. I've had quite enough of this not talking and not looking each other in the eye. Stop pretending that nothing has happened and let us deal with it.'

Jenny rose from her place and went to embrace her father. 'I cannot tell you how awful it is to have the two men I love most in this world at odds with each other.'

'I've nothing against Edward. Except the fact that he is married. You can't pretend that isn't a problem.'

'Please don't make me choose between you,' Jenny begged. 'I have loved Edward ever since he saved us from Mr Cripps.'

'And Tommy,' Anna burst in. 'He looked after Tommy when he started at the new school; he was terrified at the thought of going. I gave Edward half a crown and swore him to silence. He never breathed a word of it.'

John got out his handkerchief and offered it to Jenny to wipe her tears. 'I chose to be your father, Jenny. When you were a little girl, left in the park, exchanged for a bicycle, we chose to keep you as our daughter.' Jenny went back to her seat, his handkerchief twisted in her fingers and a chill settling round her heart. John's emphasis on choice frightened her.

'It was not long before poor Florence started to fret that someone else might come to claim you.' John was getting into his stride now. His thoughts had cleared and he spoke with confidence. 'We were afraid that someone with a higher claim than ours might come for you.' He paused. 'Well now someone has. That someone is Edward Carter.' He looked enquiringly across the table at Jenny.

She nodded; her head wobbling precariously. Her neck was swollen with emotion.

227

'I have tried to be a good father,' John began.

'You are. Oh you are.'

'Sometimes it is hard to know what a good father should do. Would a good father give his blessing? I don't know. I cannot give you my support yet but I know I will smile on you and Edward on your wedding day. Until then, this is your home, Jenny. Be in no doubt, this is your home.' He looked to Anna for confirmation. She smiled her approval.

Jenny wept grateful tears.

———————————————————

Six months is a long time to carry a secret. This one didn't survive the first hour at work on Monday morning. Mavis wormed a brief account of the events of Sunday from Jenny. 'I guessed the minute I saw you two together,' she whispered as they exchanged confidences in the cloakroom. To her credit, the notoriously outspoken Mavis kept the secret as close as an oyster conceals a pearl for almost the whole 6 months.

Mr Frederick returned from Germany and work began on the power plant, a project that occupied the minds of all the local men. Some were not keen on the idea until they realised that it brought work to the town; the power station would be fuelled by coal.

It was the leisured ladies of the town who first remarked on the absence of Dorothea. She had been a thorn in their flesh for long time. They soon stopped saying how peaceful it was without her and began to look for information on her whereabouts. She was spotted on a flying visit to her parents. At the same time Edward Carter went to stay at his mother's. His car was seen parked outside her house overnight. That was all the information the ladies needed to work on.

When Dorothea made a second visit she brought cuttings of newspaper reviews raving about her performances, and mentioning the title of one of her admirers. Mrs Woodward was too modest, or embarrassed, to show off the newspaper evidence of her daughter's success when she made her social calls. One of her neighbours voluntarily took over the task in her place. The woman had come across Dorothea's name in her husband's newspaper and proceeded to spoil his evening by taking her scissors and cutting it out. To compensate for the telling off he gave her, she passed the cutting round the next at home she attended. After Dorothea made a third visit and provided her mother with details of the interior furnishings of a ducal residence Mrs Woodward saw it as her duty to pass the information on herself.

Mr Martelli wisely decided not to accompany Dorothea on her visits home.

When Edward judged that the Woodwards were sufficiently recovered from the blow that the divorce proceedings had dealt them, he told them that when the divorce was made final, he hoped to marry Miss Truesdale or Jenny as he preferred to call her. If Mr Woodward was dismayed to see his daughter so quickly replaced he took the blow with stoic calm. He treated Jenny with the courtesy she deserved as the future bride of the man he had begun to regard as a son.

Mrs Woodward remembered Aunt Anna's kindness to her in the days of her darkness and invited both of them to tea. Jenny took the opportunity to see where Edward planned to build their house at the edge of the paddock. As he never started a big project without involving her in the planning, they agreed that it would be tactful to delay building work until Jenny was officially Mrs Carter. In the meantime they could discuss ideas and add some improvements to make living above a garage more comfortable for Edward. With pride he showed her where the ground had been dug out to accommodate the drains for the flushing toilet. 'I knew that would be your top priority,' he laughed.

As the weeks passed into months John Truesdale grew reconciled to the unusual circumstances of his daughter's secret engagement. The end of the 6 months of waiting was in sight when Anna suggested that they invite Edward to join them on Sunday. John welcomed the prospect, thinking it would be a good day for the conversation he had in mind. The Truesdales attended the Church of England in the morning and Edward accompanied the Woodwards to the Methodist chapel. They met for lunch.

When the meal was finished and Anna and Jenny were washing up in the kitchen John squirmed with indecision as he sought a way to raise the subject tactfully. 'Perhaps the time has come for us to talk about this wedding for my daughter. Most fathers expect to lead their daughters up the aisle of their customary church.' He glanced at Edward, looking for signs of annoyance. Edward was wondering if he could offer John a cigar in his own home. He decided not.

John hmphed and coughed. 'Obviously that is not going to happen for Jenny.' Edward tried to look suitably penitent and braced himself for the complaint that was likely to follow. It did not happen. John continued, 'When the law changed to allow me to marry Anna I went to the vicar to ask him to call the banns. We were both his parishioners and had attended his church for years. It was only when I was standing in his study that it really struck me that the vicar had the right to refuse to perform the ceremony. The Bishops had insisted on that. I wondered what I would do if he did refuse me.' He paused for effect. ' I had a terrible suspicion that I might hit him. I could feel my anger growing and my fist clenching as he delayed answering while he faffed about with the paperwork.'

Edward was silent as he digested this new side to John Truesdale. John continued. 'It was all right of course. He was perfectly agreeable. I'm only telling you because at first I did talk of walking Jenny up the aisle. I want you to know that was just a figure of speech. Not a firm belief. When, the time comes for Jenny to marry, I wouldn't want that to be a problem. After all, civil weddings are my day job.'

'Thank you for that.' Edward had done his homework and knew that for a divorced man a wedding ceremony in the Church of England depended on the decision of the clergyman. He had not even raised the question with the Methodist minister; the Woodwards had suffered enough. 'Jenny and I have talked about it and we both would be very happy if you were to marry us. The civil ceremony ties the knot just as tight as the church does.' He managed a wry grin. 'As I know to my cost.'

230

CHAPTER 24

At last Edward held in his hands the document that declared him free to marry. The King's Proctor, whoever he might be, had found no reason to stop the divorce proceeding to its conclusion. Edward and Jenny presented themselves to the Registrar's Office to arrange their marriage. John smiled on them, as he promised he would and handed them over to his assistant.

'Better not to have a family member do the paperwork,' he murmured as he slipped away. 'Just in case there are questions later'. The assistant filled in the forms, describing Edward as the 'divorced husband of Dorothea Woodward', a phrase which caused Jenny to pull a face. She pulled a longer face when she learned they would have to wait 28 more days before they could marry.

'Is there no way we can speed things up?' asked Edward who was considering offering a £5 note in the hope of jumping this final hurdle.

'You can apply to the bishop for a special licence, but I don't recommend it. People will talk,' said the deputy registrar cryptically while looking everywhere except at Jenny's waistline. Jenny saw why her father had left his assistant to do the dirty work.

"We will wait and your father will smile on our wedding day.'

John greeted the arrangements for the wedding with approval. He was pleased that the formalities had been strictly complied with. He even offered Edward a glass of sherry before lunch on Sunday and accepted cheerfully that he would not be walking Jenny up the aisle of the church.

Their relationship was no longer a secret; it was written up on the wall of the Registry Office. Mavis could now set free the tongue she had kept under strict control for months. She upbraided Edward for not providing Jenny with an engagement ring to mark the occasion; there was no jewellery for Jenny to inherit from a conveniently deceased mother-in-law. Edward promptly took Jenny to the jewellers where she found a sapphire ring that met with her approval and, as the wedding was only weeks away, they bought the wedding ring as well.

The engagement ring succeeded in diverting everyone's attention from the past, the marriage that no longer existed, to the wedding that would soon take place. Jenny and Mavis spent a lot of time in their cloakroom exchanging confidences. The men assumed that they were planning their dresses. They were not. Jenny had something more important on her mind. She was getting close to finding out about **it**, and thought Mavis would be a mine of information.

'It's no use, Jenny, I can't describe **it**. **It**'s different every time. You really love Edward so **it** will be wonderful for you. And he should know what he's doing. He's been married.'

News came that Dorothea would be visiting from late on Saturday until Monday evening. Edward thought he'd better make himself scarce in case Dorothea put a spanner in their wedding plans. Upsetting other people had been one of her hobbies for years.

'When we are safely married, I'll go and meet her but not until then,' he told Jenny. When he turned towards her he saw that she was giving him a very special look that took his breath away. It was the look that Mavis had tried to teach her, that made her look as if she had swallowed a frog when she practised in her bedroom. This time the look told Edward that she wanted to be naked in bed with him, that she wanted his breath hot on her body and his hands on her breasts. She wanted to **it** to happen to her and she wanted it soon. The desire came from the very centre of her being and passed to Edward in a bolt of power that stunned him. He was still dazed when she stretched up to whisper in his ear, something about anticipating matrimony. His face lit up.

'If you are sure,' he said.

'We've waited long enough already,' she said. He could not argue with that.

There was no point in delaying. Their plans were a model of discretion. An overnight visit to her sister, Margaret, in Manchester provided Jenny with her cover story. John and

Anna gave every appearance of believing her, as they waved her off to the station with her little suitcase. Once they were safe behind their front door Anna embraced John with a special warmth.

'What a blessing we don't have a telephone.'

John frowned at her. He had stopped trying to understand the family jokes about his reluctance to welcome modern conveniences such as the telephone and electricity.

Anna explained to him. 'Margaret cannot ring us up, so she won't have to lie to us.'

As Jenny emerged from the entrance of Victoria Railway Station, Edward's sleek car drew up. She enjoyed the admiring eyes lavished on the car as she climbed in the front. Half hidden by the windscreen they smiled shyly at each other. Edward took her left hand and produced the gold wedding ring. He slipped off her engagement ring. 'You'll need this for the receptionist,' he told her as he slid the wedding ring on her third finger. Jenny sat speechless, admiring the effect. It was a detail of the planning that had escaped her.

'I'd forgotten about that,' she told Edward, who looked smug. 'But then I don't do this very often.'

Edward turned to her and touched his forehead as a professional chauffeur would do to his employer. 'Where to, ma'am?' he asked in his broadest Lancashire accent.

'The Midland Hotel,' said Jenny without hesitation.

ACKNOWLEDGEMENTS

I am grateful to my daughter, Rebecca, for her scrupulous editing and for holding my hand for the technical bits.

Liz Harris has generously taken time from writing her own novels to provide me with invaluable advice.

The contribution of the many writers of history who manage to produce really enjoyable books is beyond measure. I am particularly indebted to Joan Perkins for her Victorian Women and Women and Marriage in the Nineteenth Century.

The research into their forebears by members of the Lancashire and Manchester Family History Society have provided invaluable glimpses into the lives of working people in Lancashire in times past.

The cover was designed by J D Designs using a painting by Eugen Bracht.

By the same author

Thornfield Hall, Atlantic Books Ltd.
His Wife's Sister, Richmond Press

Printed in Great Britain
by Amazon

25517412R00138